What the critics are saying:

"Brings together two strong characters in a situation where fast-paced suspense and danger parallel the sexual tension. Readers who enjoy alpha males in their erotic fantasies will feel Luca's powerful sexual attraction in nearly every scene of this page-turner." --*Romantic Times Bookclub Magazine*

"The Dare, is highly recommended from this reviewer. Ms. Agnew captures your attention from the beginning to the end just wanting the story to continue and never end. All together, this is a story worth reading and keeping as a favorite author and a story that just gets more exciting? Way to go Ms. Agnew! I can't wait for her next novel, seeing as how talented this writer is." - *Sizzling Romances*

"Isabella and Luca explode on the pages of THE DARE. Luca grabbed my attention with his masculinity, his sexy, cocky attitude and a gentler side the love scenes between these two. Oh my gosh! They simply burned up the sheets...incinerated them...turned them to dust. Ms. Agnew certainly packs a powerful punch in THE DARE. I fell in love with her characters and the storyline perfectly created and executed. Luca is definitely an alpha male but with a gentleness that brings tears to your eyes. So grab your man or your toys, or both and have an orgasmic time." - *Reva Moore, Just Erotic Romance Newsletter*

"When you read THE DARE, you will find that these two make this story worthy of reading and that this book is about as hot and as titillating as they come. Ms. Agnew does a good job of keeping the suspense in the background, though not letting us forget it. We are enthralled by the sexual compatibility of Luca and Bella. I think the readers will be pleased on both stories . . . the suspense is wrapped neatly, while Luca and Bella realize that they need each other on every level that counts." - *Robin Taylor, In The Library Reviews*

Discover for yourself why readers can't get enough of the multiple award-winning publisher Ellora's Cave. Whether you prefer e-books or paperbacks, be sure to visit EC on the web at www.ellorascave.com for an erotic reading experience that will leave you breathless.

THE DARE
An Ellora's Cave Publication, September 2004

Ellora's Cave Publishing, Inc.
1337 Commerce Drive, Suite 13
Stow, OH 44236-0787

ISBN #1-4199-5018-5

Other available formats: MS Reader (LIT) Adobe (PDF),
Rocketbook (RB), Mobipocket (PRC) & HTML

Edited by Martha Punches
Cover art by Syneca

Warning:

The following material contains graphic sexual content meant for mature readers. *The Dare* has been rated E–rotic by a minimum of three independent reviewers.

Ellora's Cave Publishing offers three levels of Romantica™ reading entertainment: S (S-ensuous), E (E-rotic), and X (X-treme).

S-*ensuous* love scenes are explicit and leave nothing to the imagination.

E-*rotic* love scenes are explicit, leave nothing to the imagination, and are high in volume per the overall word count. In addition, some E-rated titles might contain fantasy material that some readers find objectionable, such as bondage, submission, same sex encounters, forced seductions, etc. E-rated titles are the most graphic titles we carry; it is common, for instance, for an author to use words such as "fucking", "cock", "pussy", etc., within their work of literature.

X-*treme* titles differ from E-rated titles only in plot premise and storyline execution. Unlike E-rated titles, stories designated with the letter X tend to contain controversial subject matter not for the faint of heart.

THE DARE

Denise A. Agnew

Dedication

As always, to my very own hero, Terry

Acknowledgements

To Kate Douglas for giving me the final nudge toward Ellora's Cave and for her valuable critique.

To Karen Morris and Susan Tatley for their critique skills.

To MaryJanice Davidson for inspiration.

Chapter One

Police Say Serial Killer Stalking Women in Piper's Grove.

Isabella Markham read the headline in the paper and swallowed hard. A cold shudder ran up her spine and made the hair on her arms prickle. By old habit she pushed her glasses back onto the bridge of her nose.

For one unnerving moment she wondered if she couldn't venture anywhere without the specter of fear haunting her night and day. "Great. Just great. I go on vacation and look what happens."

She'd been here, cloistered in this luxury one story condo in this town several miles south of Denver, for two weeks. In that time she'd read about murder and mayhem in a town that never saw atrocities committed like this in its hundred year history.

She reached for her coffee and almost knocked over the fat green mug. Her hand trembled as she gripped the ceramic cup and brought it to her lips for a healthy swallow. She read more of the disturbing article.

Police are baffled by the sudden and devastating series of murders that began three months ago in Piper's Grove. Three women have been brutally murdered, and now the townspeople are starting to question whether the police can protect them. Many young women have left this quiet town in the last two weeks and headed for Denver, saying they actually feel safer in the big city than in this normally secure hamlet.

Bella shivered.

All you need is a good jolt of caffeine. Everything will be all right.

As she sat there reading at the breakfast bar in the gourmet kitchen, she admitted she had everything she needed and nothing to worry about. Yes, it was quiet here, but she needed the time and the peace to think. She brushed her fingers over the cool, dark blue granite countertop. Cooking for one in the light oak, brightly lit, kitchen seemed lonely, but she couldn't complain on the whole. She laid the paper on the breakfast bar and tried not to let old memories explode in her brain. Thinking about the murders and what happened at her father's estate in recent months would ruin her vacation and peace of mind. She'd escaped to Piper's Grove, Colorado, thinking it must be safer than Denver. She would stay the entire month in the rented vacation condo or be out the money. All she needed to do was be cautious, and she could still enjoy her time here.

Adjusting her glasses again, she inhaled deeply. That is that. She refused to second guess herself.

After another sip of coffee she felt better. Today she'd take advantage of the warmer temperatures predicted and soak in some rays. She shifted on the bar stool and glanced out the kitchen window into her next door neighbor's window.

What she saw there made her mouth drop open and her eyes widen. "Boy howdy, I don't believe this."

She didn't often shuffle, half asleep, into her kitchen in the morning and see a gorgeous naked man through the window. She praised whatever gods or goddesses made her neighbor either uninhibited, an exhibitionist, or incredibly unselfconscious about his body.

How could she be expected to maintain disinterest when the man paraded in full view with nothing more on his body than a smile? No man had a right to be so damned beautiful. No. Beautiful sounded too girly-girl for him. This guy didn't approach feminine in any way, shape, or form.

Hottie.

Hunk.

Edible.

Tasty.

Whatever she called him, she could stare at him all day and never have difficulty explaining what made her want to spend the next twenty-four hours staring at him. Or maybe licking him from one end to the other.

The man simply turned her on.

He looked just out of bed, tousled and maybe thoroughly satisfied by a night of hard sex.

Her face flamed.

Now your imagination is running away with you.

She drank in details as he moved. His rich, wavy ebony hair tumbled around his shoulders in disarray. Small, white streaks of hair touched his temples. Unusual, but the white hair gave him an added mysterious lure. She imagined how it might feel to slide her fingers into those thick strands and tug him down for two hungry kisses.

Hah! Who says she'd stop at two?

His nose looked strong, almost hawkish from this angle. From this distance she couldn't see as many fine points about his incredible face as she would like.

Yesterday she'd caught a glimpse of him in a muscle shirt and a pair of ragged denim shorts. His butt, tight and perfect, had snagged her gaze and refused to let go.

She'd pulled into the driveway as he'd leaned over to pick up his paper. He hadn't looked at her or waved in greeting, so for all she knew he could be an unsociable bastard. A white picket fence surrounding his front yard and hers didn't keep him from seeing her front yard or vice versa. As he'd walked back to his house, his incredible body had caught her attention and held it. The way he'd moved suggested primal male animal, and a dangerous man with an agenda.

Wrenching herself back to the present, she zeroed in on his form again. Her neighbor opened his fridge and reached inside. Muscles in his naked back rippled and bunched along his wide shoulders. She imagined running her fingers over smooth skin and hard sinew. When he grasped a bottle of water and twisted off the top, she watched his biceps and forearms move. He tipped the water to his lips and took a long drink.

Her gaze slid down, down, down. She couldn't see naked proof this man had one world class butt, but Bella imagined it might be solid and oh-so-squeezable. She flexed her fingers and smiled as she remembered the old commercial with the funny man who squeezed toilet paper.

When he turned slightly towards Bella, her breath caught in anticipation and her gaze coasted down his physique. She could tell he had a powerful chest and that at least a sprinkling of hair covered his pectorals and down over a ridged, flat stomach. Below that...

She couldn't see the entire package because the bottom of the window obscured her view. Unfortunately, her outstanding imagination conjured an explicit image. She stood up on her tiptoes to continue her inspection. While nothing could be guaranteed, she'd bet her next Alaskan cruise the man sported a healthy-sized cock.

Cock.

Isabella blushed again. The brazen, hard-core explicitness of the word made her feel...horny. *Good deal, Bella. You're spending valuable vacation time staring like a love-sick puppy at a man who wouldn't look twice at you.*

Who would? Her gold metal glasses needed fixing so they wouldn't slide down her nose. Her hair needed a trim, her purple gingham cotton pajamas wouldn't be mistaken as sexy in any county, and she wore a frayed green terry robe and fuzzy pink bunny slippers. All a part of the cover, she'd told her father a few days ago when she'd left the Markham estate for a long needed retreat from a hectic and boring social life.

Who am I kidding? My life in the last few days hasn't been boring, it's been terrifying.

She couldn't tell him the truth.

Not if it meant blurting out she felt a menacing presence in their house, and the last few weeks' events reminded her of something dark and unnatural lingering nearby. Old memories resurrected and revealed to her shades of the past. She'd run from her father's estate to escape those memories, as well as assert independence.

Bella needed a break, and she would have one, even if it meant dressing in a habit like a nun and pretending she didn't have much money to her name. She would have a few weeks with good books, an occasional glass of wine, and nothing more to worry about than painting her toenails if she felt like it. *Yeah, that's the ticket.* She could forget that she no longer felt safe at her father's compound. Inhaling deeply, she looked again at the man in his kitchen.

Mr. Tall, Dark, and Perhaps Well-hung started to turn toward the window, and she realized if she could see him buck-naked, he could see her. Stepping back from the window, she ducked out of the kitchen. She headed to her bedroom and a quick shower.

While warm water pounded her skin, she tried to push the image of the man next door out of her head.

Fat chance.

She could hear her sister Madeleine. *You don't know anything about him. He could be a serial killer. A pervert. Or a serial killer and a pervert.*

A wild, scary idea flew through Bella's head.

What if the man next door is the serial killer?

Bella groaned. Now she really had allowed her imagination to go batty. What were the chances a serial killer happened to live next to her? Astronomical?

Bella smiled. She heard her sister's voice trilling in her head. *Why on earth would you want to stare at a naked man, Bella?* Madeleine would sputter and stutter. *How could you be so…so…so… brazen?*

Anyone with a healthy sexual appetite qualified as a pervert in Madeleine's *Book of Life Rules*. If Madeleine had seen the man next door in the nude, she would have screamed and run into the living room to hide her virgin eyes. Okay, so Madeleine didn't have virgin eyes; the woman had been married for fifteen years. On the other hand, it wouldn't have surprised Bella if Madeleine and her rich, boring, puritanical husband had sex in the dark and half-clothed.

Of course, half-clothed could be sexy. She tried to imagine Madeleine and her husband having kinky sex. *Nah. Not possible and not appetizing.*

Instead, she allowed the warm water to ease away her troubles and fill her with a wild fantasy. She closed her eyes and pictured herself running her hands down the naked man's chest. Hair would tickle her fingers as she detoured with deliberate slowness over the hard contours of his pectorals. She imagined the tight outline of his muscles, steel-like and immovable—able to cradle a woman with tender attention, or take down the meanest bastard. He looked like a man who knew what he wanted and how to get it, and as she looked up into his eyes, her fantasy flamed like an afterburner.

Heat built and moistened the folds between her legs with surprising quickness. With pure delight she'd slide her fingers to his biceps and trace the smooth skin stretched taut over solid muscle. Bella tried to picture slipping her hands through the hair on his six-pack stomach and converging on the erect, long length of his penis. What would it look like? Thick and long? Long and thin? Somehow she knew it would not only be thick, but long, too. A tight, steady ache strengthened between her legs and she almost reached down to touch herself. Almost. Something held her back, a tiny reluctance to admit a man could have this much potential to turn her on.

Especially a man who might be a world-class asshole.

An honest-to-God, Grade-A choice male didn't come along often. She would get whatever pleasure she could out of the voyeuristic delight she'd experienced watching the real man in the window. Who cared if he didn't know her from Eve and might laugh in her face if she suggested they do the two-backed beast?

Holy Toledo. Bella switched off the water and leaned against the shower wall. Her hands seemed to reach for her breasts almost against her will. Sometimes self-conscious of her body, she'd always thought her breasts mediocre, neither large nor small. They suited her fine. Bella slid her fingers upward until they brushed with featherlike precision over her big nipples. Gasping, she took each nipple and tugged. Instantly they puckered, and she shuddered as warmth flooded her body and centered between her legs with a pounding ache.

As she allowed herself this one indulgent pleasure, Bella reached between her legs and passed her fingers over the soft, wet flesh. Surprised at the level of her arousal, she imagined the mystery man once again. She envisioned hard, unforgiving eyes turning warm with passion, showing her how much he cared and adored her. His hands would coast over her body with a light but possessive appraisal. Each lingering brush of his fingers would make her hotter until she wanted him against her, surrounding her, inside her.

Making her forget.

She touched her clit and a bolt of white-hot pleasure stung and burned and made her writhe against the shower wall. Cold tiles beneath her back ceased to exist as she manipulated one nipple and brushed her middle finger over her clit again and again. She took the moisture between her legs and applied it to her clit, starting a new feeling and a new texture. Each pass over her aroused tissues made her sigh with pleasure.

God, it felt so good to let go and forget no man had ever made her feel this good.

Again the mysterious stranger entered her imagination. Without preliminaries he lifted her against the shower wall, and Bella felt his steel-hard penis slip between her legs and ram home. He felt harder than rock and bigger than any man she'd experienced before, stretching, reaching high to her womb. Immediately he pounded into her center, thrusting deep and hard and unrelenting into her depths. She moaned with every imagined thrust, every flicker of her fingers on her nipple and each touch on her clit.

Rising higher and higher by the second, her excitement erased worry under a torrent of blinding need. Again she tugged on her nipple. Again she manipulated her clit until she panted and moaned and urged her fantasy lover onward.

Forbidden words she never dared say during sex with a man or any other time slipped from her lips.

"Fuck me," she whispered. "Fuck me harder."

Her dream man growled with arousal and complied to her will, grabbing her butt and squeezing as he drove inside her with a furious pace. She panted, driven crazy by an overwhelming need to come and come hard. Heat rose in her chest and throat and skyrocketed into her face as staggering pleasure erupted between her legs, sending an almost unbearable orgasm through her body. She shook as her entire body throbbed and incoherent gasps and whimpers came from her throat as the scorching pleasure burst inside her. Moments seemed to lengthen in to eternity as she panted, shivered, then eased into a sensuous languor.

She sagged against the wall. "Damn."

She couldn't remember the last time she'd either touched herself or had an orgasm that strong and that fast. Trembling from the force of her spent desire, she left the shower and toweled off. Every nerve seemed hypersensitive as fluffy material slid over her skin, sending vibrations of heat radiating through her. Last aftershocks of arousal ebbed, but she knew this impromptu self-manipulation satisfied her for the moment.

Unfortunately, her mind reverted to wondering what Madeleine would think of masturbation. Bella sniffed and shoved the thought away. Now that Bella had spent several days out of Madeleine's presence, and experienced relief from the rest of her overbearing family, Bella felt free. Free for as long as it took to decide what she wanted to do with the rest of her life.

Deciding that she spent far too much time thinking about Madeleine's hang ups, Bella dressed in cotton shorts and tank top, still feeling the pleasure of her orgasm as her bra touched her nipples and her panties touched her clit.

After returning to the kitchen to make breakfast, she realized her morning appetite hadn't resurrected. She grabbed another cup of coffee, a travel magazine, and sauntered outside to the small covered porch. After planting her butt on a lounge chair, she inhaled the fresh morning air. June in Colorado promised to be unusually warm. Even now puffy clouds spilled over the Rocky Mountains, assuring a good chance of thunderstorms.

The little back yard spoke of peace with its potted pink verbenas. A couple of aloe vera plants nestled in pots near the porch overhang. Tall pines soared behind the wall of the condo. Birds chirped and a squirrel skittered from one branch to another. She took a sip of coffee, opened her magazine and started reading.

A deep, husky male voice purred with enjoyment. "Oh, yeah."

Bella froze. She listened, certain the raw, sexual tone came from her neighbor's back yard.

"Oh, baby." A moan. "Oh, shit."

Bella stopped reading the magazine again, stunned into stillness by the pure lust in the man's voice. She'd never heard 'oh shit' sound sexy before, but this guy managed to make it so.

She glanced at the small open knothole in the brown wood fence that bordered their property. Could he be making love with a woman in broad daylight in the middle of his back yard?

Two feelings burst upon her. First, a weird, uncontrollable jealousy came over her in a rush. Second, overwhelming desire to see what he was doing. She hesitated maybe all of a minute before she stood and walked toward the fence.

* * * * *

Luca Angello imagined soft, tight warmth as he slid deep inside the woman. At last he held her in his arms. He didn't plan on letting her go until he'd fucked her into the next century. He slid his hand into her red hair and allowed his fingers to tighten on the strands. He thrust again, feeling her slick walls grip his cock with a mind-blowing fit.

He groaned. "Oh, yeah."

Heat splintered through his body as she surrounded him with liquid desire. His thoughts turned to jelly as body sensations took over. He pulled his hips back, then shoved forward. Her body jerked upwards as she gasped.

Hot muscles grabbed his cock, and he sucked in a tortured breath. "Oh, baby. Oh, shit."

He slammed forward again and his hips started a hard, steady pumping as he drove toward climax.

Some inherent instinct told him they weren't alone.

Luca vaulted out of the dream with a grunt.

Lying on the chaise lounge, he felt the sun pouring down on him, and realized he'd been dreaming about the woman again. The illusive woman he'd wanted all his life but never could seem to find; she tormented his nights at least once a week, calling to his body and driving him mad with desire. His last girlfriend hadn't given him the real satisfaction he wanted. In bed and out, their relationship had lacked a vital force. Sexual compatibility they possessed, but as time went on the fire and passion didn't give him what he needed. He needed real—

Don't go there. You can't do love.

Maria Concita Dominquez took care of that possibility a long time ago and proved to him he couldn't trust his instincts when it came to so-called affairs of the heart.

He sat up and decided he'd better drop into bed. He had work to do later and couldn't afford to fall asleep on the job. He glanced up and saw an eye peeking out at him from a knothole in the wood fence. "What the hell?"

Every muscle went on alert, and he sprang into action as he shot to his feet. His hand went for his weapon on the table next to him.

The eye disappeared. The woman next door. He chuckled and remembered the look on the woman's face as she'd seen him in the driveway yesterday. She'd appeared almost offended as he strolled out to get his paper. His training assured he noticed everything he could about her in those few seconds. She had wavy chili-red shoulder length hair. Small nose, full lips, and pale skin. Evenly-spaced beautiful brown eyes. Eyes covered with glasses that gave her an intellectual appearance. Thinking back over the years, he realized he'd never dated a woman who wore glasses. They either had twenty-twenty vision or wore contacts.

Red hair? He realized his special dream woman looked like his neighbor. Intrigued, he thought about what he could do to meet her other than walking up to her front door and announcing that he'd like to take her out for a test drive. He didn't have sex with women he didn't know, and she'd probably slam the door in his face. Still...

Back off. Not while you're working.

He knew plenty about the redhead because he'd gathered intelligence on the people in the units around him. The background check told him everything about her short of her bra size.

He knew that his neighbor, Isabella Markham, was thirty. She lived with her father in an expensive estate on the outskirts of Denver, and she had an older sister. But, hell, he could think of more interesting ways to discover her bra size than doing a background check.

A crash and a cry of pain, and then curse came to his ears. Worry vaulted through him, and he hurried to the connecting door in the fence. He unlatched the door, opened it, and rushed through.

Isabella's head snapped up, and her mouth opened in surprise. Her neighbor, dressed in an emerald green muscle shirt and black denim shorts, strode toward her across the lawn. She couldn't move, mesmerized by the combination of anger and worry mingling in his rough-hewn features.

She sat on the cold concrete of the patio holding her throbbing side. Hot tears of pain and embarrassment trickled down her face. She realized his image looked blurry because she'd smeared her glasses. Yanking them off her face, she wiped at them furiously with the hem of her tank top, then plopped them back on her nose.

Embarrassment burned her cheeks. He'd caught her looking through the fence at him, and when she'd turned away and headed back to her chair, she'd tripped on the concrete step and slammed right into the table like a total klutz. Oh, God. She didn't peep at men through fences and she didn't cry at the drop of a hat. Had she lost her mind? She stifled the urge to sob. No doubt about it, the guy would think she was nuts.

Then she saw the gun in his hand and everything within her froze. Old fear slid into her like a knife. She stood, and a prickling pain shot through her left side. She gasped. To her relief, he stuffed the gun into the back of his waistband.

Once she straightened, his height dwarfed her. At five feet, six inches she never considered herself small, but this guy must be at least six four and carried two hundred pounds of ripcord muscle. Every inch of him looked coiled and ready to spring.

As she took a deep breath, his clean scent enveloped her. With hints of bergamot and maybe musk, his scent slid into her awareness with gentle persuasion and sensual touches. A mellow aroma that didn't overpower, but teased just the same. Wonderful. Of course, he would have to smell like heaven and sex and sin. Sex? Well, he didn't smell like sex, even if a few minutes ago it had sounded like he was engaged in the hunka chunka at full throttle.

"Easy." His voice sounded rough and dark, the rasping quality sexy and deep. "Are you all right?"

"Yes." Pain rippled through her left side, and she winced. "It's not that bad."

"Then why are you crying?"

Damn. "I'm not."

"Okay, have it your way. What happened?"

"I tripped and hit the table. I'm fine now."

Skepticism lined his features. She'd never seen eyes as black as his, and their intensity pinned her to the spot. His scrutiny held a mysterious heat, a lingering fire she couldn't remember ever seeing before. As if he knew every last one of her secrets.

"You were just holding your side."

"I'm all right." She heard the defensive note in her voice.

Up this close he looked good enough to eat. As she remembered her wild imaginings about him just that morning, she realized the reality of being near him was far better than fantasy.

The man screamed masculinity. Stubble on his jaw gave him a hard, unforgiving edge, and his high cheekbones added sharp punctuation. Wind ruffled the silky, thick waves of hair away from his forehead, and the jagged edge of a scar touched just above his eyebrow. Immediately she wondered what kind of situation he'd encountered to get such a scar in the first place. Heat flooded her stomach, and despite the ache in her side, a strange, breathless excitement made her take a deep breath.

Overall, he looked thoroughly disreputable.

He touched her shoulder. "Let me see your ribs."

Even the light brush of his fingers over her skin sent a weird combination of thrill and panic flaring through her. "What?"

His eyes narrowed. "Your side."

Bristling, she stepped away from him. So the guy hadn't been doing the two-backed beast with a woman. She still didn't like the gun tucked in his waistband.

"Excuse me, but I don't know who you are. Why would I just pull my shirt up for you?"

"You might have bruised or cracked a rib."

She sniffed. "Hardly. It doesn't feel that bad."

"You ever cracked or bruised a rib?"

"No."

"I rest my case." He crossed his arms and his biceps bunched. Bella's gaze snagged on the powerful structure of his arms, then her gaze landed on the determined, firm line of his mouth.

"Why were you running way?" he asked.

Defiant, she straightened. Pain rolled through her side and back. "I wasn't running."

"Yeah. Right." His irreverent grin eliminated the cool expression he'd worn when he'd first appeared. "Look, I'm not some jerk trying to get his jollies." An arrogant grin touched his lips. "I don't need to do that to get female attention. As for pulling your shirt up, I didn't think you'd mind, since you're were peeping through the fence to see what I was doing."

Embarrassment flooded her face with heat. "I'm sorry, but it sounded like you were—"

She shut herself off and floundered around in her mind trying to think of what to say.

He shifted a little closer, his gaze curious. "I was what?"

"You were dreaming. Crying out in your sleep."

Comprehension covered his face, but she didn't see any sign of mortification. "What did I say?"

She couldn't resist giving him a disapproving look. "Oh, shit, I believe, was one of the statements."

His soft, husky laugh drifted on the air. "I was dreaming."

"It didn't sound like it." As soon as the words came out, she wanted to bite her tongue. "I mean, I thought maybe you were having a…"

When she couldn't seem to keep her tongue working, he lifted one eyebrow and said, "Having what?"

"A fight."

Lame. Totally lame. She knew it, and he knew it.

"Uh-huh." His gaze did a sweep over her, and she saw undeniable heat in the depths of those obsidian eyes. "I was dreaming about having sex."

Hot waves of awareness walloped her in the gut. "That's a damn cheeky thing to say to a woman you just met."

He shrugged, and mile wide shoulders rippled. "Sorry, but I tend to call it like I see it."

"A fine excuse for being tactless."

A new fire seemed to ignite in his eyes; this one said he'd had enough. "So now I'm an unfeeling, tactless bastard?"

"I didn't say that."

The big man shrugged and raked her with an assessing gaze that tipped the scales toward insolent. But, oh, that look sent messages straight to her underfed libido. Intense and hot, his eyes said he liked what he saw and maybe wanted to sample. For a crazy moment she almost considered letting down her guard and being friendlier. Then old caution kicked into high gear.

"Look, I don't even know you." She kept an edge in her voice.

He put his hand out. "Luca Angello."

His voice resonated with grit and restraint and hinted at the slightest bit of east coast.

Reluctant to touch him, she inched out her hand to clasp his. "Isabella Markham. Most people call me Bella."

His large hand enveloped hers, and while his grip felt firm, he didn't mash her hand the way so many men often did. As his fingers slid over hers, the slightly callused texture sent a tingle through her palm and straight into her stomach. In her fantasy he'd gripped her butt in those big hands, and now she felt so aware of him she wanted to scream. What on earth was the matter with her?

"Pleased to meet you, Bella. Now you know me. Let me see your injury."

"What are you? A doctor?"

"Paramedic training in the marines."

Ah, the marines. That explained the hard, unflappable tone in his demeanor and voice.

"Trust me." A soft rumble in his voice, coaxing her to conform, felt like a potent drug chipping away her will. "I'm not going to hurt you."

Reluctantly, she lifted her shirt with slow deliberation. She looked down at her side at the same time he did. Five reddening welts, outlining red scratches, peppered her side.

"Would you look at that?" he asked. "You did a number on yourself."

He peered at the damage, his mouth drawn into a hard line. With quick, gentle pressure, he touched an unscathed patch of skin. She gasped as his slightly callused fingers tickled her flesh.

"That hurts, I take it?" He drew back, his gaze demanding answers.

"No."

'Then why did you gasp?"

Because your touch sent a shiver straight down to my gut? Oh, sure. She could say that out loud. No problem.

As if.

"It startled me."

He didn't look like he believed her. He touched again, his hand sliding over the bottom part of her rib cage. "Is the pain sharp and continuous?"

"No. Just a little throbbing."

He nodded, and when he caught her gaze with his, she dropped the shirt back into place. "I don't think there's anything cracked or broken. If the pain gets worse, call me immediately."

She grinned in spite of her irritation, amused around the edges at his take-charge tone. "I don't have your number. Are you always this bossy?"

One corner of that gorgeous mouth twitched upwards. "Yes."

His gaze did a slip and slide from the top of her head down to her sandaled feet, and a simmering slow blaze ignited in her stomach. Attraction plowed over her like a steamroller as her breasts felt warm and full, and a tingle darted through her belly. She didn't like the sensations; it meant she must stay on guard. No man would distract her from her goal of an uneventful vacation.

When she didn't respond to his inspection, he scowled. What did he expect? Did he think she would invite him into her bedroom to join in a live version of the dream he'd been enjoying earlier?

"How long are you going to be in town?" he asked suddenly.

Despite the scowl on his face, his question took her off guard and she spoke without thinking. "A few weeks. I'm on vacation."

He nodded and put his hands on his hips. "Well, try not to ruin your entire time by getting hurt again."

Offended, she decided she'd finish the conversation. "Thanks for the advice. I've got to go."

"Hey, wait."

His hand dropped on her shoulder, and for a split second she almost panicked. She stiffened and he immediately removed his hand.

Turning, she caught the intrigued, intense look on his face. "Yes?"

"Have dinner with me tonight."

His request stifled the cool rebuff she wanted to give him. *The man is gorgeous. Go for it, Bella. What can you lose?*

My life?

"That's rather sudden." She put a few steps more between them. The door wasn't far away, and if he pulled anything, she could rush for the back door.

"When I see a woman I want to get to know, I act on it."

She didn't know whether she liked his directness. She did know she didn't need complications in her life right now. "You're certainly sure of yourself, aren't you?"

He nodded, and that granite-hard face warmed into a grin that gave his features a stunning, knock-you-to-your-knees impact. "I like to cut to the chase."

She put her hand on the doorknob. "Well, Mr. Angello, there is no chase."

"Call me Luca."

She simply smiled and went into the house.

Luca watched her go, then decided he'd better retreat to his condo before she got suspicious and called the police. He knew he'd have to tell her what he did for a living, because if he didn't she'd maintain distance because of fear. And if he admitted the truth to himself, he wanted to get to know her.

Screw consequences. Fuck complications. From his first glance at her the other day, until moments ago when she turned and walked away from him, he felt an inexplicable connection to her. In the three weeks he'd been at his condo, he hadn't seen her outside before. During his investigation, he discovered she'd been at the condo two weeks.

His gut clenched with a hot, undeniable need as he marched back to his condo. Luca knew he walked a thin line. Used to riding a bucking bronco to the end, he decided he would learn more about this woman.

He located his cell phone and put in a call. Less then five minutes later he'd found the man he needed to speak with.

"You want to do what?" Damon Kravis's voice grated harsh and deep across the phone line.

Luca's partner in the police department always sounded like he was grinding gravel when he spoke. His rough, rugby player face went with his voice, too.

Luca stalked around his kitchen feeling restless and a little unnerved. "I need another background check on the woman next door. She fits the profile."

"You sure it isn't your Johnson leading you around by the nose again?"

"Shut up and do it."

"You already know a lot about her. What more do you need to know? Whether she wears a Miracle Bra or what?"

Luca chuckled as he strode into his living room and looked through the window. "Don't worry, I'll find that out for myself later."

The woman in question stood in her driveway by a sleek, new looking BMW. She sprayed the car with water and her clothes looked damp. Oh, yeah. He'd like to help her wash the car all right. If he hurried up, he might get a chance.

"Pretty confident, aren't you?" Damon asked.

"Are you going to do this for me or not?"

"Yeah, yeah, I'll do it. For a price."

"What now?"

"You know that pretty little secretary down in the chief's office?"

Damon's voice sounded way too chipper. Luca knew the man had a plan, and he could guess the target. "Debra Fundett?"

"You got it. She's about the hottest piece of ass I've seen in a long time, and I'd like to get me some."

Not for the first time in his life, Luca felt mild disgust with his friend. At thirty-seven Luca sometimes felt like he boasted more experience and understood women better than his older friend did. Not only that, but Damon tended to fall flat on his face with women. He didn't know how to seduce them into giving him what he wanted. The guy might be a good cop but when it came to finesse, women tended to give him a D for dickhead.

"Hey, take it easy, Cochise." Luca retreated to his kitchen so he would quit staring at his neighbor. "Debra seems like a nice woman. I don't think she's likely to jump your bones any time soon."

"Bull shit."

Luca didn't have time for his friend's crass behavior right at the moment, so Luca hurried him along. "Okay, what am I suppose to do about your love life?"

"She's been asking a butt load of questions about you for days now. Apparently her panties are mighty wet for you, Angello."

Luca chuckled as he went back to the living room, unable to resist another look at Isabella. "You don't know that."

"When you get done with this case you've gotta come back here and show her you're not interested."

"Who says I'm not interested?"

His friend grunted. "You'd better not be. Just because all the women around here think you're a sex machine—"

"Just do the background check, and I'll forget that Debra's panties are wet for me. Okay?"

"Yeah, yeah."

Luca started to hang up, but when he heard Damon's voice again, Luca put the phone back to his ear.

"Just don't get to into this woman, Luca. If you blow this case, the Captain will have your hide."

Luca peered out the window again and saw Bella spraying more water on the luxury car. She bent over and her butt-cupping shorts rode up the back of her thighs. Luca felt his cock twitch.

"You there, Angello?"

"Yeah, I'm here."

"You sure you still want the background check?"

"Yeah. I've got a strange feeling about this woman. If the killer is still in the area, Isabella Markham fits the description of every other woman this prick has murdered. I want details and I want them now. I have a feeling she's in danger."

Chapter Two

Bella heard the steps coming up behind her, and she whirled about, garden hose clutched in her hand.

Water hit Luca Angello right in the head and chest. He grunted in surprise as he ducked away from the stream of water.

With a gasp she brought the stream back to the car. "Oh, God! I'm sorry." Irritation lapped at her heels. "What do you think you're doing sneaking up on me that way?"

Instead of growling at her as she expected, Luca frowned and ran his hand over his dripping face. His hair, damp and tangled, fell around his shoulders. "What do you think you're doing washing your car? You're hurt."

Determined this cocky man wouldn't unnerve her, she gave him a slow smile. She reached to push her glasses up her nose and then realized she'd put in her contacts.

"My side doesn't hurt anymore. Besides, my car needs the wash."

"I'll finish washing it."

"What?"

"You're in no shape to be stretching and bending. Let me finish it up."

Bella, exasperated, ignored the dull throb in her side. "Haven't you got other things to do besides save damsels in distress, Mr. Angello?"

"Call me Luca."

"Luca." The word slipped off her tongue before she could stop herself. "I don't need your help."

When he moved toward her with a slow, deliberate pace that reminded her of a carnivore stalking prey, she almost stepped backwards into her car. Her heart pounded with sudden alarm. He stopped less than a foot from her and slipped the hose out of her hand.

"Wasting water." His velvet and brandy voice rippled over her senses like hot liquid as his gaze searched hers. Definite interest, and maybe a little amusement flashed through his intense gaze.

More water splashed on his muscle shirt, and the material molded to his hard pecs and stomach. His shorts had taken a dose of water, and the clinging denim molded to his package. Man alive, the guy was — she tried pulling her mind back from the gutter, but fell in anyway — *built*. Yes. Built would be a good euphemism for the man's body, no matter what part of him she might talk about. She tried sucking in an entire breath and failed.

He turned off the hose and let it fall to the ground. Then she forgot his hot bod and became angry with herself for ogling him. She couldn't let this guy push her around one more minute.

"Get out of my yard."

Ignoring her request, he grabbed the bucket and sponge and moved toward her car. "I'll do the scrubbing, you do the rinsing."

God, the man's got —

Cheek.

He bent over and started scrubbing, and she got a full view of his world-class butt encased in those sexy black shorts. She gulped. Dragging her gaze away from forbidden territory, she wondered how she'd lost control of the situation so fast.

With a speed that surprised her, and without saying a word, he sponged the entire car. As he worked, Bella decided she'd ease back from her consternation and enjoy the show. The mystery man owned the best ass she'd ever seen, and his entire body held her mesmerized as if she hadn't already seen all of him naked. Well, almost all of him naked.

In the nude, Luca exuded virile power. Clothed, that power multiplied. She imagined many women looked at him this way, and not all of them became lucky enough to have the guy in their front yard.

Lucky? Maybe not.

Her father had called her in the interim between her meeting Luca and the car wash. His words of caution rang in her head. *You ought to come home, Bella. At least here you'll be safe. There are all kinds of predators out there. Dirtballs of every order. Including this murderer that's on the loose.*

She knew what he thought. Little Miss Isabella may have gone to college, become a first rate painter and even sold pieces of her work for quite a sum. Along the way her inspiration had dried up. *Father, that's why I'm on vacation. Renewal and relaxation. It'll give me back my creativity. And to chase away the feeling I'm being watched.*

He'd sputtered and argued until for the first time in her life she'd hung up on him. She'd flipped on the answering machine.

"Beamer 500 series. Very nice," Luca said, breaking into her thoughts.

What could she say to that? "I got it last year."

She half expected him to quiz her on her job. How could she afford such a nice car? Instead he said, "First rinse."

Following his command, she turned on the hose and let the water spray over the gleaming and now clean blue surface. "Surely you've got better things to do than help me wash the car."

"Nope." He grinned as he started a second rub down on the car. "I'm a very tactile guy. I like getting my hands on things. "

Pure heat ran through her stomach. "What kinds of things?"

He turned around, still holding the dripping sponge. While his clothes had started to dry, they clung in damp spots to his torso. His gaze caressed her without remorse. "Smooth, silky surfaces are the best."

Primal urges rose out of nowhere and slapped her in the face. She felt a hot tickle deep in her belly and knew exactly what the sensation meant. For once she resisted the urge to back off. If the guy thought he could intimidate her by sexual innuendo, she would fry his cookies. She snatched up the hose, turned the water back on, and aimed a spurt of water right toward him.

He darted out of the way, a wicked grin on his lips. "Stop or there will be consequences for your actions."

"I think you're flirting with me, *Mr.* Angello. And that can get you in a lot of trouble."

He waggled his eyebrows. "What? You've got a boyfriend who's going to beat me up?"

Beat up Luca? None of her former boyfriends would have stood a chance against this man. Rippling muscles moved in his arms, and his height alone commanded obedience.

A bold premise came to mind. "Who says I couldn't beat you up?"

Before she could blink, Luca snatched the hose from her and water went everywhere as their fingers battled for the device. He won, and one direct blast of water caught her right in the chest. Water splattered up around her face, and suddenly she was glad she'd worn her contacts. She let out a squeal of protest, then laughed. Luca let the water nozzle close again and the freezing water stopped. He stepped forward, and she bumped against the car.

Bella sucked in a gasp. They stood with a hair's breath between them. His gaze took on an assessing quality that combusted into slow-burning fire. His attention riveted on the front of her tank top, and she realized the water soaked clear through her sports bra. Under his scrutiny, her breasts tingled, her nipples tightening into points.

Luca smelled like sunscreen, soap, and that delicious musk scent she'd smelled on him earlier. Her gaze snagged on the black chest hair that showed above the collar of his muscle shirt.

She knew that same hair curled in a provocative arrow down over his six-pack stomach.

He dropped the hose and his hands came down on the BMW, caging her between his arms. Little tingles of forbidden fear darted up and down her spine. Apprehension battled with curious excitement. Warmth seeped into the sensitive area between her legs, and to her surprise a sweet tickle of arousal made her clit throb.

She was afraid of him, yet at the same time he aroused her like no other man she'd met. All he had to do was look in her direction, and she felt like lying down, spreading her legs, and begging him to thrust into her.

"You shouldn't have let me get this close to you." Husky and rough, his voice grated against her nerves like a touch over her body.

At his warning, her trepidation took on a new edge. She stiffened. "Why?"

Because he's dangerous. Sudden comprehension made her realize she'd been stupid. He wouldn't try and hurt her out in full view like this, would he?

His gaze, dark as midnight and just as potent, seemed to be sending her a message.

Oh-oh. He's on search and destroy mode. Man the battle stations.

"You heard about the serial killer that may be in the area?" he asked.

Her heart rate accelerated, and her breathing quickened. "Yes."

"Don't you know it's not safe to vacation in this town?" His voice turned impatient, hard-edged with disbelief. "That's not exactly a smart thing to do."

Irritation made Bella straighten her spine, even though it meant standing even closer to him. "Don't insult my intelligence, Mr. Angello. I paid for this condo in advance before the murders started. I'd lose my money if I left now."

"And you're willing to risk you life over losing some money?"

It's either that or risk my life and sanity back home.

When she didn't answer, he asked, "And you let a man you don't know get this close to you?"

His voice held accusation, and the lecturing tone annoyed her. A superior-acting male made her angrier faster than almost anything else.

"Are you dangerous?" she asked.

He grinned, and those white, even teeth gave his smile a blinding brilliance. She didn't know whether to be terrified, or angry at the game he played. "Depends on the situation."

Slowly and surely, his hands reached up and cupped her upper arms. His grip felt gentle, as if he worried about hurting or frightening her.

On her guard, she didn't relax. "Are you trying to tell me that I'm in trouble here?"

"You should never let a man you don't know get this near, especially in a situation where no one could help you if he's got evil on his mind. Do you understand?"

"I'm not a child. Don't insult me."

Luca's warm, callused fingers slid up and touched her shoulders. "I'm not insulting you; I'm making you think about safety."

"Why should you care?" Right that moment it seemed all-important to know. "You just met me."

"Because you're a woman, and I—"

"Women can't take care of themselves?"

A forewarning flickered through his eyes. "Don't put words in my mouth."

"Then why? Have you warned every woman who lives on this block?"

An exasperated sound left Luca's throat. "Of course not. The news posted a warning for all females to be on their guard."

"So what makes me different?" She liked giving him something to think about. Two could play this game. "I'm just one woman."

His lips hardened, and his next words came out gritty. "Because you're a stubborn woman who apparently needs some sense drilled into her head."

"How can you know that about me?"

His lips pressed together as if he fought to keep from saying something he shouldn't. "I'm an excellent judge of character. Just heed my words."

"Wouldn't that be as foolish as allowing a man to get too close to me physically?"

His eyes filled with frustration. "Damn, but you ask a lot of questions."

"And that irritates you."

His eyes flashed fire. Luca made a primitive sound men had uttered since they emerged from the cave, and he moved closer.

Oops. Pushed him too far.

His hands went back to the car, and this time she pressed up against the vehicle. His solid body touched hers from chest to knees with enough pressure for Bella to feel unrelenting muscles, hot and hard with tension.

Excitement zinged through her like a lightning bolt. She was bonkers. She'd never bantered with a man like this before, sparring like opponents with clashing swords. What the hell had gotten into her?

Accelerating exhilaration swirled in Bella's stomach and, God help her, she felt more heat and moisture gather between her legs. She couldn't remember the last time a conversation with a man had been so stimulating. The man's insistent, probing gaze demanded compliance. Up this close, she could see the thick lashes framing his fascinating eyes.

Oh, God. He's sexy. Luca owned the most beautiful eyes she could remember seeing on a man. His masculinity, exasperating attitude—it all made her want to grab him and kiss him until they both went thermonuclear.

Isabella, have you lost your freaking mind?

His jaw clenched and unclenched, and for a few seconds, maybe, the danger seemed to be over. "I'm doing this for a couple of reasons. First, you probably fit the profile of the women who've been killed in this area. Three other women have been murdered in this neighborhood in three months. Once a month on the nineteenth. All of them were vacationers using time-share houses or condos. Second, I care what happens to you because you're a smart-mouthed, intelligent woman and I like you."

She sucked in a surprised breath. "But—"

He placed his index finger against her lips. "I'm not finished." When she nodded, he took his finger away. "Third, you can trust me because I'm a cop."

"Cop?" Surprise almost made her voice squeak.

"Yeah."

She couldn't think of a witty comeback for this new development. "How do I know you're telling me the truth?" She allowed her gaze to drift down over his chest. "Where are you hiding your badge?"

A deep chuckle rumbled up from his wide chest, and her knees about buckled as his frown transformed to a heart-stopping, devouring grin. "I can show you, sweetheart, but not out in public."

Her face flamed, and she inhaled deeply to get oxygen. "Now who's being the smart mouth?"

He shrugged. He hadn't backed away an inch, and the insistent brush of his body against hers sent surges of desire through her. She swallowed hard.

When he didn't speak, Bella said, "So you've proved a point. If you were the serial killer, I might be in deep kimchee right about now."

"You got it."

"Is that the last reason you're telling me all this?"

"No. There's another reason, but if I tell you, you might slap my face."

"Try me."

"Uh-uh. The way we're standing I'm too vulnerable."

"What?"

His eyes twinkled. "You could ram my balls clear up into my throat."

By George, he was right. "Why on earth would you remind me that I've got that advantage?"

"Maybe you'll remember it if you ever get in this position with a man that you're not attracted to and you don't trust."

Mortification flamed in her face. Luca *knew* that she found him eye-catching. And in a weird way she did trust him. Totally. Still, she couldn't afford to admit the facts. "I'm not attracted to you, and I don't trust you."

"Okay, maybe you don't trust me. But you and I both know that you're attracted to me."

Stung that he could see right through her, and tired of playing games, Bella put her hands on his chest to push him away. When her palms encountered muscle, her fingers tingled and a deep, sensual tug filled her stomach. She knew she couldn't budge him, and her hands stilled.

"Officer, you don't have any evidence I'm attracted to you." She heard the sarcasm in her voice, and it startled her. She'd never been this wise-ass with a peace officer. "That is if you really *are* a cop."

His gaze went from slightly amused to hungry. "The hell, you say." His gaze dropped to her chest, and she felt her breasts ache again. "Case in point. Your nipples are hard and tight."

Arousal darted straight between her legs again. Moisture trickled. She inhaled deeply, trying to gain control. "Oh, come on. You spray my breasts with cold water then try to use that as proof I'm aroused? You'll have to do better than that."

His mouth curled into a one sided smile, and she knew he'd take up the dare. His attention landed on her mouth. "Right now, if I touched your breast and pinched your nipple between my thumb and finger…if I tugged on it really softly and gently…" His gaze dropped to her mouth again and stayed there. "You'd love it."

Infuriated, she felt heat rise in her face. "That's crap. Men always think they can grab a woman's breasts the moment they see her, and she'll become incoherent with desire."

His gaze burned hotter, if that was even possible. "I could make you incoherent."

She made an unladylike snort. "You are a…a—"

"Say it if it'll make you feel better." Her fingers clenched and her nails scraped over his skin. He sucked in a breath. "Whoa." He placed his big hands over her long, small fingers and pressed gently in a caress. "Easy. Just say what's on your mind."

"Fine," she whispered harshly. "You're a creep."

"Because I'm telling the truth?"

"You're a…" she sputtered. "A…"

"Yeah?"

She clamped her lips closed, frustrated to the point of screaming.

He continued in that hard-edged voice. "I'll tell you another truth. The way I feel right now, I could suck on your nipples until I made you come."

Shock held her speechless. His audacity made her want to do more than slap him and introduce his balls to her knees. For the first time in her life, Bella wanted to drag a man straight to her room and—

Fuck him blind.

Heat bloomed in her face again as she realized the intensity of what she felt.

Forceful lust rushed over her entire body. She'd lost control of the situation and hated it. At the same time the exhilaration of this dance made her want to continue. How far could she push him before the man lost it entirely? She ached with fierce need. She wanted his kiss with everything inside her.

"How arrogant," she managed to croak through her dry lips.

"Not arrogance. Fact."

Prove it to me.

"God, you really do have a tremendous ego." Disdainful, her voice should have brought him down a peg. "Is that how you get off? Intimidating women? The big bad cop with the authority to back it up?"

He laughed softly, but there was no amusement in the sound. "No. But if you want to, I can show you how I get off."

Oh, boy. She'd done it now. She could see the animal rising up in Luca like the clouds gathering over their heads. A cool breeze brushed over her heated skin, but it did nothing to quench the rising need within her. She should tell him to go screw himself, but she didn't want him to leave. She wanted…she wanted…

What?

"Push me away, honey." His whisper teased her ears. "Or I'm going to kiss you right here in full view of the neighborhood."

His statement, without any cream and sugar to cloak his intentions, set her blood sluicing through her veins like wildfire. Her fingers twitched, involuntarily caressing him.

With a husky groan, he moved in for the kill.

Chapter Three

As if weights pulled them down, Bella's eyelids fluttered closed. Luca's mouth captured hers, tenderly plying and searching. His kiss scattered her mind in twenty foggy directions until she felt dizzy.

He's so gentle.

Raw power resonated from Luca, palpable and without doubt. As his tentative exploration moved over her lips, she slid her hands up to his hair. Tangling her fingers in the silky strands, she edged nearer. His arms didn't come around her, but a primal, masculine groan left his throat, and he deepened the kiss.

Bella, dazed with pleasure, realized that her arms laced around his neck. Finally Luca's arms molded her against his ripcord body with gentleness, as if he worried about hurting her. Tension coiled in his muscles, and she knew instinctively he wanted her nearer. To accommodate him, she shifted and snuggled closer. With a fierceness that surprised her, she wanted his tongue in her mouth. She ached for it. Was dying for it.

As if he could read her mind, he gave her what she needed.

His tongue swept over her lips, asking permission and with a surge he dipped inside. She gasped into his mouth, and his exploration went deeper. With stabbing strokes his tongue rubbed over hers. The sexual rhythm caught her up, and a hard, relentless pulsing beat between her legs. Overwhelmed by a pounding ache of sexual excitement, she returned the sensual friction, moving her tongue against his. Ravenous and knocked over by the ferocity of her desire, she clutched and strained against him.

His palms swept over her back in a continuous searching, molding and caressing manner until she thought she might go crazy. Luca arched his hips against hers in the smallest increment.

Oh.

Long, thick, and stone-hard, his penis pressed against her.

Reality grabbed her by the throat. She was outside in the plain light of day, undulating against this stranger like a wild woman.

Panicked, Bella yanked out of his arms and pushed against his chest. She fell back against the car. Putting her fingers against her swollen lips, she stared at Luca.

A flush reddened his high cheekbones. His eyes possessed a hooded quality that made him seem dangerous beyond words, and his chest rose and fell in deep exhalations. His hands clenched into fists at his side, and he tightened and released them as if trying to hold back. As if he almost couldn't keep his hands off her. New fear arose inside Bella, threatening to grow out of all proportion.

"Please," she whispered without knowing why.

"Did I hurt you?"

Shaking her head, she took her hand from her mouth. "No. No."

He took two steps back. After a deep breath, the raging tension seemed to slide from his body. His gaze went from ravenousness to hard. Other than the heightened color in his face, he no longer seemed affected by what they'd done.

She, on the other hand, couldn't ignore the throbbing in her belly and the heat rising continuously in her face. Unbidden emotions rose, threatening a cloudburst. The man made her so crazy she couldn't think coherently from one moment to the next, and this made her furious.

"How are your ribs?" he asked softly. "Did I hold you too tightly?"

His obvious concern wiped away all irritation. "I'm fine. They don't hurt."

Relief flooded his face. "Good. On another topic, please believe what I said, Bella. You're not safe in this neighborhood. Don't talk to strange men."

"I talked to you, didn't I? What makes you so different?"

He jammed his fingers through his hair. "I'm not a serial killer." Worry flickered in and out of his expression so fast, she thought she might have imagined that grim expression. "Look, I'll bring over my badge and my phone number later."

Before she could say another word, he walked back toward his condo.

* * * * *

Luca rummaged through the dresser where he'd pitched his badge and identification. For the first time since he started on the force ten years ago, he felt out of his element.

All because of a woman.

"Damn," he whispered harshly.

His erection refused to go away. Hard as a spike and screaming with need for release, his body protested that he'd walked away from Bella without slipping deep into her heat. She'd been hot all right. The way she'd moved in his arms, her soft moans of pleasure echoing from her throat said it all.

Oh, yeah. She'd almost been willing to let him fuck her right there and then in front of God and country without so much as a by-your-leave.

Bella's Little Miss Righteous act might be just that. An act. A protection device used to keep men away. When she'd ripped out of his arms though, he thought for one terrifying moment that he'd gone too far and held her too tightly.

Despite the overblown reputation he had around the department, he didn't screw any woman who would lift her skirt for him. But with the way he'd acted with Isabella Markham a few minutes ago, he almost believed his own publicity.

Luca caught a glance of himself in the mirror above the dresser. His face was flushed, his hair tangled and his scar itched. Oddly enough, it always seemed to itch when he was stressed. He'd never thought of kissing a woman as nerve-racking, but Bella messed with his mind.

Closing his eyes, he remembered how great Bella's touch felt against his scalp and his body. A vision of her parted lips surrounding his cock made him grimace. Maybe a cold shower would remove the sexual daze he felt surrounding him like a cloud ready to burst.

After the water pounded on his head with a furious beat, he groaned and reached for the soap. As he lathered, his hand brushed over his cock, and the thought of Bella surrounding him in her wet heat hardened him again. What would it feel like to push his way through her tight folds until he could go no farther? Would she be hot, wet, and wild for him? As his cock filled with blood and hardened again, he gripped it and gave two strokes. Yeah, he could jerk off right now and relieve the pressure, but he resisted the idea.

No, when he climaxed, he wanted to be inside Bella, watching her come apart in his arms.

* * * * *

Bella thought she could finish drying the car before Luca appeared again. No such luck. He strode out of his house a few minutes later, his expression reserved. She'd never guess in a million years this was the man who had kissed her into the next century and set her blood on fire.

Nope. Cool as fresh watermelon, his gaze said he was all business. His wet hair and change of clothes told her he'd taken a shower. He wore a plain navy blue T-shirt and a pair of jeans. The snug fit of his T-shirt showed his wide shoulders to perfection. His almost new looking jeans skimmed his lower body affectionately, but without a tight fit. If Bella thought his ravenous kiss and brazen attitude would turn her off, she'd discovered that she couldn't be more wrong. Her body still throbbed and tingled in places she didn't want to think about, and she knew if she looked in a mirror right now her lips would be red and a bit swollen. She sucked in a breath as he arrived in front of her.

He held a black wallet out to her. "My identification."

Bella took the leather wallet reluctantly. Flipping it open, she saw it held the usual ID, including a driver's license that declared his name to be Luca Thomas Angello. Next to that she found an ID card proving he was a detective with the Piper's Grove Police Department. After skimming over the badge attached to the inside of the wallet, she also glanced at his vital statistics. Thirty-seven years old, six feet four inches tall, and two hundred pounds. Black hair, black eyes, and the sexiest aura on the planet.

Uh-huh. As if it said that on his ID.

"Do I pass muster?" he asked.

She frowned as she passed the wallet back to him. "Great. So you're a cop."

"Now you know you can trust me."

She crossed her arms and shook her head. "I think we'd better keep our distance. If you'll excuse me, I have things to do."

With an indulgent smile, he reached into his wallet and pulled out a business card. "Here. My cell number is at the bottom. "

Bella knew she had to make a fast escape or this man would take hold of her senses once again. Before she could move a foot, his hand clasped her upper arm gently.

"One more thing. I wasn't kidding when I said you fit the victim profile for this serial killer. If you see or hear anything suspicious, or if you're ever frightened, call me on the cell phone. It's on all the time."

She nodded, but said nothing. After she rewound the garden hose, she gathered up the washing items and carried them into the small utility room in the condo. Her entire body seemed to be trembling. Disgusted with her lack of control, Bella decided she would do something to get her mind off the exasperating man. Stomping into the kitchen, she fished inside the refrigerator for a glass of iced tea. She pressed the ice cold glass against her face and tried to regulate the pounding of her heart. What on earth had happened in the last few hours?

Had she ever experienced quite this much fire and fury with one man? She thought about it, staring into nothingness as she sipped her tea. As if his presence alone wasn't enough to drive her nuts, his declaration that she might become serial killer fodder made her insides tremble with sudden fear. She'd left Denver to avoid danger, and somehow it found her anyway. Part of her longed to tell him what happened to her in Denver, the other part of her said she didn't have concrete proof of anything.

No, better to keep quiet about the reason she'd left her father's estate.

Involuntarily she glanced through her kitchen window. She rushed over to the window and drew the cellular shade down, then leaned against the counter while her stomach rolled. Wanting to control the fear, she closed her eyes and thought instead of the weird combination of fear and safety she felt when Luca was nearby. Mad at herself for giving into fear, she lifted the shade again, determined no serial killer would cause her to hole up and hide. She glanced at Luca's kitchen window again.

Bella almost expected to see Luca standing in his kitchen, buck-naked again.

Rolling heat filled her face. She *must* do something to take her mind off the last few hours. She scanned the house, aware for the first time that the rental didn't say *comfort* so much as it said *mediocre*. Modern paintings on the walls and the chrome and glass furniture screamed impersonal. Her room at her father's estate had every luxury a woman could ask for — whirlpool tub, huge mirrors, large walk-in closet. You name it, she owned it.

Even there, though, she'd felt detached and as if she didn't belong anywhere.

Tears prickled her eyes, and she blinked. Bella felt adrift and uncomfortable with the raging desire and confusion rising inside her. She slumped on the couch and stared at the white walls, the entertainment center with the huge television, the tile floor and the elegant throw rugs. The place didn't speak to her, nor did the silence.

She needed something to release the real Isabella Markham.

But what?

That's why I came here. To seek and find the answers. What do I want to do with the rest of my life? How can I resolve the feeling that something horrible hovers just outside my knowledge, waiting to pounce?

"You will find the answers here." She grinned, pleased with the self-affirmation.

She set up her essential oil burner in the living room and inhaled the pleasing, relaxing scents of rose and lavender. She wandered the house, trying to work out the kinks that settled into every muscle. Several times she imagined Luca's big fingers massaging the sinews of her shoulders. Large hands held and cradled her again. She realized that she'd defeated the purpose of retreating from his proximity.

Shoving aside thoughts of his hands and body, she did a series of yoga poses designed to reduce stress. When that wouldn't work, she growled in frustration. Then she started thinking about Luca's insistence that she be cautious. If she did fit the profile of the serial killer's victims, then—

Don't go there.

Too late. Renewed fear crawled up her back an inch at a time. An overwhelming craving to call Luca and throw herself into his arms for protection almost made her reach for the phone. She resisted and gritted her teeth. She wouldn't buckle to cowardice.

Rain spattered against the windowpanes as leaves blew against the windows. The eerie howl made her shiver. She glanced around the room, uncertain of what she expected to see. Her breath quickened, and her heartbeat increased as she wondered about the safety of this condominium. Urged by her usual sense of caution, she made certain the doors and windows remained locked. If it got too hot she could use the air conditioner.

She rummaged through the tote bag of books she'd brought and selected a suspense novel. Reading a scary novel seemed foolhardy considering the trepidation running in her blood, but she decided reading about someone else's peril would make her life seem less harrowing.

Snuggling into a comfortable chair, she indulged in her favorite author's latest paperback. She loved the way the writer combined love and romance with spine-tingling thrills. The heroine stayed strong throughout the novel, though she possessed vulnerabilities only the hero could discover.

I could be this woman.

Then again, maybe not. This heroine possessed a willpower that kept her out of the hero's arms for weeks, and the tension built to a crescendo as the hero seduced her body and soul. No, the hero didn't subjugate her to his will; she let him know where she stood. Then she fell in love with the man. The author left readers dancing on the end of a tether, waiting for a love scene that assured an explosive conclusion.

Bella didn't have a hero she could rely on to assist when life danced a two-step on her head. Fantasies of throwing away all caution and getting down and dirty with the cop next door were crazy imaginings that had no basis in reality.

"That's why they're called fantasies," she said.

After reading several chapters, a long-lost sensation rolled over her. Something she hadn't felt in eons. She closed her eyes and pictured Luca again, naked in the kitchen—her kitchen this time. She imagined him standing with his hand wrapped around his own penis, holding it out to her like a prize. Closing her eyes, she envisioned a penis big enough to make her beg for a finishing climax. Somehow she knew he'd be a skillful lover, a knock-you-to-your-knees experience that would do wonders for her ego and make her forget the fear she'd left in Denver.

Just once she'd like to try a big penis on for size.

Apprehension she *thought* she'd left in Denver slowly surfaced in her mind. She drifted into half-sleep, her thoughts forming disjointed scenes as she remembered waking up a month ago with a shadowy form standing at her open door. When she'd jerked fully awake, ready to scream, the figure was gone. She would have thought it her overactive imagination, if it hadn't happened twice a week for a month.

Bella eased into a nap, the silence lulling her into a dreamless sleep. With gradual awareness, she slipped from her comfortable doze to feel something indefinable and dark nearby, watching and waiting.

Terror filled her heart. A gasp stuck in her throat and her heart pounded and she hoped against hope she'd see nothing unusual. Her heart felt ready to burst, and she begged the creeping horror to go away. Nothing in the room moved, yet a presence blanketed the area.

As she opened her eyes to half-staff, her mind saw a dark figure. With a gasp, she sat up straight in her chair, eyes wide and breathing heavy.

"No!" Bella held up one and as if to ward off an attack. "No!"

Fear tried to grip her again, but a quick glance around the room proved the figure had disappeared. *Only a dream. Only a dream.* Bella knew she needed something to leave these shadowy thoughts behind.

With urgency she walked into the sparsely furnished den. Her easel and paints sat at the ready. If she started now, let her imagination take free flow, she might relieve this tension inside her once and for all.

Minutes later, cloaked in a protective smock, she set about her work. Revitalized by the new excitement to create, she allowed her imagination to take over. For several minutes, light strokes along the canvas slowly formed the beginning of a man's features. With a foreboding that said this picture might turn into something dark and unwanted, she pressed onward. Who cared? She could destroy this canvas later if it suited her.

Instead her fingers moved faster, her heart picking up the pace, her breath rising. She felt new exhilaration in every sinew of her body as the man's face became recognizable. Midnight hair with those strange white streaks near the temples, black eyes, and a sculptured face made of angles and harshness. His mouth held firm, just as the last moment she'd seen him, a determination and strength stamped in every line that made him heartbreakingly handsome. She couldn't resist this man, and she wanted his attention with everything inside her.

Bella looked at the canvas in dismay and shock.

She hadn't created anything this wild, this fast, this *intensely* in months. She didn't need to worry about throwing this painting away. When she finished it she would be able to sell it.

But did she want to? Anyone gazing upon this rendering of Luca Angello would know how she felt about him. Her soul seemed naked on this canvas, exposed for the world to ridicule and remark upon.

So what's new? As an artist she'd experienced a healthy dose of criticism before. Any time an artist put paint to canvas they took the risk someone might not like what they see.

Could an urge to protect herself be the reason her painting had gone to hell in a hand basket lately? Had she tried to shield her feelings rather than paint what she honestly felt?

As she gazed into Luca's eyes, staring at her from the canvas, she saw the message revealed. He wanted her. He needed her.

Lust.

Passion.

Only for her.

* * * * *

A soft noise woke Bella.

At first, when her eyes popped open, she couldn't be certain what disrupted her hard, dead sleep. She remained completely still, listening. After a minute, with nothing more than the wind reaching her ears, she let her eyes flutter closed once again.

A bang near the front of the condo sent her straight up in bed. Her heart accelerated immediately, and she took a deep breath to maintain calm. *That* noise was not a part of a nightmare.

Thoughts of the serial killer came to mind, and with a lurch she grabbed her glasses and plopped them on her face. She reached for the phone and dialed Luca's cell phone number. It was a good thing she'd bothered to memorize the number, because she was too rattled to look for the business card. She didn't hesitate or wonder if she'd be making a fool of herself. Fear had taken that worry out of her hands.

"Angello." Luca's voice sounded hard and awake, even though her clock said three in the morning.

"Luca, this is Bella Markham."

"What's wrong?" His immediate, rough tone jerked her to full awareness.

"I'm not sure anything is wrong. I've been hearing noises." Her voice softened as she realized an intruder would be able to hear. "Something woke me up, and now there's a loud banging near the front of the condo."

"Get out of the house." His clipped tone sounded worried and angry. "You got a sliding glass door in the bedroom?"

She wondered for a moment how he knew, then remembered he had the same house layout. "Yes."

"Get out of the house through the bedroom and wait for me in the yard—"

"But—"

"Just do it."

He hung up. Gathering her tattered courage and forgetting his bossiness, she slipped on shorts and a sports bra. If she planned on tackling with a criminal, she didn't want to do it in a nightshirt. Her mouth felt dry and her heart thumped a frantic pace.

She slid open the sliding glass door, hoping it didn't make too much noise. Well-oiled tracks allowed the door to glide smoothly, and she let out a breath.

The almost full moon rose high, sending a silver glow over the lawn. Diamond sparkling stars were painted across the inky velvet sky. A stiff breeze sent her hair fluttering. She tiptoed into the backyard and neared the side fence line between the properties. She reached for the latch on the connecting doorway—

The door sprung open, and she let out a startled cry.

A hand came through the opening and latched onto her arm just as a big body filled the gap. "Bella."

Luca's husky voice filled her with instant relief. His big biceps flexed under her fingers as she clutched at his arms. His arms slipped around her waist, and he hugged her close for one warm moment. Power and security surrounded her. As he eased her away, she saw a glimpse of the hard line of his jaw and the implacable set of his mouth.

He pulled her into his yard, then stepped onto her property. "I left my sliding door open. Go inside and lock the door. I'll check out your place."

"Wait, you can't go over there."

"Why?"

"It's too dangerous."

"I'm a police officer. It's my job. Just stay here."

He slipped through the gate and closed it.

Bella hesitated, mortified at the insult she'd given him and what he might think of her begging him not to go. Of course he could handle the situation. As a cop he could take care of anything that came his way.

Bella retreated to the sliding door to his bedroom and once inside, she locked it. She turned and noted the rumpled state of his king-sized bed, and sank onto the white sheets.

Apprehension tightened her muscles until every fiber seemed to ache. Minutes passed with agonizing slowness, and as worry began to occupy her thoughts, Bella knew she needed to do something to settle her nerves. She started with deep breaths.

Warm musk cologne or after shave teased her nose. As she placed her hand on his pillow, she imagined heat from his body still clinging to the surface. A strange thrill, part lust and part curiosity, filled her thoughts. She closed her eyes and let an image cross her mind.

Luca's hot, naked, muscular body sprawled in glorious abandon on the bed, legs parted to display his penis. His arms beckoning her to come to him, sit astride, and insert the incredible evidence of his arousal deep into her body. Her thighs twitched. She clenched intimate muscles, an exercise she had designed in the past to distract her from dark thoughts. She could almost feel every wonderful inch of him stretching deep inside her, gliding, thrusting, hammering deep into her with slick precision.

The sliding door opened. She started and gasped. She hadn't heard the key turn in the lock.

Luca entered the room, his face grim and his weapon in hand. His gaze tangled with hers. She blushed to the roots of her hair, as if he could read her mind and knew the forbidden fantasy she'd created. More self-conscious than she'd been in a long time, she stood.

"No one there," he said as he put his weapon down on the dresser.

She closed her eyes and sighed. "I overreacted. I'm sorry."

When she opened her eyes, his expression held more understanding than she would have expected. "I'm glad you called. You're in a tenuous situation, and it's better if you play it safe."

She placed her hand on the sliding door, ready to leave. "Thanks again."

He cocked his head to the side. "Where do you think you're going?"

"Back to my place."

He shook his head and crossed his arms. "I don't think so. You're staying the night."

Indignation wiped away her thankfulness. "I will not."

He advanced on her, his gaze diamond hard and determined. "You will if I have to cuff you to the bed."

Anger escalated in her mind, and she took a step toward him. She was tired of his intimidation tactics. "What are you trying to do, Detective Angello? Harass me?"

He stopped his advancement on her, and she inhaled deeply to try and slow her heart.

"What?"

"Sexual harassment. You know, it's pressure for sexual favors—"

"I know what the hell it is. I'm not sexually harassing you, Bella." He entered her personal space, and this time she held her ground. "Make no mistake, Bella, you're a very attractive woman. Hell, attractive doesn't even begin to describe how hot you are. But I don't have to harass women to get what I want." His voice dropped to the deadly, husky tone she'd heard him use more than once. Luca's gaze held inferno heat. "When a woman comes to my bed it's because she wants to have sex with me, not because she's been coerced into doing something against her will."

His gaze coasted down to her sports bra, and she realized her nipples made a clear, aroused outline against the fabric. She felt her breasts swell under his attention.

"Keep pushing my buttons, baby, and you'll find out how persuasive I can be."

Angered by his assumption, she made a scoffing noise. "I wouldn't sleep with you if you were the last man in town."

With a sweeping look that devoured her breasts, Luca stared at those tight, puckered tips clothed in white cotton. His gaze darted back to her face. "Oh, yes, you would."

Her blood pressure felt like it might skyrocket. In defiance she crossed her arms over her breasts. "Get a life, Detective. You aren't as sexy as you think you are."

He stepped forward, a grin forming at the edge of his lips. She could smell the heat of his body, warm, masculine and unbelievably affecting. The muscles in her belly tightened.

"So you think I'm sexy?" he asked huskily.

"Huh."

"That isn't an answer."

"It's all you're going to get."

He shrugged. "Well, at least I know you're lying about one thing, Bella."

"Oh?"

"You do care about me, at least a little."

"Now I know you've lost a few brain cells."

He chuckled. "You didn't want me to go over to the condo. Why do you suppose that is?"

A slow burn heated her face again. *Damn him to hell.* "Normal human caring."

"Uh-huh." He sounded doubtful. Luca's lips parted, then he pinned her eyes with another intent gaze. "I think you were worried about me."

Before she could say another word, he led her to the guest bedroom and supplied her with fresh towels. "Sleep tight."

He closed the door with a thud, and she stared at the white wood with incredulity.

Chapter Four

Bella woke up in the morning and Luca Angello popped into her thoughts the first minute she peeled open one eyelid. She groaned against the intrusion of morning.

She left the room and found a note on the coffee table saying he'd been called to the station. He'd left her condo key along with the note. Relieved, she left his condo.

As she stepped through the back door, she looked for signs that anyone could be around. She heard nothing, and realized she'd allowed her fears to dominate, just the way she'd allowed the detective to rattle her cage last night.

She had to stop fantasizing about him. Watching a naked man through a window didn't mean she wanted to sleep with him in reality. Yesterday morning she'd allowed those fantasies, but now she'd met Luca, she couldn't allow him to take this much control of her thoughts.

Bella left the house and picked up a paper at a nearby gas station. She found a mom and pop diner that served breakfast and indulged in a hearty meal. She hadn't munched down on bacon, eggs, and hash browns in an eternity, and her taste buds enjoyed every minute of it.

She looked at the front headlines and the fork stopped halfway to her mouth.

Killer Claims Another Victim.

Her gaze dropped to another smaller story below the main feature. The headline screamed *Neighborhoods Lock and Load Against Killer.*

Bella read the first article with a sick sense of fascination, and with each word a chill stepped up her spine one vertebra at a time. While the story seemed sensationalized, she couldn't stop reading.

Residents of the Sun Hill Heights area were stunned this morning to learn that twenty-seven year old Diana Marie Geller of 24 Montebellow Place, was found strangled and beaten to death in her apartment. Her roommate, Jennelle Swergenbaugh, discovered the nude body when she came in from a few days out of town. The last time Miss Geller was seen alive was when she left her job at about eleven o'clock last evening. Miss Geller's car was also vandalized and graffiti with the serial killer's distinctive message, was sprayed on the car. Based on evidence, it is suggested that this murder is indeed the work of the serial killer.

Sarah was part owner of the elegant downtown Italian restaurant, Capricio's.

Bella stopped reading the article and skimmed down to the second article on the murder. According to the second article, some residents of Sun Hill planned to take extreme security precautions. In fact, some young women had moved from the area temporarily until authorities caught the killer. Many women purchased guns and installed security systems.

She didn't have either.

The thought of running away flitted through her mind. She glanced up at the sparsely populated restaurant and took in the appearance of the men in the grouping. An old man slurped his coffee two booths away. A man with the grimy nails and hard look of a laborer dug into his breakfast with gusto. Along one wall of tables a handsome man in a three-piece suit read the same paper that she did.

He doesn't have to worry. The idea whispered through her mind, slipping inside like a dark proposal in her ear. Suspicion made her twitchy, and she decided that she needed to do something else to take her mind off the murders. After paying her bill, she left the restaurant in search of diversion.

As Bella drove down her street toward the mall and a serious bout of shopping, she realized clouds had built in the late morning sky. Great. Rain to screw with the wash she'd given the car yesterday. She groaned. *The Car Wash.* That's the way she'd always think of the event from this day forward.

What if his over protectiveness was just an act to get her into bed? Humiliation burned her face as doubts ran rampant in her mind. The last two men she'd dated had plotted, planned, and attempted seduction like mountain lions on the prowl. Her instincts told her all she needed to know about these guys. They wanted her in the sack and then wanted her money, and not necessarily in that order.

Face it. All men seem more interested once they realize you're richer than God.

Well, maybe not *that* rich. But she never had to worry about working as long as she lived, and she could always afford the best. At the same time, how could she alleviate the gnawing knowledge that she could never know if a man could love her for herself? Some men didn't know when to quit, and Luca fell into the relentless category. She'd do well to stay away from him.

She'd driven about a mile when she realized a black sedan with smoky windows crawled up her tailpipe with inches to spare. Any closer and the dip-weed would be in the front seat with her. Bella gritted her teeth. She hated people that tailgated almost more than she disliked gold-digging men with uncontrolled hormones.

As another mile went by and the sedan continued to adhere to her ass, Bella decided she would increase her speed. At one stoplight she zoomed through the yellow light and left the sedan in the dirt.

As she turned into the covered mall parking lot, she made furtive glances at her rear view mirror. No sign of the sedan. She released a sigh of relief. An ache started between her shoulder blades, and she rolled her shoulders to relieve the tension. She glanced around the sparsely inhabited parking area. A strange unease rolled through her, despite her deep breathing and personal mantra that said everything looked all right. She couldn't allow Detective Angello or newspaper headlines to rile her up over serial killers.

Detective Angello.

Yes. That's how she'd think of him. It was safer that way.

She tried to imagine him as a sedate, pussycat of a police officer without a sexually charged bone in his body.

She failed. There was nothing kitty-like about the man. Maybe a Rottweiler? Or a German shepherd with a husky build and watchful temperament. Shaking off traitorous thoughts, she decided the day wouldn't get any younger.

After leaving the car, she hurried toward the mall entrance and went inside. She welcomed the air conditioning on her heated skin and the illusion of safety in numbers. Since serial killers didn't commit murder in full view of the public, she knew a few mindless hours in the mall would be safe. Even the elevator music sounded soothing.

She wandered around the department store, looking without seeing. Luca continued to occupy her mind until she pushed away thoughts of him and concentrated on shopping. She'd picked up a pair of shorts that looked fit for a stripper, when the hair on her neck prickled.

Expecting to see someone behind her, she whirled around.

An old woman, bent over and using a cane for support, rifled through a stack of T-shirts that looked way too *young* for her.

"Whatever," Bella muttered to herself.

After Bella tried on a couple of T-shirts, she returned for the shorts she'd eyed earlier. Without thinking about motivations, she went back into the dressing room and tried the barely legal garment. The shorts, cut high on the leg and cupping her butt, screamed sex. She'd never worn shorts like this before, and as she looked in the mirror, she assessed the picture she presented. She might be tall, but her delicate looking structure made her look smaller. She looked curvy and maybe a little slut city. Hell, why not pair the shorts with a top designed to drive a man mad? Maybe someday she'd want to use this clothing as ammunition.

Against whom?

She returned to the dressing room a few moments later with a sleeveless screaming- red top that boasted a low neckline. Lean over too far and her breasts would fall out. Micro fiber material hugged her ribs and waist. She licked her lips and smiled in satisfaction. A wild thought bloomed in her head.

What would Detective Angello think of this outfit?

She imagined his midnight eyes turning to molten appreciation, and the way his mouth would dip into the cleavage and lick between her breasts. Heat warmed her face again as she stripped off the top and shorts. Oh, yeah. Detective Angello would appreciate this, all right. Would she have the guts to wear this in front of him? Part of her wanted to show him she had the nerve and could wear this outfit without blinking an eye. The other part of Bella knew she played a dangerous game if she tantalized the man with a promise she couldn't fulfill. It amounted to swinging a hook of meat in front of a starving carnivore.

But why would a man like him care about having sex with her? Plenty of beautiful women roamed this town who wouldn't mind lying on their back for a man as good-looking as Detective Angello.

Damn him. He'd managed to creep into her mind no matter what she did.

Exasperated, Bella made her purchases and continued shopping for a few more items. She walked up to a counter that sparkled with jewelry. She wanted a necklace to compliment the shimmering green tea-length dress in her closet. Although unsure why she'd brought the dress with her on vacation, she decided better to be prepared than sorry.

A variety of diamond necklaces caught Bella's eye, but she didn't want or need another diamond. She asked the saleswoman for any sterling silver or white gold jewelry featuring cubic zirconium. A few minutes later Bella bought one that would work with her dress; a beautiful one carat cushion-cut stone that flashed like the finest diamond and hung on a long sterling silver chain. She also picked up the matching earrings.

Thirsty, she headed to the food court. Although not hungry, she got a cola and then headed back to her car. A sense of accomplishment and relaxation, something she didn't often experience while shopping, overcame her. She felt free, energized, and ready to tackle anything her family or the irascible Detective Angello could throw at her.

As she entered the parking lot, she again felt that weird sensation of being watched. Instead of turning around, she quickened her steps. The scent of moisture-laden air teased her nose. Rain lashed the ground outside the covered parking. A flash of light and immediate clap of thunder made her jump. She didn't look forward to fighting torrential rain, but she understood the vagaries of driving in Colorado thunderstorms. Once she entered her car, Bella immediately pushed the center console lock button. Safe and snug, she left the mall.

She hadn't gone far when she glanced in her rear view mirror. Her breath caught in her throat. The sedan trailed behind her once again.

* * * * *

The phone rang and Luca jumped about a foot. Disgusted with himself, he grabbed the phone by the bed. He'd better get back his edge. He couldn't afford to start jumping at noises and shadows like an unseasoned rookie.

"Yeah," he barked into the phone.

"Whoa, partner. What's up with you?" Damon asked.

"Nothing. What have you got?"

Damon chuckled. "Isabella Markham is a real princess. She has more money than Queen Elizabeth."

Luca sat down on the bed. "What's that got to do with anything?"

"If she'd done much dating lately, there's no way to tell. She's a painter by trade and has raked in even more money with that."

Luca allowed himself to fall backward onto the bed. "Humph. A portrait painter? Landscape painter?"

"Well, she sure as hell ain't a house painter."

Luca chuckled. "Tell me more."

"She's got a rep as an upstanding citizen, too. Almost enough to make me puke, she's so squeaky clean. Doesn't have a traffic ticket to her name. She was rear ended by an old woman about six months ago. Practically totaled the old lady's puddle jumper car, but only about five thousand dollars of damage on Princess's BMW."

"Only five thousand," Luca drawled. "What else?"

Luca could almost hear his friend shrug. "Nothing that I can tell. Like I said, she's clean as a whistle. As pure as the driven snow. As—"

"Yeah, yeah, I get the picture." Luca sighed and then regretted how weak it made him sound. "But I think she's hiding something."

Damon slurped a drink. "Like what?"

"I don't know."

"I don't know isn't going to do us a hell of a lot of good." The sound of fighting erupted in background. "Jesus, Mary and Joseph."

"What's up?"

"Rowdies at the front desk. Two biker dudes with egos bigger than their dicks."

"Charming."

"I'm sure they think they are."

"Back to the problem at hand. I think Isabella is in danger. It's a feeling I've got."

Damon slurped his drink again. "We know you're hunches are usually right, so I say we follow 'em."

Luca finished the call and a couple of minutes later his cell phone rang. He snatched it off his coffee table and answered. "Angello."

A breathy sigh of relief reached Luca's ears. "Detective Angello, this is Isabella Markham. I think I have a problem."

All Luca's systems went on alert. Muscles tensed and he stood. "Where are you?"

"I just left the Sun Hills Mall, and I'm being followed."

"Damn."

"Exactly my thought. This black sedan with smoked windows followed me on the way to the mall, but I thought I'd lost him. I went shopping, but I didn't see anyone. Then he turned up out of thin air as I was making my way home."

"Keep on populated roads and don't take any short cuts. When you get here, pull into my driveway, and I'll come right out." When she didn't say anything, a thread of worry pierced him. "Bella?"

"He seems to be backing off. In fact, I think I've lost him again."

"How far are you from the house?"

"A couple of miles."

"Stay on the line."

She made a soft noise that sounded like a strangled laugh. "It would be just my luck if a police officer pulled me over for using the cell phone while driving."

He could hear the nervousness in her voice. "You'll be fine as long as you come straight to me. I'd send a unit to trail you, but you're too close to home. The unit wouldn't get to your location in time."

"Guess your phone number is coming in handy after all."

Luca heard disdain in her voice, as if she hated the idea of calling him. Consternation made him frown. He paced the living room floor. "Is he still back there?"

"I don't see him."

"Keep watch."

"Aye, aye, sir." Humor laced her voice, but it sounded forced.

Damn her little hide. She wouldn't reveal real fear to him, at least not in a sincere way. "We'll have to take other protection measures."

Luca couldn't believe what he was thinking. His supervisor, Captain O'Hara, wouldn't approve. Damon would think he was nuts. But he knew what he had to do to protect Bella.

"What kind of measures?" she asked.

Spit it out, Angello. Now isn't the time to go weak in the knees. "Full time protection."

"Full time as in what?"

"Around the clock." Luca made sure he tucked his weapon into the shoulder holster, and then he went outside. "I'll explain when you get here."

She didn't argue and a short time later, her BMW pulled into the driveway. Rain pounded the house, and he plunged into the torrential weather. He didn't see a dark sedan trailing her, but he ran to the end of his driveway. A quick scan revealed no suspicious vehicle in sight. Relief made him take a deep breath.

Bella's stomach did a nervous dance, nausea and tension filling her with a prickling awareness of danger. Thunder rattled the air, and she jumped. Now that she'd found sanctuary, she wondered if calling Detective Angello had been another overreaction.

Since she couldn't sit in the car all day, she left the car and slung her purse over her shoulder. Rain pelted her body, drenching her in seconds.

Detective Angello surveyed the area, his stance as lethal as the weapon in his holster. The man looked like a restless renegade prepared for any contingency. Rain soaked his green polo shirt and dark navy jeans. As he turned, she caught her breath. His wet hair clung to his neck, and water plastered his clothing to his made-for-sin-body.

The cop stalked toward her, and before she could say a word he clasped her arm and marched her toward his condo. "Come on."

"What—"

"We'll talk inside."

Thunder pounded her ears, and she flinched in reaction. She couldn't blame him for wanting to get out of the rain. His fingers tightened on her arm just above her shoulder, but his big hand didn't bruise. The warmth of his skin burned into hers, and the strength of his grip made her feel safer than she expected.

First impressions flew at Bella as he closed and locked the door. Although his condo featured the same floor plan as hers, everything had been switched to the opposite side. A burgundy leather sectional couch and chunky dark wood coffee table took up one corner of the room. A slouchy matching chair and ottoman sat nearby. A large fireplace nestled on the other side.

Her gaze swept over the orderliness and apparent cleanliness of the place. Surprise made Bella pause; she hadn't pictured him as a tidy or organized individual. Her misconception, the fact that she'd made an assumption about him without giving him the benefit of the doubt, shamed her. Her hunches about people were so dead on most of the time, she didn't expect to be off in her estimation. She wondered what else about this dangerous-looking, virile man wasn't as it appeared.

He marched to the window and looked out of the mini-blinds. He kept his weapon in his right hand, and she felt that tiny frisson of fear all women experienced when around a predatory male. Whatever flirting, kissing, and fondling he'd done yesterday, he seemed to be one hundred percent lawman right now.

His hair tangled against his neck and around his face, and she realized with a flash of inappropriate timing that now she knew what he'd look like during a shower. Damp, mussed, and ready.

Ready for what, Bella?

She also recognized that she'd misplaced all functioning brain cells. A strange car followed her twice today, and she stood here thinking about what this cop would look like fresh from the shower?

"See anything?" she asked, feeling baked-over-lame.

"No sign of the sedan." He reached for the cordless phone on the coffee table and punched in some numbers. He eyed her wet tank top and shorts, and Bella felt the long, slow sizzle of his attention. "There's a robe hanging in the master bath. You can get undressed in there."

A trace of alarm tingled through her. "Get undressed? I'm not getting undressed."

He sighed. "You're dripping all over my floor, sweetheart. If you take off the clothes I can toss them in the dryer."

Sweetheart? She wanted to tell him he had no right to call her such an intimate name, but the gentle sound of it on his lips, overlaid with caring, made her pause.

"I'm not staying here. All I need to do is go home. I can get dry once I'm there."

He gave her a stony look, then reached the party he'd dialed. "Yeah, Damon."

His conversation ran to filling in details and asking for information. When he hung up, she hadn't moved from her spot on the rug near the front door. He pinned her with a frustrated gaze.

He came toward her faster than a blink. Bella gasped and backed up to the wall near the window. His hands came down on either side of her, pinning her between his arms. Thunder rattled the condo, punctuation to his swift movement.

As he looked down on Bella, she felt the faintest quiver of arousal mixed with a wallop of complete fear. Her stomach felt like gelatin, her legs not much stronger. A breathless, heady anticipation seized her throat at the same time caution tried to stop it. *Bella, you've gone insane. Keep your guard up.*

A strange thrill she'd never experienced before made Bella pause and evaluate the message in his dark, measuring gaze. She could deduce three things from his expression.

Number one, he thought she was a pain in the ass.

Number two, he wanted to tell her where to go.

Number three, he wanted to fuck her.

It was that third, absolute certainty that stunned her down to her shoes. Instead of acting on that desire, one that she knew would sweep her away into fulfilling *his* need, she decided to reaffirm his belief in number one.

"What kind of twisted game are you playing, Detective?"

"I deal in facts. Maybe you haven't figured it out yet, but there's a good chance the serial killer is after you."

She shivered with cold and a frisson of alarm. "We don't know that for certain. For all I know it might have been my imagination that the sedan was following me."

"Right. You wouldn't have called me if you believed that." His fathomless eyes cut into her, read her, and made her feel more susceptible than she'd ever been. "Why did you call me if you thought you could handle this yourself?"

Feeling rebellious and reckless, Bella blurted the truth. "I was scared. Satisfied?"

"God." His chest heaved as he inhaled. "I'm not a sadist. I want you cautious, alert, and ready to take my orders. I'm a professional, and unfortunately I've dealt with scum like this before. Wrong move and you're dead. I'm not doing this because I want you scared spitless."

Years of being treated as if she had the brain cells of an amoeba made her sensitive to any slight. She knew she shouldn't bristle up like a cat ready to fight, and also realized conditioning threw her into an automatic reaction.

"I'm not an imbecile, Detective. I've taken self-defense, and I heard all the tips about how to protect myself and how not to be a victim." Bella tilted her chin upward. "In fact, considering how close you are to me, you should be a little worried about your family jewels."

His eyes narrowed, and his entire body seemed to tighten. Oh, yeah. He knew she could attack his cock with a quick jab of her knee. She could see his realization in every muscle as he glared down at her. "That would be assaulting an officer."

She let out an unladylike snort. "Defending myself is assault? I thought you were a professional, honorable man?"

To her surprise, he smiled. "Touché, Bella." The way he said her name, husky and with extra heat, made curls of desire swirl in her midsection. "Later we'll see just how good you are at self-defense."

Rather than try to get away, she drew a deep calming breath and softened her voice. "I've never heard of the police keeping people against their will if the protection is unwanted."

His granite expression didn't ease and his nostrils flared a little. For once Luca was speechless.

"I don't need your protection." She heard herself saying the words, but didn't believe it. "And your intimidation tactics are way over the top. Do you usually force women against the wall and hold them against their will?"

He didn't back off. Instead, a dangerous, predatory smile came to his mouth. "You're not pinned against a wall. You backed into it. And if you're so damn knowledgeable about self-defense, why did you let yourself get into this position in the first place?"

He has a point. You've allowed him to get you in this position more than once.

Ashamed, she frowned, blazing with renewed anger. "Most women don't expect police officers to act this way. Your behavior is unethical to say the least."

He moved away, and she felt relief and a weird sense of regret.

"I'm afraid my rep in the department confirms that, *Miss Markham*. I don't always follow the party line, but I always get the job done."

"Are you corrupt?"

His fisted his hands in anger at his sides and his frown grew deeper, boiling in his eyes. "I'm an honest cop. Always have been, always will be."

And don't you forget it. She could almost hear the unspoken words ringing in her ears.

Their little tête-à-tête seemed to have taken some of his fizzle. He jammed a hand through his wet hair. "There's something about you that drives me up a wall, Miss Markham. I'm afraid it's gone to my head."

She twitched one brow. "Miss Markham?"

"As long as we're being formal. You insist on calling me Detective Angello."

"It's the professional thing to do."

"There's that word again. Professional. Do you always do the safe thing?" The velvet quality of his voice caressed her ears. "Or can you be persuaded to loosen up?"

Exasperation mingled with a desire to slap him. Bella had never met a more infuriating man. But at the core of her anger, she felt out of control. Never once could she recall allowing herself to lose all propriety and bust free. The temptation teased and taunted. What if she did let go? What if she reached for him and tried something totally foolish? If she kissed him, would he accuse her of a ridiculous crime? She dangled on a high wire of uncertainty, urged inside by a little demon to try something insane. But what and why?

In spite of the turmoil roiling inside her, she kept her voice low and modulated. "For many people loosening up is an excuse to be irresponsible."

His eyes were touched with regret and worry. "That's true."

She didn't expect him to agree, and the sudden compliance made her look at him closely. Though he bristled with a hazardous edge that made her insides warm, she didn't feel scared. She knew he would never hurt her physically. At the same time, a woman could get torn to pieces by the rushing emotions that seemed to bounce around him, creating a whirlwind of instability.

His gaze dropped to her mouth and rested there for a disconcerting increment before trailing over the rest of her face at an excruciatingly slow pace. "What is it about me that makes you so uncomfortable?"

"You're…" What could she say? That he drove her to within an inch of screaming? Could she be that honest with him and survive the consequences? "Okay, I'll tell you the truth. You're one of those alpha males. The type who thinks a woman is good for one thing. Conquering and seducing and leaving her on the corner when you're through. Like a jock trying to screw the popular cheerleader. You may be a good cop and you may be concerned about keeping me from getting killed. But that doesn't make you a nice man or a particularly good person. So don't expect me to play defenseless female to your big, strong male. It isn't going to happen."

She took a deep breath at the end of her speech, startled down to the core that she'd babbled her thoughts to him and almost revealed one of her deepest secrets. Then she smiled. It felt damned good to let it hang loose as he suggested.

"And another thing." She stepped forward, almost touching him. She stabbed him in the chest with her index finger. "Don't call me sweetheart or Bella. Only my close friends call me by my first name, and I don't know you well enough for you to call me sweetheart."

If she expected him to yell or get angry, he proved her wrong once again. Instead he chuckled. Small lines formed around his eyes, and a little dimple formed in his left cheek. Even that scar on his forehead, which dared her to ask how it was formed, didn't look so intimidating. The fiery quality in his smile turned him from surly to devastatingly handsome.

Her heart did a tumble, tripped, and almost went under right there. *God, the man is so sexy. I can hardly get my breath.*

"You really want me to believe you're a prude, don't you, *Miss Markham*?"

Contrary to what she'd just told him, a formal rendering of her name sounded ridiculous and stuck up. Still, if it kept him at a distance… If it would keep his sinful, off-the-charts face and body away from her, well that would be dandy. She didn't want or need the complications of a physical attraction. Brawn didn't always equate with brain, Bella knew as well as anyone.

His gaze roamed her body, doing a meticulous flourish from her lips down to her legs. "You also want me to think there isn't an inch of real woman under that soft skin, right?"

Way too personal, bud.

She poked him in the chest again. "This conversation has nothing to do with police work, professionalism, or serial killers."

He nodded. "You're absolutely right. We're way off track." He captured her finger and held it in a strong, but gentle grip. Then he turned his hand so that her entire palm pressed against the unyielding mass of his chest. She sucked in a breath at the strength she felt under her fingers. He cupped her fingers gently, placing them right between rock solid pectorals. "If you keep poking me in the chest, we'll have a serious problem."

Deep inside her, a little imp jumped up and demanded to be noticed. Again, her nebulous control started to unravel. "What would you do if I poked you again?"

He shook his head, and the drying strands moved about his shoulders in a dark sweep that looked lustrous and touchable. She swallowed hard as he moved her hand higher on his chest, and her fingers tangled in the small bit of dark hair that peaked above his collar.

"Uh-huh." He grinned, slow and wicked. "I don't give away my strategies to anyone. Consider yourself warned."

She tugged and he let her hand go. Her fingers tingled and pleasure slid up her arm. She wished now she hadn't been so impulsive. Everything she tried seemed to dig her deeper and deeper into a mud hole.

He glanced at the clock on the wall. "It's getting late, I'm getting hungry, and we need to secure your condo. We'll go next door and get an overnight bag packed and then you're coming back with me."

"Detective—"

"Twenty-four hour protection. Starting now."

Heat filled her face. "I don't believe this. Are you saying you want me to stay here all night with you? Do you think I'm crazy?"

"Crazy has crossed my mind more than once."

She sniffed. "Well, I'm not comfortable with your motivations. This can't possibly be authorized by the police department. They aren't going to allow you to be my personal bodyguard for this. Every woman in this town that fits the killer profile would have a bodyguard in that case. "

He closed his eyes a second, as if gathering his patience. When he opened his eyes he looked more determined than ever. "You're right. I'm not authorized as a personal bodyguard. I was placed undercover in this neighborhood since most of the women were murdered within a few blocks of this section of town. "

She swallowed, her throat dry and scratchy. "Then why the personal attention for me?"

"Because this is personal to me. I know you fit the profile, and I'm worried as hell about you. I want to protect you."

Warm, gentle appreciation filled her, along with new excitement. She could hear it in his voice and see the truth on his face. He was doing all this because he cared about her.

Before she could apologize, a scoffing laugh left his throat. "Wait a minute. You think I'm doing this to get into your bed?"

"The thought crossed my mind at one time."

She expected fury to light his eyes, but instead a mild weariness played over his features. "No games, Bella. Sure, I think you're one of the hottest, sexiest women I've seen in a long time. But I'm a cop, and I'm a good one. I'm talking about your personal safety here. That's what matter's most to me. Add that to my professional duty and you have the total motivation."

Shocked by his admission that he thought she was hot and sexy, she allowed her mouth to pop open. Nothing came out.

When Luca had mentioned full time protection, she'd felt the worry creep up on her like a monster in a movie. As a child she recognized the weariness in her older sister's eyes as her personal bodyguard had followed her from place to place. As a child Bella also had a bevy of nannies that might as well have been bruisers. She knew her father had hired them as much for their tough exterior as for their child rearing capabilities. She hated being cloistered like a horny nun. More than anything, she despised the power that some bodyguards had used to try and intimidate her.

Luca reminded her far too much of those men.

If a serial killer watched her, though, whom else could she turn to?

"All right." She hefted her handbag higher on her shoulder. "Let's go."

Chapter Five

Luca stood by the fireplace in Bella's condo, his gaze riveted to the pictures lined on the fireplace mantle. Bella made the condo her own; the photographs showed an older man, and a woman who appeared a little older than Bella and resembled her around the jaw line. Another photograph showed a young boy of about twelve, his red hair and freckled nose similar to Bella's features. She might not have the freckles, but the tilt at the corner of her eyes, and that smile that said she knew something you didn't—yep, she must be related to the boy.

Her kid? The background check he'd done on her said she'd turned thirty, six months ago. She wasn't old enough to have a kid that age unless she'd had him at a very young age. Suddenly the idea of Bella having a child, in love with a man enough to have sex with him—

Whoa. Hold it right there. He continued his scrutiny of the condo as he forced his gaze away from the photo. For one irrational, gut-wrenching moment he'd felt a spurt of animal jealousy. As if he wanted to find the man who'd bedded her, got her pregnant and left her to raise the child alone.

Then he shook his head. The dossier said nothing about her being married, engaged, having a boyfriend, a favorite fuck...nothing. And no indication she'd ever given birth.

He scrubbed his hand over his jaw and grunted. "Give me a break. I'm losing my fucking mind here."

She sauntered back into the room in time to hear his mumbled self-deprecation. "You're just now figuring that out, Detective?"

Man, if she didn't look so hot and have such a sweet smile, he'd be half tempted to get mad again. But he couldn't. She'd changed into a short-sleeved top that molded her high, small breasts, and a tight pair of shorts that snuggled her ass like a surgical glove.

Luca did what any red blooded male would. He stared.

Bella's garments curved and touched and called to him so loudly he wanted to scream. She didn't have the princess slut look many women acquired when they wore provocative clothes. No, she held the regal bearing of a virgin queen. Sexual without being touchable.

That didn't keep him from wanting her.

He wanted to strip her clothes off, lay her down on the floor, and ram inside her until she came so hard she drained his balls.

His cock jerked, then began to harden. He gritted his teeth.

Oh, shit.

What the hell was the little wench doing? Trying to drive him mad?

He almost told her to change her clothes again, but before he could say a word, the phone rang.

"I'll get it." Sitting down on an antique looking telephone stand, she snatched the cordless phone out of its cradle. "Hello." He saw her stiffen, her back going poker straight. "Father."

Father. Somehow her tight-assed way of greeting her old man didn't surprise Luca.

He tried not to listen, but he couldn't do anything about it. Instead he wandered around the room absorbing the types of odds and ends she'd brought to the condo. Her identity didn't grab him, though. Since the condo was a vacation rental, it didn't tell him as much about her as he would like.

After a significant pause, Bella rolled her gaze to the ceiling. She looked like she was holding back a primal scream. "Yes, Father, I heard the reports about the serial killer. But you know what, you can be completely at ease." A man's voice, loud enough so that even Luca could hear it, poured from the phone.

Bella's pretty features, muffled somewhat behind her glasses, twisted into undeniable anger. "I am not coming home. We agreed that no one is to bother me here. Not my sister, and not you. Like I said, I'm safe. I've got protection."

Surprised that she'd mention it, Luca waited to see how she'd qualify the protection. "My own personal bodyguard. He's a cop." She looked up at Luca and smiled with pure conspiracy. "That's right. I have twenty-four hour protection while I'm here. Why? Well, because the serial killer may have followed me from the mall today."

Luca heard the man's unmistakable yell into the phone. God, didn't the guy have a volume control? Wondering where the conversation would lead, Luca paced in front of the fireplace. He shoved his hands into his jeans pockets.

"I'll be perfectly fine, Father. And don't you even think of sending some of those goobers to act as my bodyguards."

Luca almost laughed. Isabella Markham owned some layers of serious coercion. Her words didn't always suit her actions, and that made Luca more determined than ever to discover what her tough words, and dressed-to-screw clothes meant. His glance went down to her seventies style platform sandals. Not the traditional screw me shoes, but the nice long line they gave her legs made him sweat. She'd painted her toenails a shocking candy pink. His cock hardened again and he winced.

Luca realized that she'd paused in her conversation when she cleared her throat. He caught Bella's gaze and saw the flush in her cheeks. She'd seen him giving her a once over, and maybe even noticed his hard on. He focused on those nice tits and saw her nipples had hardened into sweet little beads. What would she do if he reached over, cupped those luscious breasts and simply held her nipples between his thumb and finger? An overwhelming urge to suck on her nipples made his cock grow to impossible-to-miss status.

Holy shit, if I don't get a grip soon—

"Want to talk to him?" she asked the carping man on the phone.

With an unrepentant grin, Bella held out the phone to Luca, and he could hear the griping coming over the line. Luca took the phone, not so sure he wanted a conversation with her pissed-off daddy. On the other hand, it might be what he needed to get rid of this raging hard on.

"Mr. Markham?"

"Who is this?" a deep male voice bellowed into Luca's ear.

Luca winced. "Detective Luca Angello of the Piper's Grove Police Department."

"How the hell do I know you're who you say you are? For all I know *you* could be the serial killer."

Luca grinned. "A reasonable question, sir. All you need to do is call Captain O'Hara." He gave Mr. Markham his badge number and the Captain's phone number. "You can confirm my identity."

Luca described the situation without holding anything back. Rich daddy would check him out with the Captain and rant and rave about his precious daughter's safety. Not that he could blame Markham for being worried. With a precision he'd honed from years of police work, Luca managed to calm the hyper father. After reassuring Markham he could protect Isabella, Luca hung up the phone.

He stood near the telephone table and looked down at her. "From the look on your face, it appears you're planning a mutiny."

She shook her head and for a second he saw sadness and resignation on her face. "I should. But I think my father's usual brand of manipulation has worn me out for the moment."

"Manipulation?"

"You heard him." She stood and brushed by him. She slung her night case over one shoulder and her purse over the other. "What Father wants, Father gets."

Luca thought he understood a little more of the missing puzzle pieces of Isabella Markham. "So you're running away from home."

She shook her head. "Vacationing and figuring out what to do with the rest of my life. The next time I go back home, it will be to pack my bags and move out once and for all."

Thirty years old and stuck with a domineering father and what? An empty life? Luca's curiosity notched upward another level. "What else are you running away from?"

"None of your business, Detective."

Firm and no-nonsense, the statement put him in his place. Temporarily.

He edged closer to her and sank into the light, golden brown of her eyes. A soft color, copper in tone, shadowed her upper eyelids, and it gave her a mysterious quality that he liked and hated all at once. He wondered how often she slipped the glasses on her nose to hide from the world. When she'd worn those glasses on her small nose the other night, he'd wanted to pluck them off and toss them aside so he could dive in and take a kiss. He'd wanted her breasts in his hands. His tongue in her mouth. His cock buried as far inside her as he could go.

That's it, Angello. You are one hundred percent fucking certifiable.

Clearing his throat, Luca dragged his mind off her body. "Who is the little boy in the picture on the mantle?"

Her features saddened. "My little cousin David. He...he died two years ago."

"Oh, man. I'm sorry, Bella."

"It was a freak accident. He was actually visiting us one night when it happened. For some reason he fell out of bed, hit his head and...and that was it. In a blink he was dead."

Luca wanted to wrap his arms around Bella and whisper words of comfort to her. "I'm so sorry. You must have loved him very much."

He saw her chest rise and fall as she inhaled. "He was more like a brother. My Uncle Robert married later in life to a younger woman and they had David."

Silence hung between them for a long time until he spoke again. "I'm surprised you told your father what's going on. Are you sure he isn't going to send—what did you call 'em—a goober down here to guard your body?"

"That's why I told him about you. Otherwise there would be several thick-necked gorillas stumping along behind me watching my every move."

Ah, motivation. Now he knew better than ever why she hated his protection. "You prefer an alpha male with a thinner neck following you everywhere?"

Her gaze danced over him with a quick but one-hundred percent thorough appraisal. The admiration behind that once over shell shocked him. *Damn.* She played at being oblivious to him, but maybe a little bit of the woman in her liked him.

Alarm, strong and without remorse, ran through his mind. *Hell, I don't need her or want her to like me. I've got a job to do.*

Thunder interrupted his internal dialogue. He reached for her overnight bag, sliding it off her shoulder before she could protest. "Come on. I've got a pizza in the freezer with my name on it and it's calling to me."

* * * * *

Rain drenched Bella again as she dashed into the cop's condo.

Her stomach decided to growl as soon as he closed and locked the door. She didn't realize how hungry she'd become until Luca mentioned pizza.

"Hungry?" He gave her an almost boyish grin.

She snatched her overnight bag from his hand. "Pizza sounds good."

"Sorry it's not gourmet, but it's all I've got right now." He tossed her a cocky grin. "Don't worry, it's a big pizza."

"Good. Hope it has lots of cheese." She headed for the bedrooms. "I'm getting out of these wet clothes."

"Miss Markham."

She turned around. He leaned against the kitchen door jam and tucked his thumbs into waistband loops. His movement drew attention to the front of his jeans. She tried not to look, but her gaze landed there for a millisecond. Earlier, when she'd been talking to her father on the phone, she saw Angello develop a full-blown hard on right before her eyes. Surprised and secretly a little thrilled, she'd turned her attention away. Right now he didn't look aroused, but the package under all that mystery kept drawing her back. Hell, she couldn't remember being obsessed with thoughts of sex with this intensity before.

The detective looked serious, all trace of banter and teasing gone. "I meant what I said earlier today. This is no game. The man who killed those women is a ruthless son of a bitch. If you want to stay alive, you've got to do what I say, when I say. Understood?"

Complying grated like sandpaper against her ego, despite the wisdom of his words. She hesitated long enough for him to walk toward her. Once again he stood too near, crowding into her personal space. Even with her platform heels she felt small and a bit overpowered by his strength. Almost against her will, she looked at his powerful arms and wondered what they'd feel like wrapped around her once again. Not to restrain or dominate, but to hold her close like a man did when he loved a woman more than his own life.

Face it. You're never going to know what that's like.

Besides, Luca Angello had probably never fallen in love with a woman. He didn't seem the type. Love 'em, screw 'em, leave 'em. That would be his forte and motto.

She stood up to the scrutiny in his eyes, afraid if she looked away first he'd detect that she found him way too attractive. *A hottie beyond all hotties.*

She almost giggled.

The big cop's expression went hungry, as if he wanted something more from her than a quick roll in bed. As soon as Bella thought she recognized that look of desperation, it disappeared into the cynical, hard-bitten lawman. A hunger to know him, to experience him with a soul-searing intensity, rose up and nipped her.

"I'm not going to let anything happen to you." That warm, coaxing quality in his voice about curled her toes. "And you don't need to be afraid of me. You're safe with me."

Yeah, right. As safe as she could be in a cage with a woman-eating lion.

Without warning, she remembered two months ago, when she'd been lying in bed at her father's mansion. Her bedroom door had swung open. A silhouette of a man had stood at the entrance, massive and impenetrable as a fortress. Fear had drained her ability to move. Like a trapped animal, she'd been immobilized by memories.

And she knew some day, if she didn't leave her father's house, she would die.

Her breath snagged in her throat. She must have made a sound, for his hands cupped her shoulders. His gaze looked worried. "Bella?"

"What?" Her voice sounded thin and a little shaky.

"Are you all right?" He reached up and caressed her cheek with a tender touch.

Sweet comfort slid through her body like brandy, heady and potent. For a reckless moment she leaned into that hand, enjoying the gossamer touch of his thumb over her skin.

Bella surrendered to that exquisite feeling and pretended he meant the sign of affection. "I'm fine."

"You look scared as hell." His eyes narrowed. "Why?"

"Not every man is as safe as you."

"Obviously not. The serial killer rapes his victims before he kills them. This guy doesn't just want power over them, he wants them gone forever. But he's not going to get near you. I promise."

"Take the promise back."

"What?"

"You can't guarantee my protection. Nothing is ever certain. As a cop you should know that."

He frowned, more concern etching lines between his eyebrows. "I guarantee your safety."

"There are more ruthless men out there than this one serial killer."

"Well, I'm workin' my way through the bastards one at a time, sweetheart."

If she'd heard dishonesty and sarcasm in that one soft utterance, she could have resisted him. Instead the way he said it made Bella feel like he meant it down deep. Remembered pain unfurled inside of her. She thought she'd wiped it away after she decided to leave her father's estate before something worse happened and the next silhouette standing in her doorway succeeded in hurting her for real. A shudder went through her.

Almost as if he read her mind, the detective's gaze turned harsh. "Wait a minute. Did someone hurt you? Have you been—"

When he stopped, she heard the question in his voice even though he didn't say it.

"Raped?" she whispered her question, almost afraid to say the word. She shook her head and dislodged his touch. "Um…no. But there was a little…incident a couple of months ago at home…" She didn't want to talk about it right now. She shrugged out of his grip. "Excuse me, I need to get out of these wet clothes."

After he showed her where his bedroom was, she slipped inside and closed the door. Dominated by a huge king size bed with a monstrous light oak wood headboard, the room held Luca's masculine scent. Running shoes stood by the bed, and a pair of jogging shorts and t-shirt littered the navy blue plain bedspread.

"Better not dawdle."

Knowing this man, he'd barge inside and demand what took so long. With her luck she'd be naked as a newborn babe when he did it. Propelled by urgency, she left her damp sandals on the bathroom floor.

She striped naked in record time. As she slid into the huge, green terrycloth robe, she sank into the warmth it provided. Chilled, she stood in front of the mirror and tried combing her wet hair into a semblance of order. Bella sniffed when the bouncy strands refused to go into any order. She contemplated redressing and running from the condo back to her car. Retreating to her father's estate where armed guards and trained dogs meant security might be the answer.

The idea lasted all of a second. No, going home to her father wouldn't solve her problems. Not if she valued her new-found independence. He would tell her that he'd told her so, and then he'd place a bodyguard on her like so many times before. His precious little girls wanted for nothing, including the best money could buy.

At the same time, her father couldn't save her from the men who were supposed to protect her.

A blast of thunder made her twitch. Rubbing her hands over her face, she sucked in a tired breath of resignation. One of her first adventures, as a woman without real ties, and now she'd run up against a serial killer and a cop who thought he knew best.

She smiled at the mirror, aware that her mind rolled in the gutter, wallowing in the image of Luca Angello's massive penis.

Assuming he had a massive penis. As minds will do, hers ran in circles contemplating how it would feel to have him inside her.

While she knew size didn't matter when it came to lovemaking technique, it didn't stop her from being curious. Two men had plumbed her depths, and she'd never experienced an orgasm. They'd been normal-sized men, and they'd made all the right moves. Massaging her breasts, sticking their tongues down her throat, rubbing her clit, and yet nothing had happened. She couldn't come. Both men had screwed her nonetheless, urging her to climax as they'd thrust into her. They'd goaded, probed, and done everything their male minds said they could do. Again, she failed to orgasm. Finally, unable to hold back, they ejaculated. They assumed it was her problem, and so did she.

She didn't think *it* would ever happen. *Frigid be thy middle name.*

It wouldn't matter if Detective Luca Angello had an erection the size of the Eiffel Tower, she couldn't orgasm during intercourse.

Well, it was nice to fantasize, anyway.

She went back into the living room and found him on the phone again.

"Yeah. No problem. I'm hoping this case will be done in a few days. Then I can drop by and see the kids."

Kids?

Her gaze latched onto his hand. No wedding ring that she'd somehow missed, and no tan line that suggested he wore a ring at other times. A lump, tight and hot, grew in her throat. If the creep had been coming on to her and he had a wife and kids —

"I'll see you then. Love you, too."

His smile and the soft way he said the words, made her heart lurch with crazy jealousy and warm appreciation. If he did have a wife and kids at least he told them he loved them. *What would it be like to have him say those words to me? Softly. With passion. With meaning.*

After he hung up, he walked toward her, and Bella clutched her purse to her chest like a shield against the writhing, conflicting feelings inside her. Trying not to look defensive or vulnerable, she slipped the strap of her handbag over her shoulder and went for the casual look.

He laughed. "Now that's a new fashion statement."

Realizing that a bathrobe and purse must look ridiculous, she flushed. She put the bag on the coffee table, planted her hands on her hips, and glared. "There. That better? I wouldn't want to offend your sensibilities."

He grinned. "Where are your clothes?"

She muttered a curse under her breath and headed back to the master bath in his bedroom. She'd looped her clothes over the shower door, forgetting that he offered the dryer.

Bella grabbed the clothes and started out of the bathroom. Coming back around the corner, she stepped on the robe's too long belt and tripped. The violent tug pulled the robe apart and exposed her body.

He walked around the corner in time to see Bella lose her footing and the clothes go flying from her grip. She let out a startled cry, and he lunged forward to catch her. His muscular arms slipped around her naked waist. As he yanked her upright, she landed against his chest, her bare front pressed to every inch of his hard body. Big hands slipped to her back, and as he moved they caressed her involuntarily.

All the air sucked right out of her with a whoosh.

Holy shit.

Stunned into silence, she waited as his arms tightened around her and everything inside her stilled. Her hands lay on his chest, and she could feel his muscles tighten and release. She didn't know what to do, and by the intrigued, half-amused look in his eyes, he didn't either.

"What are you trying to do?" he asked. "Break your neck?"

Hating the teasing quality in his voice, she glared at him. "Oh, sure. Didn't you know it was on my agenda for today? I couldn't go on any longer and figured this was a good way to commit suicide."

Her tone held contempt, and he decided to take offense. "Next time I'll let you fall on your pretty little face."

"Please, don't do me any favors." Bella knew she sounded like a bad imitation of a thirties era private investigator—or a snotty, spoiled brat—but this man brought out every crass instinct she possessed.

"Are you always so damned contrary?" He sounded amazed and exasperated, and the pinched look between his eyes confirmed it. "Or are you hiding under all that sarcasm? Who is the real Isabella Markham? The hot woman in my arms right now, or the straight-laced bitch in high heels and a strident voice?"

Truth hit her in the stomach like a punch. Again he managed to see inside her the way no one else could. Anger bolted through her. "You...you..."

"Yeah? Spit it out, baby. Don't hold anything back."

Baby.

Oh, great. First he's called me sweetheart, and now he's added another endearment into the mix. Instead of insulting, his tone sounded so gentle, caressing and sexy, that it melted her down to her bare toes.

"Maybe I'm both of those women."

A seductive smile added to the power he seemed to possess over her. "Think so? Should we experiment and find out?"

With a feather light touch, his hands slid down, down until they rested above her buttocks. Only the robe separated his hot hands from her naked skin.

"Oh." Her voice lost power, and she wished she didn't have this overwhelming desire to writhe against him.

His gaze went mellow and aroused, the glassy quality in his eyes evident. "Bella, you gotta move away from me right now, or I'm going to do something drastic."

She could slap him. Knee him good and hard. Instead, she made the mistake of looking into his eyes.

Without hesitation he moved his hands over her naked back. Luca established a seductive rhythm, his fingers gliding down to right above her butt. Every pass over her body made her warm and tingly, and she arched into him. His big hands thrilled her straight to the core.

His eyes narrowed, the pupils dilating. Luca's breathing increased, and his arms tightened around her. Then she felt the unmistakable evidence as he pressed his growing erection against her stomach. Her own breath picked up speed, as a tight, persistent tugging began in her lower stomach. Lord help her, that sensation signaled one thing. With a look that spoke of defiance, he cupped each butt cheek in his palms and gave a gentle squeeze.

She gasped, her lips parting in surprise and outrage. "Let me go."

When she shifted against him, his gaze dropped to the top of her breasts, and his eyes turned hot with appreciation. "I don't think that's such a good idea. Not if you want to keep your modesty."

"What I want is—" She shifted again, and his warm palms caressed her butt with gentle arousing stokes. "Oh, my God."

"Yeah." Feathering, stroking, and cupping, he filled his hands with her rear end. Overflowing with arousal, his voice and his expression indicated that if she didn't run and run fast, they would end up on the bed. He closed his eyes, the furrows in his brow giving him the look of a man in pain. "Don't move."

"Why?"

"Because you're killing me."

With wicked satisfaction, Bella realized she possessed some control over him. This big, tough cop would be putty in her hands, perhaps, if only she would move against him one more time. Everything about the moment expanded with kaleidoscope sensations she couldn't say she'd experienced so intensely before. Did one second seem to last a minute? Or was it the hot, determined look in his eyes that held her enthralled. Heat rolled through her limbs as she absorbed the tension, the spellbinding feeling of solid man along her body.

So, she disobeyed him and moved her pelvis a little, wriggling against his palms.

With a hooded, almost drowsy look, and before she could utter one protest, his mouth came down on hers.

Luca let his cock do all his talking, his little head taking over when his big head should be shouting for him to let her go. Just one taste and he'd release her.

The warm, sweet bundle in his arms felt soft and so feminine he couldn't resist. As his lips coasted over hers, Luca tried to rein back and keep the kiss light. If he did anything more, if he let his libido kick into full overdrive, he'd be all over her in a heartbeat.

A soft moan came from her throat as he gently tasted her. Hard and throbbing, his body had other ideas. He pressed and rotated against her flat belly, all the while testing the pliability of her ass with a continual massage. Soft whimpers reached his ears, and he made sure he didn't hold her too tightly.

Bella heard the groan deep in his chest, as if he struggled to hold something back. She exploded into need, wrapping her arms around his neck. He pushed his fingers through her hair and his mouth worked hers with a gentle persuasiveness she wouldn't have expected from him. Tender, repetitive touches of his lips kept her on edge, unable to think of anything but the next kiss, the next stroke of his warm hands on her skin. She thought the kisses would never end, and she wanted him to take her to the next level. As she touched her tongue to his lips, he growled deep in his throat and slanted his mouth over hers.

Before Luca could plunge his tongue deep, she slid hers into his mouth. The hot interior tasted like mint, and she moaned softly. He turned his head, searching for another fit, and he took over the kiss. His tongue moved, stroking and thrusting until the rhythmic slide started a firestorm in her stomach. Bella arched, wild for the idea of more enticement, more of everything.

Primitive and without remorse, her libido said goodbye to inhibitions as he plied her mouth with the deepest, most erotic kisses of her life. Sparks of deep arousal burned, sending liquid need between her thighs. She ached inside for something, a woman unleashed.

Before she could take another breath, he pulled free, stepping out of her embrace. Breathing hard, he gazed at her nakedness with untamed eyes. "God, Bella."

He pushed his hair out of his face and took another deep breath. To her utter surprise he backed away and left her standing in the bedroom.

Chapter Six

Bella followed Luca a short time later, a curious mingling of disappointment and amazement keeping her steps slow. Her body continued to throb with need, and she wanted to roar in frustration. Why had he stopped? She heard noise in the kitchen and stepped inside.

He looked up at her, his face now hard and expressionless. What had gotten into him? A few minutes earlier he'd been ready to go to bed with her. She couldn't have mistaken the way he held her, his kiss, or that massive erection. Instead of speaking, she held his serious gaze until he looked away.

Surprise, surprise. The big, bad cop looked away first.

He seemed to relax, the tenseness slipping from his hard, sharp features. "I've got iced tea, cola, water, milk, you name it."

A quick glance around the room showed that his kitchen looked like hers. She remembered that moment when she'd seen him standing here drinking out of a carton, his butt as naked as could be.

Bella cleared her throat. "Cola will be fine."

He opened the refrigerator and reached inside. He brought out two cans, then headed for the cabinets and retrieved two tall glasses. His nonchalant attitude made her want to scream.

"What are you thinking, Detective? You don't think I'm going to stay here with you until you catch this serial killer, do you?"

Instead of handing her the drink, he crossed his arms and planted his feet apart in that semi-military stance that spoke of authority and assurance. "I obtained full approval from my Captain to be your bodyguard. I wasn't lying to your father or you. Hell, the Captain almost tore a strip of my ass off in the process."

She felt a keen sense of satisfaction mixed with a desire to choke the detective. "Why would he do that?"

"He thinks I may have compromised the investigation."

"Oh?"

"He doesn't think I have a good enough reason for putting you under protection. I told him I did."

"And just like that he said okay?" Bella suspected this man could argue anything away from anyone given the incentive. "I don't believe you."

He reached for the phone and held it out to her. "Call and ask for Captain O'Hara. He'll tell you what I said and how I said it."

When Bella ignored the phone, he put it back into the cradle.

Uncertain, she reached for the cola and took a long sip. The cold liquid soothed her tight, dry throat. She coughed, choking on the cold liquid.

"You okay?" he asked softly.

He stepped closer, and with a gentle sweep of his fingers, he brushed her hair back from her face. The heat of his touch made her stiffen, surprise rolling through her like the thunder outside.

He cupped her cheek. "Those other women had two things against them."

"Name the first thing." She put the cola down on the counter and stared at the condensation ringing the clear glass.

"They didn't know there was anyone after them, so they weren't cautious enough."

She didn't feel the least reassured. "And the second reason?"

His hand brushed through her hair, his fingers touching her earlobe. Heat rolled down from where he'd touched her to her belly.

"They didn't have a bodyguard. Whoever this creep is, Bella, he'd have to go through me to get to you. That isn't going to happen." He released her and headed back to the fridge. "Let's cook that pizza."

Arousal sprinted through Bella as primitive longings clawed deep inside her. This man would protect her with his life, and that said something more than just his job. Sure, police officers put their lives on the line every day for citizens. She knew he would take a bullet for her any day, and that concern ground inside her at the same time it made her feel safe.

As soon as they sat at the small kitchen table to eat, she felt some of her tension ease, and she discovered she couldn't wait to dig into the pepperoni and sausage deluxe.

"Pizza on china. What a concept." He winked. Using a spatula, he slipped a second piece of hot pizza onto her plate. "Eat up."

His gaze twinkled, and Bella had a strange reaction. Unexpected tenderness.

For about the hundredth time that day, she decided insanity ran rampant inside her. How could she feel anything extraordinary for a guy she'd known forty-eight hours?

"You're being bossy again." She gave him a wry smile. "Tell me about your time in the marines. The part that made you bossy. Or were you just born that way?"

His smile returned, unrepentant and charming. She blinked. He looked almost boyish when he let down that hard-as-nails exterior. A woman could get all mushy over a guy if he kept throwing her curves and angles like this.

"I was a marine medic for six years. I decided that wasn't what I wanted to do for the rest of my life. When I got out, I finished my bachelors in criminal justice at New York University."

"I thought I detected a slight accent."

"New York City. And here I thought all these years in Colorado erased the accent."

"It's still thick enough. Must help when you want to sound authoritative." She bit into her second slice of pizza. Sauce caught on her chin, and she dabbed at it with a paper napkin. "So what made you want to be a cop?"

"My uncle Delio is a cop in New Jersey. He's one of my heroes. A great guy."

This man had heroes? "It's satisfying to hear your idea of a great man doesn't include WWF wrestlers." She stopped eating and tried to keep a straight face. "I hope."

"Shit. I can't stand wrestling."

She stifled a laugh.

He took a bite of pizza. As his gaze turned speculative, he appraised Bella in a way that made her feel naked again. "Tell me more about your life on daddy's estate."

Unease ate at her. "I came here to escape from it for awhile, not talk about it."

He leaned back in his chair and crossed his arms. "What are you running from?"

"From family and old memories. From new nightmares."

"That's too bad."

"No, it's good. Take my word for it." She took his example and finished her pizza in record time, enjoying the momentary silence. Outside the storm began to diminish, filling the air with occasional small rumbles of thunder. "Who knew last night that tonight I'd be nesting with a cop and eating pizza?" Renewed anxiety blossomed inside her, and she twisted her napkin between her fingers. "Do you think the killer is watching the condo?"

"It's difficult to say, especially if he lives nearby. Damon is keeping surveillance on the area. If anyone starts creeping around, we're going to know it."

"Shouldn't you be out detecting? Jack-jawing with me and eating pizza won't help you solve these crimes."

He swept his hand through the white strands of hair at his temple. Edgy anger returned to his features. "If you don't like how I'm doing my job, Miss Markham, you're free to file a complaint."

"That's not what I meant."

He narrowed his eyes, as if he didn't believe her. "You can go at any time. But I recommend that if you leave, you head to your family's home where the goobers can guard you. Hell, I'll deliver you right into your daddy's arms if that's what you want."

"No." Adamant, she shook her head. "I won't go back. In case you haven't figured it out yet, my father lives in fear that something will happen to Madeleine and me. He's overbearing, demanding, and stubborn."

"Not at all like his daughter."

"Maybe the stubborn part."

A smile quirked one corner of his mouth, and he gave a soft chuckle. Deep, masculine, and husky, the sound reached a ten on the sexy-sound-o'meter. The only thing she could think of that might sound sexier was the way he'd called out to the woman in his dreams. She could still hear that groan, that raspy request for more ringing in her ears.

A desire to hear him ask her for that same thing rose high inside her.

She realized she'd been staring at him, and his gaze stayed pinned to her, hungry and alert. Hungry all right. He looked like he wanted to eat her up.

With a shuddering breath, she continued. "My sister lives in fear of me turning into an old maid."

"You're kidding?" He sounded beyond incredulous. Indignant, perhaps. "Why?"

"Because I'm thirty and I don't have prospects for marriage."

He leaned his elbows on the table. His strong, broad, long-fingered hands lay on the table. "She thinks you have to be married to enjoy life?"

"Madeleine and I used to be close until she married her megalomaniac husband. A very conservative, pious sort. He's molded her to his will and has her thinking he's the only one who has any brains. She now thinks sex is dirty."

"Do you think sex is dirty?" He leaned forward, his lips parting slightly.

She looked at his mobile, expressive mouth and remembered how his lips had felt on hers. She wanted his tongue in her mouth. His lips touching her nipples. Sucking on them. Nibbling.

Help.

She felt her nipples push against the robe and knew she had to get away from him before he saw the evidence that he'd turned her on again.

What she'd told him about men pulling her nipples and repulsing her was true. She'd yet to have a man arouse her by touching her breasts. Maybe, like her last boyfriend suggested, she had a serious sexual dysfunction.

She stood and went to the kitchen, carrying her empty plate and her utensils. She put her glass and plate on the countertop. When his hands cupped her shoulders, and his heat invaded her space, a gasp slipped from her throat.

"Tell me about the man that hurt you." His hands caressed with gentle swirls down her arms, starting a firestorm of tingles from her elbows down to her wrists. He kept a soft touch on her hands for a moment, then settled his hands on her waist. He drew her back until she leaned against him. "Tell me his name."

"No one hurt me. Not really."

"Not really?"

"Is there an echo in here?"

"Shit. Just tell me who he is," he growled softly.

His rough, demanding tone should have pissed her off. Bella tried summoning offense at his over-the-top insistence and his touch. She failed.

When she didn't answer him, he said, "If you weren't raped, then some asshole must have scared you pretty badly. You're as jumpy as a jackrabbit." His breathing deepened; she felt the rise and fall of his chest. "The idea of a man hurting you makes me crazy. I couldn't bear it if anyone harmed you."

Whoa. A tender feeling emerged deep inside her that she didn't want. But it was there anyway, invading her thoughts.

"If a woman and I have sex it's because she wants it. The idea of any guy forcing himself on a woman makes me ill, Bella."

Bella. She'd asked him not to use her first name, but it didn't seem imperative anymore. Not when his voice held that gentle, raspy tone.

"If I'm so jumpy, why did I let you kiss me?" she asked.

She felt him shrug. "Beats the crap outta me. I was pretty surprised you didn't try and cram me in the nuts right then."

A laugh broke from her, close to a giggle, but not quite. She didn't want to sound silly, so she slammed down the urge to erupt with a belly laugh. "Well, I've still got time."

"Hmmm."

Again, he shifted against her, and this time she felt the evidence. Nestled hard against her back, his full-blown erection proved he wanted her. Uncontrollable desire pooled in her stomach and melted her loins.

Hot. Oh, God. He felt so warm and solid against her she wanted his arms holding and reassuring her, removing all doubt and disappointment. But she also knew no one else could give her the satisfaction of knowing she'd made it on her own. Maybe in a weird way this incident with the serial killer would propel her into making the decision about what she wanted.

Excitement, anticipation, and fear warred inside her as his touch lingered along her waistline. Then he slid one hand to her belly. She could feel his touch all the way through the terrycloth robe. Her stomach muscles jumped, sensitive and ticklish. She inhaled sharply as he pressed the slightest bit, bringing her butt up against him. Shock rippled down her spine at the realization that she wanted more attention. More caresses. Fear and excitement warred with common sense inside her.

His breath puffed against her ear as he leaned closer. "Tell me."

"Being rather personal, aren't you?" She tried to keep the warble out of her voice, but it didn't work.

"Trust me."

"You're asking me to trust you while you're feeling me up?"

"Yes." A soft chuckle filled her ear as his lips touched the sensitive lobe. "Tell me the creep's name."

When his tongue touched Bella's ear for a whisper of a second, she almost groaned. Hot fire darted deep in her stomach, almost hard enough to make her womb clench. She had to inhale deeply. "Why do you want to know so much?"

"Because then I can track him down and kick the shit out of him."

A tiny, forbidden thrill raced through her. "You'd do that for me? I mean... that's criminal."

He laughed. "Yeah, I'd do it for you. I'm protective of women, and I won't apologize for it. I don't like to see women hurt or in pain."

"So you think they need to be babied?"

His hands wandered along her body as she spoke. The robe didn't keep the heat of his touch from her. He seemed to be touching her everywhere at once. "Now you're putting words in my mouth. I like independent, confident women. But I also know that it's a biological fact of life that a man can overpower most women."

The tone in his voice, rough and whispery, rumbled in his chest and vibrated through to her.

Now I am in trouble. Trouble down to the soles of my feet.

She fumbled around for conversation that might take her mind off the hard press of his fantastic body, and the way his lips teased her ear.

His mouth touched the side of her neck as he nosed his way through her hair. "God, you smell good."

"Thank you," she whispered. She swallowed hard. She had an overwhelming need to distract him. Otherwise he'd do more, and she'd let him do more, too. "My father smothers his women with his protection."

"His women?"

She fingered the counter in front of her. "Father is on wife number four right now. My mother was wife number two."

"They divorced?"

"No. She died when I was four. Heart complications."

"I'm sorry."

"I don't remember much about her, but I sometimes wonder if she would have counterbalanced Father's over enthusiasm to protect his daughters."

"Did he overprotect Madeleine, too?"

Of course an investigator would try this angle. The idea that he knew so many things about her remained disconcerting, and she tried to resurrect anger and couldn't. Maybe exhaustion explained why she didn't care.

"Yes, he did," she said.

In the back of her mind a warning tickled. She didn't know him. Not honestly and deeply. Before she let a man touch her like this she had to see inside him and know he wasn't playing with her.

"Why are you really doing all this?" Bella asked.

"This…what?"

"Don't play innocent. Why are you fondling me one moment and in the next second telling me you're a hands-off, respectful cop. It doesn't fit. When we were in the bedroom you shot out of there like someone blew you out of a cannon."

If she thought she'd provoke irritation, it didn't work. His chest moved against her again. "Because I care about you." His arms went around her waist and tucked her against him tight and sure. "Because I'm having a hell of a time keeping my hands off you. You smell great, you feel wonderful." He kissed the side of her neck, his hot breath and warm lips sending shivers of sweet desire straight into her limbs. "I want to show you that not every man is the same. Besides, you never answered my other question. Do you think sex is dirty?"

"No. Of course not."

"Then something else is wrong. I think there's a hot, sexy woman under all that reserve, but I don't think you let yourself enjoy it. Why?"

"Because I don't think that every impulse should be acted upon." She knew her voice sounded irritated.

He laughed softly. "You're right about that. My day is filled with people who don't hold back their impulses."

"Then you know how dangerous it is."

His fingers tightened a little on her arms, but not enough to hurt. "A little danger sometimes is good. Stimulating."

Stimulating. Oh, boy.

"And I suppose you think you can give me that danger?"

"I could."

Luca's arrogant tone made her bristle, but she refused to turn around and meet his gaze. She knew what she'd see there. Assurance. Confidence. Everything she didn't feel right now. "I don't think so."

"That was the wrong thing to say. I like challenges."

"I don't think you really are any different from other men. You think you can do a little stroking here and there and a woman is going to come all over you. Well it takes a lot more than fancy talking and a few quick passes over a woman's breasts."

He broke out in hard laugh. "You're right, sweetheart. Absolutely right. Is that all your lovers ever did for you?"

Somehow the damned man seemed to keep getting into her psyche before she realized what he was doing.

From deep inside her, Bella felt her own challenge burst forth, propelled by anger. "So you think you could fuck me senseless?" She didn't care if she spewed four letter words, angry with his presumptuousness. "I don't think you could seduce a tree stump."

He chuckled again. "No, but I could seduce you. Right here, right now. And then I'd fuck you senseless."

That did it.

"Fine, Luca Angello. *I dare you.*"

Chapter Seven

"You're on," Luca whispered, his voice husky with promise.

Bella shivered as his hands slid up the sides of the robe, then landed right under her breasts. "Is this a seduction technique—?"

Her breath gasped out as Luca slid one hand into her robe and touched her bare stomach. Sparks of arousal tightened the muscles between her legs. She moistened even more, aware her naked flesh was already highly aroused.

Again he pressed her against his groin. "Yes? You were saying?"

She couldn't say. Her senses went traitor, turning her knees to putty and her heart jumping in her chest. He took his index fingers and with a delicate touch that amazed her, drew wide circles around her breasts. He didn't cup, and he didn't reach for her nipples. Just those few tender brushings on her naked skin sent more deep stirrings into her stomach and her nipples went taut. With an agonizing pace that turned her senses to melted butter, he brushed his hands over Bella's hips, her butt, the sides of her breasts, all the while kissing her neck. On and on he tantalized, his warm breath puffing into her ear.

It seemed he'd been soothing her forever when his hands cupped her breasts with the barest of touches. She stiffened. "Detective…"

"Luca," he whispered, with a hot, drugging tone. "Call me Luca."

He cupped her breasts without doing anything else, holding them with a gossamer pressure until her nipples grew even harder.

She couldn't believe it. She wanted more. More. "Luca, I need...I need you to..."

"What, sweetheart? This?" As if he'd read her mind, he drew his fingers up until he clasped her nipples between thumb and forefinger.

"Oh," she gasped, a soft moan escaping her.

He didn't move his fingers. He simply held her nipples between his fingers, exerting the tiniest of pressure. "Like that?"

"Oh, yes." The sigh escaped her mouth before she could hesitate.

His fingers clasping her hard nipples felt so damned good she couldn't believe it. She wouldn't have imagined, even minutes ago, that she would feel this wild for more, wanting him with an explosive urgency that made her writhe against him.

A splinter of heat raced from her breasts down to her loins. Luca kissed her ear, then stuck his tongue inside. She shivered in pleasure, and a deep, rumbling laugh of pure male satisfaction came from his wide chest.

He let out a soft groan as he rotated his hips against her, a continual, sensual thrust of his erection against her back. She required that hardness nestled between her legs with a sweet ache that made her want to scream. Pounding, sudden need obliterated all hesitation.

He released her breasts long enough to pull her robe apart and lift the hem above her hips. Air-conditioned coolness blew against her skin, but the heat of his body more than made up for it.

"That's it," he whispered against her ear. "Remember what I said earlier about making you come by just touching your breasts?"

In an agony of wanting, she pressed back into him. "Yes."

"Do you want to come now?"

"Yes."

Damn the man! He'd driven her to within an inch of meltdown, her throat raw and aching, her breathing shallow and rapid, and her heart ready to pound out of her chest.

She cared about nothing but getting to that big O she'd heard about so often and never experienced while making love with a man. A woman's own finger never rejected her and always got it right. Nothing said this man could or would provide her with that illusive ecstasy.

She still had her doubts.

Her body didn't seem to care what she thought as warm moisture trickled between her legs. She pressed her legs together in a special agony reserved for the sexually frustrated. A moan of pleasure parted her lips, and when his hands clasped her naked breasts, she jerked in surprise.

"Easy. Easy," he murmured into her ear. "We're going to do this nice and slow, and soft." Seconds later he cupped her butt and said, "Oh, baby. This is a cute little tattoo." He chuckled softly. "A heart. When did you get it?"

She couldn't think for a moment. "When I was nineteen. On a dare."

He caressed her butt with tender touches, soothing and arousing all at once. "I love it."

His thumbs and forefingers returned to their gentle pressure and clasped her nipples with the lightest touch. Instead of the expected revulsion or the instantaneous irritation she expected to feel, pleasure blasted into her like a firestorm.

"Luca, please." She didn't know what she needed, but she burned with a desire stronger than anything she'd felt before. "Please."

"Tell me what you want."

His soft request, said with a gentleness and pure pleasure that seared her to cinders, made more than her flesh tingle. Her heart blew wide open.

"I want to come."

"Bella, I guarantee it."

His tone held a male conceit she would call irritating if she hadn't found it all out erotic. She knew he meant it. Luca intended for her to have a good time.

Inhibitions did one last gasp, then expired.

She twisted against him, and he replied with a sinuous twist of his hips and a rotation against her butt. His fingers tugged her nipples.

"Oh, God," she gasped.

"Again?"

"Please."

He plucked her nipples once. She shivered. He plucked again. She moaned.

"Again?" he asked.

"Yes."

Luca tugged at the sensitive flesh, rolling her nipples with a gentleness that made her crazy and surprised all at once. Emotions welled inside her, threatening to overwhelm the raging excitement. She could panic and shove him away. She could beg him to fuck her. Bella didn't know which she wanted to do more.

Then his skillful fingers plucked her hard nipples again, and she had her answer.

She wanted him inside her, thrusting inside her like a pile driver, removing all doubts, all fears, all cares.

He stuck his tongue in her ear and started a motion that mimicked sex in no uncertain terms. He continued the tempo, so carnal that she thought it might drive her straight out of her mind.

Tug. Pluck. A soft brush of his thumbs. Tug. Pluck. Tug. Pluck.

"Luca." She heard the pleading in her voice and didn't care.

He continued to torture her until she thought she'd go mad. Suddenly he twirled her around. With a slow movement he removed her glasses and put them on the kitchen counter. His hands landed on her breasts at the same time his mouth took hers. His tongue plunged into her mouth, thrusting and tangling in a primeval ritual of stroke and retreat. Every gentle but persistent stroke of his fingers over her nipples, each pump of his tongue against hers, made her moan with heightened arousal.

Luca ground his erection against her stomach, and broke off the kiss. He whispered against her ear. "You want me between your legs, Bella?"

As he thrust against her, she couldn't deny she wanted each inch of that hardness buried deep up inside her. She licked her lips.

"Say it, Bella. Say it."

"I want you between my legs."

Groaning with satisfaction, he bent down and kissed the valley between her breasts.

His right hand slid across her belly, circling and brushing with tantalizing sweeps that made her muscles jerk and flutter. His fingers touched between her legs, and she gasped as sensitive tissues enjoyed the gentle stroking. With a light movement he slid his fingers over her labia and caressed in a continuous circle. Spreading her wetness, he allowed his fingers to dance and flick. He pressed and rotated against nerve endings that tingled and throbbed.

As he looked into her eyes, liquid desire dampened her again, and he moistened his fingers with it. Seconds later, he barely touched her clitoris. One brush across the surface made her shiver in his arms as hot pleasure rocketed through her. Another pull on her breast and a soft strum across her clit made her writhe. Shocked by the enflamed desire dancing through her with such ease, Bella kept the last bit of control. Luca seemed to sense it and started a consistent pressure on her clit.

Unable to resist, she closed her eyes and gave in to extraordinary delight. Incoherent words slipped from her throat, and Bella heard her voice begging. She knew that any minute she would come unglued. His hand left her mound as he returned to torturing her breasts into stinging hard points. Luca shifted and his tongue flickered across one nipple with a continuous caress that sent her libido up another inch.

"Want more?" His hot breath gusted over her breast, and when she nodded, he returned to his sensual onslaught. "You're going to come, Bella. Come for me."

His tongue bathed her nipples, laving them with wet, long laps of his tongue over and over, and then he drew one captive nipple between his lips and sucked hard. She moaned and then clawed at his shirt, trying to find some shelter in the relentless storm against her senses.

Never in her life would she have thought the relentless attention to her breasts, the persistent licking and sucking, could make her experience that illusive orgasm. Yet the climb began until it rippled and flowed between her legs like a tide. As he kept one nipple clasped between thumb and finger, his mouth continued to suck the other. With ravenous attention he attended to her breasts until the throbbing between her legs became an almost painful pounding need for release.

A hot bolt of indescribable pleasure jolted through her loins without warning, and she gasped in astonishment. She grabbed his shoulders and her fingers tangled in the sleeves of his T-shirt as she held on for dear life. The thunderbolt sensation died as quickly as it began, and she moaned in startled pleasure.

"Oh, God, yes," he whispered as she shuddered and moved in his arms. He chuckled softly as he released her breasts and looked down at her tenderly. "Want more?"

Bella could choose to be embarrassed that the man had seen her come. Never in her life could she have imagined getting off from having him play with her breasts, but the damn man had done it. She'd dared him and he'd given her what she'd desired for so long.

He smiled, cocky and apparently satisfied that she'd climaxed. He kissed her forehead with a gentleness that made her heart ache. "What do you want? Tell me, and tell me in no uncertain terms."

Well, since you put it like that, Luca Angello.

Her hands clutching at the powerful sculpture of his arms. "Please."

Again his fingers slipped down to her clit and strummed. She moaned as sensitive tissues cried out for a finishing climax.

Bella had never begged for sex before, and had *never* asked for a man to fuck her blind. But that's what she wanted, and she wanted it now with such a rampant frenzy she could barely see straight.

"What do you need?" His voice went rough, his arousal evident. The continual stroke of his fingers would make her rocket into the sky again at any moment. "Tell me."

He gently inserted two fingers deep inside her, and she panted and groaned. Rubbing and thrusting, Luca used a motion that caressed high and deep. Then he withdrew slightly until he hit the proverbial G-spot. She'd heard of it, even knew where the damned thing was supposed to be, but she'd never received any pleasure from rubbing it or having it stroked.

He kissed her, hard and long, the carnal movement of his tongue setting off new explosions of wild need. He stopped kissing Bella and let his fingers slide from her, and she almost launched a protest. Feeling greedy, she almost shoved his fingers up her vagina again and asked point blank for a G-spot massage.

"What do you want?" he asked again.

Just say it, Bella. It's what you want. Lose the pride. Gimme a G-spot massage.

No. That won't be enough.

"Fuck me," she whispered.

"I can't hear you." His voice, sexy as hell and full of teasing, brushed against her ear warm and pleasing. "Tell me again."

"*Fuck me.*"

Her own words aroused her, and she enjoyed telling a man what she wanted in blunt terms. It freed her in a way she never experienced before.

Luca drew back just enough so she could see his smile. He chuckled against her lips, and then stepped from her arms. "With pleasure. Don't go away."

Bella leaned against the counter, her breaths panting as she struggled for control. She'd allowed a man she hardly knew to touch, stroke, and suck her in ways she'd never allowed another man to do. A man who frightened her in strange ways, and who seemed to have a magic touch. She closed her eyes, aware there were no covers on his windows in the kitchen and like the day when she'd ogled him, anyone could see what they were doing. A wondrous, forbidden thrill pulsed between her legs, rebuilding the deep, hungry desire. She glanced at those naked windows and smiled.

A condom landed on the counter next to her, and he strode into the room. She looked at his crotch and saw that his arousal hadn't abated. Feeling empty and ready to throw him on the floor and ride him, she watched as he approached with a catlike intensity. His grace and strength, evident in every powerful movement of his body, notched her arousal into the stratosphere.

Screw consequences.

His dark eyes blazed with renewed interest as he cupped her face tenderly. He placed sweet kisses on her face, starting with her forehead, her nose, and her chin. The unexpected gentleness made her need for him grow another inch, and she felt the muscles between her legs clench and release, clench and release.

If she expected him to immediately enter her, she was wrong.

Instead, he got down on his knees in front of Bella. Anticipation made her grip the counter tightly. "Luca."

He smiled up at her as his hands clasped her thighs. "Mmm. I think I like the sound of that. Open wide."

Willing to do anything to reach another climax, she parted her thighs. He wedged between them and began to savor her inner thighs with sweet, delicate kisses. When men had given her head, she pretended to like it. Not that she abhorred the idea, but it never seemed to be as exciting as everyone made it out to be. Her thighs quivered, and she tilted her head back as he licked along one fold of her labia.

"Oh, God. Yes!" She couldn't keep the words in as he licked with gentle, teasing sweeps. He seemed to lick her for an eternity before he drove his tongue inside her. A string of curses left her lips as desire shot her upward a few more degrees. As he fucked her with his tongue, each stabbing movement made her vagina contract and release. For what seemed forever, he tormented and thrust, again and again.

Then he did the most mind blowing thing of all.

With a touch so light she barely felt it, he parted her and opened her clit to full exposure. Sensitized from previous stimulation, she didn't think she could stand it if he—

Lick.

He tapped her clit with his tongue and she whimpered. Each pass of that wicked tongue seemed to find new territory. She buried her fingers in his hair, holding him in place. Another stroke over one side of her bud led to another flicker of his rasping tongue on the other side. He never pressed too hard or too often in one spot, stimulating and tantalizing. When she thought she might scream, he covered her bud with his entire mouth and began to suckle.

"Ah!" She thrashed against his mouth until he grabbed her hips.

He released her clit from his mouth and grinned up at her. "Like that?"

"Holy son of a—do I like it?"

He laughed and placed his mouth over her again. He sucked gently. He added to the excruciating pleasure when he reached up and started pinching and rolling her nipples.

Just when she thought she'd come again, he pulled away.

Panting for breath, she managed to speak. "Luca, if you don't—"

"Don't worry, baby. We're going to make love now." His eyes smoldered not only with lust, but a growing tenderness that made her heart accelerate with fresh desire.

Make love.

She never expected him to say those words in such sweet terms. As if he took her like a woman he loved and not for a screw designed to prove a point. As if she'd never dared him to fuck her.

But that he wanted with his whole heart and soul, to make love to her forever.

Luca stood and kissed Bella's lips, and she tasted herself on his mouth.

He turned her around so that her hands landed on the counter. She heard him fumbling with his belt and zipper, then watched as he reached for the condom.

With soft persuasion, he urged her to part her legs. With guidance from his hands, he drew her back so that she bent over the slightest bit. He dipped down a little to align his hips with hers. She moaned when the hard, hot tip of his penis touched between her legs. Luca moved his left hand up to her left breast and took her nipple between finger and thumb and exerted a soft pressure. She writhed against the prickling pressure.

Then he thrust.

Slow, gentle, but inexorable, he slid deep until he could go no further, and she gasped and pushed against him in astonished pleasure. Hard and hot, his arousal sent a pounding throb throughout her vagina. And he hadn't started to move yet.

Oh, my God. He feels even better than in my fantasies. Hotter, longer, wider. Just plain bigger.

Panting, she moved against him, wanting his possession with a wildness she'd never experienced before. She moaned. When he slipped his hand in a lingering caress down her belly, then stroked down to her clit for a languorous massage, Bella thought she'd die.

She wanted him to move, to show her what his penis could do, but Luca refused. He kept his penis pushed high and deep; his fingers started a new dance on her breasts. He crimped the helpless nipples, drawing on them softly like his mouth might suckle. Sliding his middle finger down her belly again, Luca initiated a stroke around and over her clit.

"Oh, please, please, please!" At one time begging would have seemed unimaginable to Bella, but now she would do it until she got what she wanted. "Please."

He kissed her neck. "Slow. I want you ready again."

"I *am* ready." Frustration showed in her voice, but she took deep breaths and tried to calm down.

He rotated his hips against her, grinding inside her. Her heart pounded as the slow rub of his penis created the most mind-blowing friction she'd ever experienced. Luca's harsh breath blew against her neck as she felt his excitement mount.

She begged, she pleaded, she tried to push back against him to make him thrust harder, but he wouldn't. Finally he stopped stroking her hypersensitive clitoris and cupped her breasts.

"Damn it, Luca," she growled, surprised by the force of her need. "If you don't finish me, I will die."

"You got it, sweetheart."

He grabbed her hips and drew out of her. He rammed inside her and held deep.

She jolted with the next powerful thrust. Another deep, hard stroke almost sent her over. By now she was whimpering, almost crying with the need for release.

Luca increased the pace until he jack-hammered, pounding his penis into her with such fury she knew she'd reached the end of her limit.

She chanted. "Oh, God. Oh, yes. Oh, my God!"

Tiny orgasms sparked and tingled in her vagina. Feeling slick, hot and more aroused than she could have imagined in a million Sundays, she allowed the earth-shaking sensation of his hips pounding between her thighs to send her over the final precipice. She was panting so hard, she feared she'd hyperventilate.

Fireworks exploded between her legs.

Her belly tightened, her legs stiffened. She seemed suspended on the cusp for one moment. Then…

Bella came.

A scream ripped from her throat as everything broke away and roared through her body in a melting rush of incredible heat, spreading from loins through her belly, up toward her face and throat.

As she hovered on an incredible wave of pleasure, he continued to fuck her without pausing, his breath rasping.

His body lurched, thrust hard and held. Then he started thrusting again, his breathing harsh. She thought there was nothing left within her to give, but as his penis continued a merciless hammering, the rush built again.

Not in a million years. I don't believe this.

Luca's fingers found her nipples again and danced over them as he thrust high and deep inside her.

Bella's vagina began to twitch and clench in another building climax. As his gyrating, pumping hips slid hot and slick between her legs, Bella screamed again.

Bone-melting pleasure struck her like a blow. Her hips jerked, and she bucked as shards of mind-splintering excitement blew her apart.

His guttural cry of fulfillment echoed in her body as she felt him shake. She felt his penis swell and explode as a series of masculine growls issued from his throat with each remaining thrust.

Chapter Eight

Bella sagged against the counter, her body aware of Luca's rapid breath against her neck, his arms tight around her ribs, his penis buried deep inside her. Fine tremors twitched through her skin and shook her in ways she'd never been moved before.

Emotions threatened to invade. Gratitude, amazement, and to her surprise, tender sentiments.

"God, Bella." He uttered a ragged groan, then cleared his throat. "I've never had a fuck like that in my entire life."

Luca's blunt words, in the aftermath of a head-splitting orgasm, somehow sounded crass. The "F" word to describe what they'd done offended her last prudish cell. What sounded sexy earlier now became detached and cold. She'd had sex with a man she barely knew and it hadn't even been face to face. They'd rammed away at each other like animals. *God, how insane can I be?*

He shifted and his still-hard penis moved inside her sensitive tissues. She involuntarily squeezed him and contracted. He gasped and pulled out. Her rear felt cold without him, and then her robe slid over her butt again, and she no longer felt the air conditioned breeze on her bare areas.

"Be right back," he said softly.

She continued to lean on the counter, her mind turning to mush at the prospect of understanding everything that transpired between her and this cop.

Never in a million years would she have guessed that within two days of meeting this man, she would have made love with him until she felt dizzy. She straightened and tied her robe together. Thirsty, she went to a kitchen cabinet and searched until she located a tall glass. After slugging back a large amount of water, she sighed in relief. She never knew sex could make a person so parched. A satisfied smile curved her lips. She never knew sex could be this exciting. Period. Gratification took a little of the edge off the niggling feeling she'd just done something she shouldn't have.

Luca returned, dressed in a pair of relaxed cotton pants and a sleeveless black t-shirt that clung to his muscles. His grin held a tenderness that belied the bluntness of his words earlier. He didn't approach, put his arms around her, and whisper undying love. No one did that within two days acquaintance if they had their head screwed on straight. She'd been damn lucky he'd remembered a condom, because she'd been so out of her mind she would have taken him without one.

A frown creased his brow. "What's wrong?"

She took her glasses, which lay on the counter, and plopped them on her face again. He came into fine focus, and now looked even more incredible with his hair tousled and the glow of satisfaction radiating from him. His animal grace and power meant sexual energy poured from him. A fine, overwhelming sensuality that other women experienced and understood and could take or leave. Craving for another round of hard, hot sex started to grow inside her, and she knew right away she'd made a mistake allowing this man to touch her in the first place.

He moved closer. "Bella, what's the matter?"

She walked passed him. "I'm going to bed."

He caught her arm above the elbow and held her back. "What? It's not that late."

She licked her lips. "I'm tired. Let me go, please."

With a heart far heavier than it should have been, she stalked away to the guestroom.

That night she dreamed. A dark figure hovered near her bed, and she lay helpless. Her entire body felt paralyzed. She wanted to scream, and in her dream she did, her heart pounding so hard she thought it would burst from her chest.

She awoke with a start and sat straight up in bed. Reaching for the bedside light, she glanced around the room frantically. No one was in the room. She'd locked the door before she went to bed, half-assured that Luca would try and seduce her again in the night.

Bella shivered as old memories crept forward again. Deep inside she knew why she dreamed about a figure hovering over her in the night. But it was so much simpler to forget. Sinister thoughts homed in on her, desiring a return of her fear and worry. Instead she shoved them away, knowing she couldn't add one more problem to her life.

She could deny nightmares. She could forget her family troubles.

How would she forget Luca Angello when the time came?

* * * * *

Luca jumped when the phone rang. He threw his magazine onto the nightstand and grabbed the phone.

"What's up?" Damon asked as soon as Luca picked up the phone.

"Unfortunately, everything."

"Huh?"

"Long story."

Damon laughed. "If it has something to do with all the time you've been spending lately with Isabella Markham, then I believe it."

Luca grunted. "Tell me something promising. Like you've already caught the serial killer and I don't have to worry about the bastard any longer."

"Wish I could. Hey, I wanted you to know that Mr. Markham called the Captain earlier to check up on you."

Luca shifted back onto the pillows. "Figures. Bella and I had a conversation with him earlier. I assured him his little girl would be in safe hands."

"Your hands?"

Damon's insinuating tone made Luca wish his partner was right there, so he could shove a fist through his face. "Screw you, Damon."

"Sorry, buddy, you're not my type," Damon said in a pseudo-falsetto voice. "What's with the aggression? Did I hit a little too close to home? I mean, she's okay if you're just looking for something to fuck—"

"Shut up. She's a smart, courageous, gorgeous—"

He strangled the words, but he'd already done the damage. A few telltale terms slipped out and doomed him forever. Damon would never let him live this down. He gritted his teeth and closed his eyes.

"Hey, you haven't uh...you're not starting to fall for her or something are you?" Damon's voice, to Luca's surprise, didn't hold a hint of teasing. "You know, the 'take home to momma' type of serious?"

Luca didn't know. For a few seconds he let silence hang on the line, well aware that not speaking condemned him, too. An outright refusal should have flown from his mouth. Instead his brain tried to form the right words that meant that she'd been a good lay, but nothing romantic or long-lasting. Instead he received silence from the part of him that should have shouted *hell no.*

Luca cleared his throat. "She's a classy lady. All right?"

Not a one-night stand, not a love-and-leave-'em fuck. That's what he'd wanted to say, but it would be hypocritical. He had taken her once, but he didn't plan to again. That made her a one-night stand. Shame boiled up.

As if realizing he wouldn't receive a straight answer anytime soon, Damon continued. "Seems the illustrious Mr. Markham was impressed with you, Sport."

118

"Ha. Right."

"No, really. Heard Captain O'Hara going on about how his men always did a good job. I guess Markham must have sung your praises; otherwise the Captain would have your head on a platter by now. You're not exactly assigned to protect her, you know."

"I'd say the Captain is keeping kissy-face relations going with a prominent citizen but Markham is in Denver. I wouldn't think Markham would have that much influence here in Piper's Grove."

"Yeah, the Captain has made a fine art of butt kissing. Wonder if he could give me lessons?"

"There's an image."

Damon's laughter grated against Luca's nerves in a way it normally wouldn't. Luca's encounter with Bella left him raw, his skin feeling as if a thousand pinpricks danced over the surface. Damn Isabella Markham for getting under his defenses. Now that he'd tasted, touched, and felt the tight, hot clutch of her body, he wanted more. He couldn't have some, no matter how much he wanted it. Because down deep he knew if he took her again, he'd want her over and over like opiate in the blood.

Moments later, conversation completed with Damon, Luca turned off the light. He eased his thoughts away from the gut-wrenching excitement and pleasure he'd experienced as he'd made Bella climax. Seeing the flush of her skin, the gasps, the moans, the tightening of her body over his hard dick, almost sent him over the edge far earlier than he'd wanted. Her challenge, that he couldn't make her senseless with pleasure, that he couldn't fuck her until she screamed in orgasm, had spurred him like a madman. He couldn't recall ever being that horny and out of control.

He hated it.

From this point forward, he would ease back into the formal zone, refusing to allow his libido to dictate a dangerous path. His destruction would come if she pressed sexual harassment charges or got it into her head that she wanted more from him than a casual relationship.

He must keep his head on straight and his hands off her to perform his job with professionalism. As Luca closed his eyes, though, the memory of holding her in his arms haunted him.

* * * * *

Golden light touched the horizon when Bella tiptoed out of her bedroom. She peeked around the guestroom doorway, hoping Luca hadn't gotten up yet. When she didn't see or hear a sign of him, she started down the hallway.

This morning she wore a conservative short sleeved top and chino pants. No more skin-tight shorts or breast-hugging shirts for her. She'd dared a virile man to a duel, and he'd won hands down. She yawned as her tired body took the hallway at a dragging pace. She'd remained wide-eyed most of the night as her brain refused to forget the most stunning sexual experience of her life. After tossing and turning for hours, she'd read a nature magazine lying on the bed stand. Even that diversion hadn't cured her need.

Bella wanted to be taken by Luca again and know again the relentless ecstasy of his hips pumping between her thighs. She flushed just thinking about how he'd made her scream. If she hadn't restrained her voice at least a little, the whole neighborhood would have thought she was being murdered.

Waves of heat flowed over Bella's skin when she recalled the exquisite feeling of Luca's erection stuffed deep inside her. Last night, nerve endings she didn't know existed flared to life, and they had a hell of time forgetting the encounter. How would she face him this morning? Annoyed with herself for running away from him, Bella knew she could save face if she confronted their sexual encounter like an adult. No more running and no pretending it didn't happen. It still amazed her that Luca had been the one to bring her to full flower sexually.

As her soft-soled sandals kept her footsteps quiet, she went toward the kitchen. Maybe she could make some coffee before Luca appeared. After filling the coffee pot with some chocolate blend coffee she located in the pantry, she leaned against the counter and listened to the machine sputter. Tempting chocolate scents wafted to her nose, and she realized that she leaned against the counter in much the same way she had last night.

The most exciting, maddening guy she'd ever met had catapulted her into a skull-splitting orgasm. *And* made her realize that her fantasies of hot sex weren't pipe dreams never to be fulfilled.

She rubbed her forehead. *I must get out of here and clear my head.* To her chagrin more erotic images, these brand new and as yet unperformed, popped into her head. Luca on top of her, sliding his hard, hot penis in and out of her with excruciating slowness. Her sitting on top of him and riding his probing hardness until they gasped for mercy. Her tongue gliding over his penis from root to tip and back again until his hips bucked and he came.

She groaned. "Oh, shit."

"Something wrong?" a deep voice asked.

Bella almost jumped clear of her skin as her heart slammed against her chest and her breath left in a whoosh. She whirled around. "Do you have to sneak up on me like that?"

Looking normal and unimposing in a dark emerald T-shirt tucked into new jeans, Luca grinned. "Don't like being caught talking to yourself?"

"I talk to myself frequently." She shrugged. "So, sue me."

He held up one broad hand, a smile still planted on his mouth and his eyes showing genuine amusement. "No, I don't think so. You could hire a more expensive lawyer than I could. I'd lose."

Giving in to his humor, she said, "Most likely. Undoubtedly."

One of his dark brows went up, and her gaze caught on the scar. She needed a diversion and jumped for the chance to change the subject. "Where did you get that scar? And that white hair?"

The coffee pot coughed and gurgled, and she reached for cups and saucers while awaiting his answer. When Luca sauntered closer, Bella felt a sensual shiver race through her as she caught the scent of warm, woodsy, cologne. Had he put the new scent on for her? That seemed hard to believe. Just because they'd been intimate didn't mean he wanted to please her. She poured them both a cup of coffee, adding cream and sugar to hers.

"Well?" she asked when he didn't speak. "Or is it a touchy subject? I'd think a big, bad cop would enjoy talking about his war wounds."

"Is that the way you see me? Big and bad?"

His even tone of voice and the unfettered amusement in his eyes made her wish she'd never crawled from bed this morning. "I think it's the way you see yourself."

Luca shook his head, and she noticed for the first time that he'd tied his thick hair back with a narrow leather strip. Nothing fancy or decorative for this guy. No, siree.

"I suppose women think it's sexy," she said without thinking. "The scar, I mean."

The last words sent red hot embarrassment into her face. *Keep it up, Bella. Open your mouth and say anything. Anything at all.*

Luca's gaze took on a sultry, hooded look that made him sexier than any man had a right to be. "Do *you* think it's sexy?"

His soft drawl, bordered with sensual nuances, made her pulse quicken. Sarcasm, though, parted her lips. "If I liked the pirate look, I might."

That brow twitched again, and he took a slow sip of his coffee. A contemplative look entered his eyes. "Okay, I'll tell you. On one condition."

She put up a hand in defensive. "Oh, no. We tried that yesterday and…"

She couldn't say it, and the fact that she couldn't made her mad as hell.

He continued. "The condition is that you go with me to the station today while I check some things out."

"Is that all?"

Luca gave her a quirky grin that probably turned hundreds of women into drooling idiots. "What? You want more conditions?"

As his gaze danced over her somewhat conservative outfit, she looked away. "No. One condition is fine."

"Good. I don't know about you, but I need some breakfast."

As Bella helped him cook eggs and toast, she also chastised herself. She'd allowed curiosity about his scar and white hair to circumvent talking about their encounter last night. Before she could tell him there wouldn't be any more lovemaking, Luca launched into an explanation about his scar.

"I didn't get this scar from the streets. At least not as a cop. When I was about ten, this bully was running around beating up little kids on my street."

She frowned as she stirred the eggs in the skillet, and he popped bread into the toaster. "He beat you up?"

"No. I was always pretty large for my age."

Her gaze insisted on passing over his solid chest and muscular arms. "I can imagine."

"My dad said he wished someone would kick that bully's ass and teach him a lesson. He didn't mean for me to hear it—he was grousing to my mother—but I took him seriously."

"Oh-oh."

"Exactly. I introduced the bully to my fist, and he introduced my head to the pavement."

She winced. "Ouch."

"All I got was this scar." He pointed at his forehead, then reached for the utensil drawer. "He got a concussion and a hospital stay."

"Did you get in trouble?" She gathered plates and sat them on the counter.

Luca grabbed the bread as it was tossed out of the toaster. "My dad grounded me for a month and the bully's parents threatened to sue our family."

She paused in the middle of buttering her toast. "You're kidding!"

"Nope. You know how it is in 'Sue-happy America'. The bully's parents said their little peach of a boy couldn't possibly be the one beating up other kids."

"Why am I not surprised? What happened then?"

"My dad had a long talk with the parents."

She grinned. "He didn't beat them up, did he?"

Luca returned her smile. "No. But the bully's parents didn't sue, and the bully never bothered another kid on my block again. Dad was a pretty big guy himself."

"Was?" she asked softly, half fearful of his answer.

"Dad had a car accident when he was forty-five. Paralyzed him from the waist down. That's when I started to grow this weird white stripe of hair. Don't ask me why it happened, it just did."

"Oh, God. I'm so sorry." Sympathy ran deep inside her. "Do you have a good relationship with him?"

After taking a healthy swallow of coffee, he nodded. "Yeah. He's a tough, New York sort of guy. Born and raised in the city. They moved out here to Colorado about three years ago because they said they needed a change. They were starting to dislike the big city atmosphere."

"And they like it here?"

He nodded. "At first they weren't so sure. They were used to a different culture. But then they realized they liked the open spaces in the west. They've got a nice old house not that far from my place."

"Do you have any other family?" She decided that since she'd slept with the guy, she had to know the answer. She blurted it out. "Kids? A wife?"

His gaze snapped to her, sharp and evaluating. Disappointment threaded across his face, a sardonic touch. "You think I would have had sex with you last night if I had a wife and kids?"

"Some men would."

He put down his coffee and stared at her hard. "I'm not some men. If I was married you can be damned sure I'd be faithful to my wife."

She inhaled deeply, relief flooding through her in a wave. "You can't blame me for asking. I heard you on the phone the other day saying you missed someone and that you loved them."

His face eased into a less forbidding expression. "That was my little sister Diana. She's got twin toddler boys. They're super kids. She's recently divorced, though, and she's been having a hard time of it."

"I'm sorry to hear that."

"She's tough. She's had a lot of things happen to her in her life and she's only twenty four. She'll make it, though, and so will her boys."

Her heart softened with sweet, appreciative warmth. A man who loved his sister enough to tell her how much he cared, and adored his little nephews—it was hard not to have twinges of deep feeling for Luca.

Oh, no. That melting sensation around her heart said he'd already wended his way inside her feelings far more than she wanted.

Curiosity kept Bella asking questions. "So you're the oldest?"

He glanced at her a moment as if he might not answer her. "Yes. All my siblings are younger than me, but not by much. I've got three brothers, Carmine, William, and Anthony. Diana is the baby."

"Oh, I'll bet you guys give her the big brother protective syndrome." She knew she sounded derisive.

"What are big brothers for? She laps it up most of the time. Except when we used to scare the crap outta her boyfriends when she was in high school."

She couldn't help but laugh when he changed to a stronger New York accent, rough and no-nonsense. "What do your siblings do?"

"Diana is a grade school teacher in New York State. She's considering moving her family out here and she's on vacation right now trying to make that decision. Anthony is a parole officer in Connecticut, William is a construction worker wherever it suits him. I think he's decided staying in Colorado is what he wants to do, though. And Carmine is a manager for Mom and Dad's restaurant."

"Restaurant?"

"Dad and Mom opened an Italian restaurant after they got married. They inherited a little money from Granddad Giovanni Angello. Granddad was from Italy and had a restaurant there before he immigrated in the last half of the nineteenth century. When they moved to Colorado they opened a new restaurant here in Piper's Grove."

Suddenly Bella imagined a big, rowdy family, all of them talking at once. She wondered if the stereotype fit. "That sounds great. Maybe I've heard of the place. What's it called?"

"Marcello's, after my Dad."

She grinned. "I know that place. I've heard wonderful things about it, but haven't tried it yet. I'd love to go some time." She blushed, realizing that it sounded like a blatant invite. "I mean, I'll have to go there some time. Your family sounds wonderful."

To her surprise, a gentle smile curved his mouth. "They are the best family a man could have."

Sharp envy spiked through Bella, and she went silent as she scooped scrambled eggs onto two plates. He took the spatula out of her hand and turned her toward him for a second. He looked deep into her eyes, his gaze attentive and searching. Wild heat curled through her stomach, and Bella wondered if he would kiss her.

That hooded, sensual look invaded his eyes. "You'd like that kind of family, Bella?"

"You know I would." She felt her throat tighten, sensitivity biting through hard-won barriers. "But that's not going to happen."

His look of curiosity fell away, replaced with gentleness. "You'll have a family some day."

"Yeah. Right." Tears welled in her eyes, and she pulled away from him.

"Hey, wait." With a tender touch he grasped her shoulders. "You're going to have that family, Bella. If you want it." She heard him swallow hard. "By the way, speaking of family, Mom, Dad, Will and Carmine are having a barbeque in two days. I wasn't going to be able to go while on duty, but I might be able to sneak it in."

A tickle of joy, so small she couldn't be sure it was real, touched her heart. "And?"

"Dad and Mom promised to cook for me. They've got some dishes that will curl your toes they're so delicious." His fingers tightened on her shoulders. "Come with me."

His voice sounded raspy, as if he had a difficult time saying the words. She couldn't believe he'd asked her to a family event. Mind racing at the implications, she tried to remain nonchalant.

She felt breathless. "Why would you do that?"

Again his Adam's apple bobbed. "Because I think you deserve a taste of good family life."

A small, insignificant fear rose inside her, and she backed away from his touch. "I can't. I may be leaving the condo by then to go back home."

Did she detect disappointment in the black depths of his eyes? "Stay a little longer. Have the best damn Italian food you've tasted. You won't regret it."

Again temptation teased her. She could meet a family that loved each other despite the ups and downs, but would it only remind her of what she didn't have?

"I wouldn't know how to act," she said.

"What?"

"Dad and my sister...they love me, but they don't know how to show it." She smiled in an attempt to lighten the mood. "I'd probably drown in all that showing of affection. You guys are probably big huggers?"

A grin resurrected on his mouth. "We are. How'd you know?"

"It sounds very *Waltonesque*. That's how I guessed."

"We're not perfect. Don't get the wrong idea. Carmine went through a lot trying to decide what he wanted to do with his life. Hell, he was a juvenile delinquent until he saw one of his best friends killed in a gang type shooting. Changed his whole outlook and made him see how precious life is. He went to school to become a chef. He decided he wanted to help Dad with the restaurant, and he's been at it ever since."

"That sounds like a minor bump in the road. I mean, in comparison to what could have happened."

"There's more. Diana got—she got pregnant when she was sixteen. She decided to keep the baby, but she miscarried at five months. She wasn't the same for months."

"Oh, no." Bella couldn't prevent her hand from covering her mouth in a display of sympathy. "That poor girl."

"She hasn't always made the right choices in life. Getting the divorce, though, was probably a good thing. Her ex-husband is an A-number-one asshole. I never wanted her to marry him in the first place, but I wouldn't interfere. She's pretty broken up about it, because she figured she'd have a good life marrying a cop. Instead he's a creep."

"A cop?" She frowned. "I'm sorry to hear that, too."

"Not as sorry as I am."

For one trembling moment she'd almost cried like a silly baby, an orphan who'd never known a home. Bella had a home, albeit it wasn't the greatest, most supportive family. No, the Markhams had never been the loud and laughing group she imagined the Angellos must be.

After they'd settled down to eat, she decided learning more about this man might not be wise. She inhaled and decided now she would talk about last night. Another sip of coffee would give her courage.

"Luca—"

"What made you decide to start calling me by my first name? You were pretty intent for awhile on calling me Detective Angello in that scornful tone."

"Why is it that men always interrupt women?"

A smile slipped over his mouth, then escaped. "*Men* always? Pretty damn sweeping generalization, isn't it?"

Irritation started to accelerate inside her, but she forced it down to remain in control. "It's difficult to call you Detective after what happened last night. As I was going to say before you interrupted, last night was…"

Bella faded, realizing she should have prepared for this.

He looked up from his plate and grinned wickedly. "Wild. Last night was wild."

Well, it was that. "We shouldn't do it again. We were thrown into this situation and things just happened. It didn't mean anything."

A grim expression took ownership of Luca's face, erasing the teasing look. "What exactly is *it*?"

"Don't be obtuse. You know." She put down her fork, the eggs tasting flat without ketchup. She went to his refrigerator. "Sex. S-E-X."

"I know how to spell it."

She located the illusive bottle of red substance and went back to the table. "Ketchup?"

"No thanks." His nose twitched, as if he couldn't stand the thought of it.

"Suit yourself."

"I usually do."

She allowed laughter to escape. "You have an answer for everything, don't you?"

"Most of the time."

So he wouldn't give up or give an inch. She didn't know why she felt like arguing, but the man brought out the beast in her. Her father's pushy tactics inflamed her sense of self-preservation, and so did this man. "And I suppose you think you're always right?"

Luca's mouth dropped open a minute, then snapped closed. "How the hell did we get from sex to me always being right? Which I am, by the way."

She glared at him.

He glared at her.

Bella turned her wrath on her eggs, pouring ketchup and digging into the concoction with relish. She didn't answer him right away, and she knew every moment that passed sent his pissed-off-meter into high gear. She didn't care. The heat pouring off the man made her stomach clench, and Bella recognized with a jolt that antagonizing him turned her on.

How very sick.

"Back to sex, Bella."

"Why?"

"Because I'm going to get a straight answer out of you one way or the other."

"What way is *the other*?"

His nostrils flared the tiniest bit. "Damn it, Bella, just be honest with me. Tell me what's on your mind."

She shoved away her plate and speared her hands through her hair. "I let myself go last night. I did things...said things I've never done or said with another man."

A self-satisfied male grin came to his mouth. "I'm glad."

"Women probably tell you that every day, right?" She allowed a sarcastic tone to tinge her words. "Is that why your ego is so monumentally high?"

"No. My ego was high enough before I had the best damn sex I've ever had."

Bella's world seemed to stop. Everything inside her froze. "*You've* ever had?"

"Yeah." He reached out and touched her hand, squeezed it with gentle pressure before letting her go. "A woman's never made me that crazy before."

His revealing words surprised her, but she didn't know if she could believe them. Sure, Luca had those puppy dog honest eyes right now, the kind that made a woman melt into a pool at his feet, no doubt. He must have been with a lot of women over the years and had plenty of women fall for him.

"But that doesn't mean I should have done it. And I'm not going to do it again, with you," she said.

He stopped eating and stared at her like she'd lost her mind...or maybe found it. "You're right. You've gotten so far under my skin, I forgot my professional ethics. From this point forward, it's hands off all the way."

Conflicting emotions assaulted her. Part of her felt relieved that he'd agreed to hands off, the other part regretted she wouldn't feel his brand of mind-melting sex again.

Chapter Nine

Bella stared at the blank canvas with dismay. She didn't know where to start. The scent of oil paint hung in the air. While she was glad she'd made a trip next door to her condo to retrieve the paints, her puzzlement made the excursion now seem less than worthwhile.

One picture of Luca and now I'm dried up again?

She'd left the first portrait of Luca hidden in the den in her condo. The idea he might recognize the raw emotions she'd captured—and as a result might see through her as well—she couldn't have that.

Now, as she stood in the mini-studio she'd set up in Luca's third bedroom, she stared at the new canvas and knew she must paint again.

Then it hit her.

Your new obsession.

Bella tended to do that when she painted; she discovered a subject that wouldn't let her go until the ravenous need to create disappeared and a new idea came to mind.

Okay, so she wanted to paint Luca again. Nothing wrong with that.

Her fingers felt wooden as she started to paint. Thank goodness the door stayed closed. She'd extracted a promise that if Luca needed to speak with her, he must knock.

Seconds turned into minutes as she drew a new outline of the man.

His fierceness, his power, absolute confidence in himself. This time the rendering came quickly, her hand moving with assurance. A smiling Luca filled with joy formed on the canvas.

She painted a more innocent face, yet not entirely void of his cocky exterior.

Bella looked into those eternally haunting eyes and saw a new emotion mirrored within. A man in love.

Love.

She put her hands to her hot face. "Oh, no."

"Bella?"

Her heart jumped at his deep voice so close behind her. She whirled around as anger spiked inside her. He stood in the doorway, and Bella wondered why she hadn't heard him come in.

She blocked his view of her work. "I told you to knock."

His lips tightened as his eyes flashed. "The door was open."

She took another breath, aware that her fears made her talk first, think later. She pushed her glasses up on the bridge of her nose. "I don't want anyone seeing this yet."

Silence stretched as his answering glare held strong. He started to turn away, but she stepped forward and clasped his forearm. "Wait. I'm really sorry. You startled me."

He glanced over her shoulder. "Was there something you didn't want me to see?"

She moved out of his view of the portrait, allowing him to see the beginnings of his new face. His expression changed gradually, showing surprise and curiosity.

"You're painting me?" Luca sounded awed.

Amazed that he looked so captivated, she drew him nearer, still holding on to his arm. *What the hell, Bella? Tell him the truth.* "This is my second painting of you. There's another I started back at my condo."

One eyebrow quirked up. "Oh, yeah?"

Heat filled her face. "Painting you the way I saw you in the kitchen the other day would take a lot of time."

Now he looked very curious. "Explain."

133

"I don't know if I should."

"Why not?"

Wicked delight filled her and removed her doubt. "You were naked."

His eyes widened. "What?"

"I looked out my kitchen window the other morning and into your kitchen. You were buck naked and drinking water right out of the bottle."

"You shittin' me?"

"No, I'm not. Don't you remember doing that?"

"Yeah, I remember it. Why didn't you say something before?"

"Because at first I thought you might be embarrassed."

He chuckled. "Me?"

She returned his smile. "It wasn't until we...you know...that I realized there wasn't much that could possibly embarrass you."

His wicked grin widened. "So my naked ass inspired you to paint?"

"You could say that."

"Nothing deep and profound, eh?"

"Nope."

Laughter burst out of him. She enjoyed the sound; at one time she never would have guessed Luca could laugh with this abandon. She tried to hold back her own laughter, but then realized she'd restrained merriment for too long. It felt good to hang loose and let it rip.

She put away her paints, feeling a new sense of discovery and release. Maybe it wouldn't be so bad for him to know and see her work. "This isn't a complete painting and neither is the first one. Just a beginning."

Luca cupped her shoulders and turned her toward him. His eyes wouldn't let her escape, capturing her with intensity and demanding answers. "Why did you want to hide this from me?"

"I don't mind constructive criticism, even from people who don't know much about art. After all, I think the proof is in what the untrained eye sees in my painting. If I can't please the casual viewer…" Bella shrugged. "I paint to please myself more than anything, and because I have to paint. I don't always show what I've painted."

He released her. "Do you paint just portraits?"

Bella smiled, her heart opening toward him in a whole new way. She felt more at ease, less on edge now that she felt he understood. "Mostly landscapes." She gestured toward his portrait. "This is definitely a departure."

A crooked smile touched his mouth, one that held mischief and maybe pleasure. "So even if no one approved you'd still paint?"

"Yes. Except lately when the painter's block came along."

"What do you think caused it?"

She suspected, but she didn't want to say. "I'm not sure."

Luca tilted his head to the side, curiosity written in his eyes. "I suppose your sister and father don't approve of your painting?"

She made a scoffing noise. "Oh, they approve all right, but only because I've proved a commercial success. You can bet if I didn't make much money at it, they wouldn't think my painting was worth squat. My studio at home is always locked when I'm inside working. At first I welcomed my father and sister seeing my work. I thought they'd see what I saw when I was painting. Instead they spent more time criticizing than encouraging. I've received no support from them whatsoever accept in public. They say and do the right things in front of other people they want to impress. To my face it is a whole different story."

"Damn, I'm sorry, Bella." He stuffed his hands in his pockets. Looking a little insecure, he glanced at his portrait again. "Is there any way I could buy this when you're done?"

Bittersweet happiness rushed through her. She never expected him to want the portrait. The sincerity and warmth in his expression melted her heart. "It's yours. For free."

"I didn't expect you to give it away. I'll pay."

"It would be pretty expensive on the market. Think of it as a gift."

His lips relaxed into another devastating grin. "Thank you."

Luca's expression took on a sheepish, almost self-conscious quality that seemed more like a little boy than a man. But it didn't take away from his rugged, undeniable masculinity, or from the warmth in her heart.

Seconds later he asked, "You always this jumpy when you're painting? I thought it would relax you and that you'd be happy that you are painting again."

Now that she'd found the inspiration, could she say happiness motivated her? Not hardly. "A person doesn't always paint because they're happy."

"Sounds a bit neurotic to me."

She smiled grimly. "You've heard of Van Gogh, right?"

His answering smile said he understood. "I see."

"Every artist is a little nutty, or so they tell me."

"You don't really believe that?"

She shook her head. "No. Some of us have mental illness, some of us don't. But I believe there is a tendency to lean toward mental problems."

Confidence returned to his face, along with a teasing quality. "Well, Van Gogh, after you get changed, we need to *go* to the office. Come on."

* * * * *

Silent and stern-faced, Luca strode into the bustling police station with Bella in tow. As he swept by the main desk, the officer at the front waved and gave a perfunctory greeting. When the man stared at Bella like she was an unusual hood ornament, Luca bristled. He didn't understand the strange compulsion to punch his fellow officer at first, but the meaning behind it tickled his brain.

He didn't want any man looking at her that way. Any man showing disrespect or leering at her needed a swift butt kicking.

"It's quiet." Bella followed Luca into a large hallway area with various open doorways leading into different departments. "Very quiet."

An almost indignant surprise tinged her voice, and he looked back at her. "We don't usually have that noisy, boisterous crap portrayed on television."

"Cop shows are for entertainment. Not documentaries."

He smiled. "Yeah, yeah. I've heard the argument."

As he gazed at her, Luca almost tripped on the short carpet. *Lift up your feet, Angello. You're acting like a star-struck fan.* How could he help it, when the sundress Bella wore showed her slim, white shoulders and the long line of her neck? Luca remembered how her breasts felt cupped in his palms and the way her nipples puckered into hard, aroused beads. His mouth almost watered as he thought about drawing them deep into his mouth and sucking.

"Something wrong, Detective?" Her eyes held a flirtatious glow, and he wondered if she knew how he felt when she looked at him like that.

Christ, she made him feel like the only man in the world for her.

Dangerous. Scary as hell.

"Not a thing." He turned his attention to not falling over his feet.

Sound carried over the tops of the cubicle walls, computer keyboards clacking and the murmur of quiet voices. Homicide didn't suffer lazy men and women. Captain O'Hara made sure "balls-to-the-wall" defined the area every day.

"So tell me again. Why are we here?" she asked softly.

Luca slowed his fast pace, matching his stride to hers. He lowered his voice. "I need to give Captain O'Hara a report. I can't send it to him with a click of a computer mouse. The man hates email. He's not exactly into the twenty-first century."

Moments later he slipped into his cubicle and looked into his in-basket.

She cleared her throat. "Is this your family?"

Luca caught her gazing at the family picture on his desk, taken when he was about twenty. "Yeah."

She made a noise that sounded like a stifled laugh. "Look at your hair. And I can't believe how goofy your smile is."

"Thanks a lot. I can always count on you for a compliment." He knew she was right. In the picture, curls massed on his head, unwilling to be tamed. "That's one of the reasons I grew it long. It pulls some of the curl out."

She glanced up at him. "No, I didn't mean that as an insult. You look fabulous in longer hair." She licked her lips and clasped her hands together as if she was embarrassed. "I'm sorry. It's just that you're so good looking now—" She cleared her throat. "You're a handsome man." Flushing, she looked damn right mortified. "And don't let that go to your head."

Her praise made his head swell, all right, and something else, too. He almost gritted his teeth to force back the arousal that sent heat rounds straight to his groin. He leaned in a little closer, his desire to kiss her almost swamping his common sense. Bella's lips parted, and he thought he saw her pink tongue. *Oh, yeah.* He'd liked to do things with *his* tongue right about now. He jerked back, blinking as he realized he'd almost given into the desire right here in the office. Not good. Not good at all.

Before he could thank her for the compliment, someone cleared their throat. "Hey, Sport."

Damon stood in the doorway of the cubicle, a shit-eating grin affixed to his broad face. Nothing earth-shattering about that. Damon often wore the mischievous face of a child. "Hey. Damon, I'd like you to meet Isabella Markham."

Damon nodded and shook her hand. "Nice to meet you. Heard a lot about you."

Her eyebrows went up. "Oh?"

Luca's partner gave a lopsided smile that held pure mischief. "You bet. Ole Luca here gave me the full run down on your...activities."

Aggravation boiled up in Luca at his partner's insinuation, and he turned the man with a frown. "Don't tell her any bullshit, Damon. I'm warning you."

Bella's surprised expression returned to low-key amusement. "Don't worry. I can handle Damon."

Damon's eyes widened with a combination of surprise and delight. "I'll bet you could."

More than a little irritated, Luca ignored the desire to give his partner a knuckle sandwich. He'd be damned if anyone would get the idea he cared whether she flirted with another man. Just because he'd had sex with her, she didn't own his emotions.

"Keep an eye on her, Damon, while I talk with the Captain."

"Sure thing."

Bella opened her mouth as if to protest, but Luca ignored it as he left the cubicle.

Captain O'Hara's glass-walled office presided over Homicide division. He sat behind his desk with a phone growing out of his ear and his loud voice coming through the closed door. Luca felt a headache coming on and rubbed his forehead. His ability to blow off his boss's pompous personality was at an all time low. Well, he'd just have to deal with it.

O'Hara saw Luca standing at the door, hand poised to knock. O'Hara waved him in. Still talking on the phone, the thin-as-dental-floss police officer looked pissed. Then again, that wasn't anything new. In fact, Luca couldn't remember that last time his supervisor had smiled. With his Santa-white thick hair and a thin face as lined as weathered rock, the fifty-something cop looked every inch his years. Life hadn't been too favorable toward this man, and because of that Luca understood the crabbiness that often came with the personality. That, and the bastard was a damn good cop.

After issuing commands in no uncertain terms to the hapless individual on the other end of the line, the Captain slammed down the phone. "Jesus H. Christ. These personnel bubbas have screwed up transfer paperwork for the last time."

Luca's head throbbed even harder. He inhaled deeply. "Bad day, Captain?"

With a growl O'Hara said, "Bad week." Eyeing Luca with irritation, the Captain crossed his arms. "What brings you in here?"

Luca handed him the folder with his report inside. "Weekly report."

O'Hara seemed to deflate a little. "Oh, yeah. Good. Sit down." After Luca complied, O'Hara narrowed his eyes. "I don't mind telling you the shit flowing down from the mayor's office is getting heavy. His assistant was in here today reaming my ass very politely and wanting to know why we didn't have a suspect in the serial killer case."

"Because he's a sneaky son-of-a-bitch, Captain."

"That's what I told him, but you know how these political types are. They've got to have someone to blame. I hate this political shit, but what's a guy going to do?"

Tell the truth. Luca knew that his boss played politics well when it suited him. "Did you get him off your back?"

O'Hara looked into a coffee cup sitting on his desk that said *'life sucks and then you die'*. "Eventually. Took awhile." He cleared his throat. "Where's Miss Markham?"

Luca grinned. "Don't look so worried, Captain. She's here with me. Damon's looking after her."

O'Hara rolled his gaze to the ceiling for a moment. "Great. You sure you trust him?"

Luca laughed. "Nope."

O'Hara launched into a discussion on how Mr. Markham had promised support to the police department if they took good care of his little girl. "I don't mind telling you that when Markham called me and said you were protecting his daughter, I about had an aneurism. Since when did you get permission to moonlight as a bodyguard? You're renting that damned condo to keep an eye on the entire neighborhood, not one woman."

Here it comes, Angello. How are you going to explain this one?

Luca tried not to smile. "Sorry I didn't get a chance to mention that. I wasn't exactly thinking straight when I talked to Markham. When I realized that Isabella Markham fits the serial killer's victim profile, I started worrying about her." He explained the noises that Isabella had heard at her condo the other night. "I've got a strange feeling about her, Captain. I know she's in danger and the only way I can make sure she stays safe is to be with me."

O'Hara stared at Luca for so long that Luca almost squirmed. "Uh-huh. Good move, Angello, as long as it doesn't interfere with the rest of your investigation."

Surprised that O'Hara hadn't ripped him a new asshole, Luca said, "No, sir."

O'Hara cleared his throat. "Her father made her sound a little unstable and maybe easily influenced."

Luca felt the pressure in his temples increase yet again, and his neck muscles tightened. "What?"

"Said she's a painter and has an artistic temperament."

"Meaning?"

"Easily upset, prone to tantrums, etc."

Luca chuckled without real amusement, half ticked-off that her father would say these things about her, especially to a stranger. "She's a hard-headed, self-sufficient, intelligent woman." As an afterthought, he said, "Her father is a dickhead."

Luca waited for his supervisor's wrath, but it never came. Instead the man leaned back in his chair and put his hands behind his head. "I agree. Man is richer than God and has an ego to match." His speculative gaze centered on Luca like a heat-seeking missile. "Sounds like you like this woman. You getting involved with her?"

Busted.

Luca kept his tone even. "What's Damon been telling you?"

O'Hara shrugged. "He said he thought you had a boner for her. That's all he said."

Luca winced at the Captain's blunt assessment. "So what makes you think I'm involved with her?"

O'Hara's careless shrug came one more time. "Saw the look in your eyes when you described Miss Markham." He lowered his arms and leaned on the cluttered desk. "Watch your back, Detective. You're not one for enjoying brainless broads. But, and this is a big, fat, hairy but, her father can put a lot of pressure on this department if he thinks his little girl is being screwed. Literally and figuratively."

While he appreciated the Captain's candor, he also didn't like the implications. "I'm keeping her safe. That's all he needs to know."

Captain O'Hara's bushy white brows moved upward. "He doesn't always deal in facts. I can tell that from talking to the guy. I get the feeling he doesn't care what she thinks."

"She's her own woman and makes her own decisions. He's got no say in what goes on in her life."

The Captain's thin lips morphed into a satirical smile. "You sound pretty sure of that. You know I could take you off this case and get her a new bodyguard. You realize that, don't you? I thought her moving in with you was a hair-brained idea to begin with."

"Then why did you give me the go ahead?" Luca asked quietly, determined not to lose his composure.

"Because I trust you to do the right thing, Angello. *Noble as shit* is written across your forehead. Probably the reason all the women around here follow you like puppy dogs. They know a good guy when they see one. They've also heard the rumors, you know."

"What rumors?"

"I heard these women gossiping in the break room one day. Queenie Jacobson said you were a virtual 3-D freaking sex machine. I don't care if you have a penis the size of Mount Rushmore, Detective. Just don't be waving it in front of some high-class lady that could sink her fangs into the department and cause a lot of trouble. Because if you do, you'll be doing more than tripping over your dick every morning. Understand?"

Retaliatory words wouldn't form in Luca's mouth. Luca knew he could be in significant trouble for starting any kind of relationship with Bella. "Yeah. I hear you."

Instead of putting Luca's head on a pike, the Captain grinned. "That's, 'yeah, I hear you, *sir*.'"

Luca allowed a smile to slip out. "Yes, sir."

"I'll read your report and get back you later this evening." He waved his hand in a dismissal. "Now get outta here."

Luca added a salute as he walked out. "With bells on, sir."

Luca's relief almost sent him walking past his cubicle, then he remembered Bella. How could he forget her? Maybe because he'd escaped having his skin ripped off and fed to him. He came to a halt a cubicle away when he heard Damon's low voice.

"You know, you ever get tired of that cynical, hard-nosed jerk of a cop, you can call me any time."

"I thought all cops were cynical." Bella's silky voice vibrated. He felt every syllable go straight into his gut. "Are you telling me you're not?"

"That's right, Miss Markham. Or can I call you Bella?"

"Bella is fine."

"Like I said. You're welcome to call me any time when you get tired of hanging around Angello."

A raw, penetrating heat filled Luca. He wanted to strangle his partner, then hang him by his nuts from a tree. His fists clenched at his side. The pain in his neck increased, and he realized that he'd let his emotions rule him again. A green-eyed monster reared to life inside him. He wasn't proud of it, but there it was.

He stepped into his cubicle to circumvent Damon's blatant come-on and to rein back his own desire to throttle the other cop. Damon hovered near Bella's slim form. His predatory look said he liked being close to her and wanted something more if he could get it.

Luca's chest expanded as he took a deep breath. "Ready to go, Bella?"

She started, almost as if she'd been caught doing something she shouldn't. "Sure." She edged away from Damon's hulking form. "Nice to have met you, Detective."

"Wait for me in the lobby, please," Luca said as she started for the entrance.

She paused, puzzlement on her face. Then she nodded and kept going.

Luca swung toward his partner, his glare full throttle and his anger simmering just under thermonuclear meltdown.

"Keep away from her Damon." Luca kept his voice low and modulated. "I swear to God, if you *ever* touch her, I'll twist your balls off and feed them to you."

Damon put his hands up and took a step back, almost bumping into a chair. "Whoa. Whoa, buddy. What the hell brought this on?"

Luca felt the tension in his head ratchet up a notch. "You were coming on to her, that's what."

Damon's face transformed into amusement and he lowered his hands. "Wow, that's what this is all about? You're worried I'm not being professional?"

"You're harassing her, that's what."

"What makes you think she wouldn't be interested?"

Luca laughed without amusement. "You don't want me to describe the reasons."

Damon's eyes went wide with surprise, then cruel anticipation. "Wait a minute. That's why you're acting so strange. You're jealous as hell."

Luca chose to ignore the anger that said he hated Damon being right and knowing it. "I told you she's a classy woman. She shouldn't be subjected to some gorilla coming on to her on two minutes acquaintance."

A flash of shame ignited somewhere inside Luca.

You're talking about yourself. What do you think you've done to her?

Damon's face went straight and nonchalant. "I'm gonna wait until you calm down to talk about this. Right now you're not thinking straight."

"I know exactly what I'm talking about. She doesn't want anything to do with you."

"How do you know?"

He couldn't recall ever being this pissed at Damon. Instead of following through on a right cross that would get his butt in hot water, he restrained his anger and jammed it deep. He took a restoring breath and tried relaxing his spring-loaded muscles.

Time to act like an adult and surprise Damon with straightforward honesty. Swallowing pride and the distinct possibility he would be mortified, he lowered his voice and spoke the unvarnished truth. "Yeah, I'm jealous. Keep your hands off her, Damon. She's mine."

Bella stood not far away from the cubicle, unwilling to head to the lobby as he'd directed her. Her face burned with a hot excitement she couldn't contain, and her breathing quickened.

Luca jealous?

She's mine.

Those two words echoed in her mind. His rough-edged, deep voice held a no-nonsense tone that said he wanted her again. *Sure gives new meaning to absolute custody.* She vacillated between wanting to brain him for sounding so domineering and enjoying his protectiveness. If she gave into feeling excited by his possessiveness, would she lose her soul?

The idea of having Luca this crazy about her, wanting her so much he'd protect her from another man's unwanted attentions, stirred primordial need inside her. It scared the living crud out of her, and at the same time sent a shivering bolt of desire right between her legs.

Oh, good. I've gone cavewoman.

When he stalked around the corner of the cubicle, the force of his anger felt like a wave. She stepped back and almost bumped into a cubicle wall. He stopped and stared at her, then dawning awareness came to his face. His eyes went stone hard. She waited for his wrath, but it didn't arrive.

"Come on." He took her elbow and guided her through the maze of cubicles and then out through the lobby and to the car. "I'm starving. I think there's a steak in the refrigerator with my name on it."

They reached the lobby when another cop flagged down Luca and asked to talk to him a moment.

"I'll wait here," she said when Luca looked at her expectantly.

When he disappeared down another hallway, Bella realized the lobby made her uncomfortable. Despite the size of the area, she felt hemmed in and watched. She slung her handbag over her shoulder and then slipped out the front door. She waited outside for some time, then glanced at her watch with impatience. Deciding that getting angry wouldn't do her any good, she took a deep breath and looked around the area. She saw a gourmet coffee shop across from the police station. Her mouth almost watered. Then she remembered she shouldn't go anywhere without Luca. Standing outside a police station would be the safest—

A sharp cracking noise filled the air, followed by another and another.

Gunfire.

Chapter Ten

A sedan hurled down the road, a police cruiser screeching after the careening vehicle.

Immobile for one terrifying second, Bella wondered if the gunfire was aimed at her. A man's arm appeared in the open window of the sedan and a large weapon came into view.

Holy shit.

Life slowed down to a slumberous crawl, almost as if nothing happened. She had a few seconds to wonder if it would be all over for her in a hail of bullets. Stark fear clogged her throat at the same time her feet came unglued from the pavement.

She lunged for cover behind a parked police car. Unyielding concrete tore at her fingers and she winced in pain as two of her nails bent back. She landed on her side and scraped her forearm on the unforgiving surface. More shots echoed as the crazy man sent his car down the street. People screamed and shouted. Stunned, she kept her head down and didn't move.

"Bella!" Luca's rough, deep voice sounded desperate and worried. Before she could move, she felt his big hands on her, his fingers tunneling through the hair at the back of her neck.

"Bella, talk to me. Are you hurt?"

She turned and levered into a sitting position, her hair flopping over her eyes. He brushed it away and cupped her face. Worry etched his face, his eyes wide.

She could barely get her breath as adrenaline pushed through her system like a rocket ship. "I'm fine."

Then he saw her arm, scraped and some blood bleeding to the surface. "Damn it. Were you hit?"

Her breath rasped quick in her throat as she held up her arm for inspection. "Pavement burn. Just what I need to go with the scrapes on my side."

"Thank God that's all it is." More descriptive curses left his lips as he slid his arms around her waist and drew her up to her feet. "What the hell were you doing out here? I asked you to stay in the lobby."

Luca's harsh tone pissed her off, and she pulled out of his grasp. Their gazes clashed. A crowd gathered as other police officers spilled out onto the street, including Damon.

Damon walked up, his usual cocky air gone. "She all right?"

"I'm fine," she gritted through her teeth as fear turned into resentment. "No thanks to that asshole that just shot up the entire street." Her legs trembled a little, and she felt nauseous.

As if worried she'd faint, Luca slipped his arm around her shoulders. "You sure you're all right?"

His solicitousness surprised Bella after his earlier irritation. She shoved back her anxiety and the recognition that she could have died. She nodded but didn't speak, and his arm tightened around her a moment before he let go. Luca and Damon listened to her explanation of what happened. A few other officers observed. Bella felt like a fish on display in a tank.

Luca rubbed his hand over his jaw. "We'll need to take your statement."

She brushed more hair away from her face, her hand trembling and the sting of her abraded arm annoying her. She nodded, resigned. All the fight seemed sucked from her for the moment. As he led her back into the office, she knew the rest of her day couldn't be any more strange and terrifying than this.

Keeping his hand locked around her upper arm as they walked, Luca pinned her with a hot, absorbing gaze. "When I heard the gunfire and realized you weren't around anywhere..." He swallowed. "It scared the shit out of me, Bella."

Her heart acknowledged his worry and reveled in it only because it meant he cared. She didn't wish to cause him pain, but a selfish part of her rejoiced. Less then five minutes after they walked back into the building, they heard that the man who'd shot up the street ran off the road and was captured.

* * * * *

Luca and Bella slipped into his vehicle, and she waited for him to start the car. She felt hot and tired and yet charged in a strange new way she couldn't define. At the police station Luca had cleaned up her scraped arm and applied a bandage, his touch gentle. The look on his face when he'd thought she'd been hurt continued to repeat in her mind. He really had feared that she'd been badly injured, and the almost terrified expression she'd seen in his eyes assured her Luca's feelings for her weren't exactly casual.

He didn't speak for most of the drive, and when she couldn't stand the silence any longer, she blurted out, "I heard you talking to Damon in the cubicle. Arguing, rather."

He nodded slowly. His fingers tightened perceptibly on the steering wheel. "I figured. Why didn't you go out to the lobby like I asked?"

"Because you didn't ask. You ordered."

Luca's grin held a hint of derision. "Okay. I guess I deserved that."

He went silent again, and she realized he wouldn't tell her anything more for the moment. She would bide her time until they arrived at the condo, then she'd ask him more about this jealousy thing. He knew she'd heard him declare she was his. If he expected her to launch into a screaming fight, she wouldn't.

She needed to understand what he felt about her once and for all, and more than that, she must clarify what she felt for him.

His gaze kept darting to the rearview mirror. Uneasiness slid through her, sinuous as a snake. "Is the dark sedan following us?"

"No."

Relief flooded through her. "Do you think the stalker won't approach me now that you're with me all the time?"

He sounded weary. "It's possible."

"But that would keep you from catching him."

"I'd rather he never come near you. I'd rather keep you safe until the bastard is contained." The glance he threw her way held unexpected tenderness.

"How was your meeting with the Captain?" she asked.

"He's about ready to roast my rear for getting involved with you."

That caught her up short. She stiffened in her seat, sliding her fingers along the shoulder harness of her seatbelt in a nervous gesture. "How did he know?"

Luca explained succinctly. "Man's too perceptive." He shook his head. "Damn, I'm no better than my idiot partner."

They pulled into the driveway, and he got out of the car before she could respond.

Once inside the house, he locked the door and took off his holster and weapon. His stoic expression told her nothing. She could remain quiet as a stone until he mentioned his jealousy, but somehow she didn't think that would happen.

Exasperated with the awkwardness, she decided she'd give him room to think. Maybe it wouldn't hurt him to stew. She moved through the kitchen. "I'll fix the steak."

He nodded but said nothing. As she cooked dinner, a concoction of steak, carrots and potatoes, he remained out of the picture somewhere else in the house.

"Bella."

His soft words and his even softer touch came to her ears as he walked into the kitchen. He placed his hands on her shoulders and gently turned her around. Warmth and compassion, something she hadn't expected, drew her closer to him. There were those damn feelings again. She wanted him nearer, and a fierce need almost made her kiss him. What would he do if she became the aggressor and showed him in no uncertain terms that she wanted his body? She imagined he'd respond, the beast inside him overwhelming common sense. She didn't know how she knew, but she did.

You promised to each other it was hands off from now on. Why can't you resist him?

"Bella, I'm sorry I left you alone with Damon."

"Ah, shucks, Detective, it wasn't that bad. He's cute in a bestial, moronic kind of way."

Unease left his face, replaced by rapid irritation. "Are you saying you liked what he said to you?"

Go for it, Bella. See what he'll do if you goad him. "In a way. It's nice to have two men in one week act like they'd love to have me for lunch. That hasn't happened to me before."

Luca's mouth narrowed into a thin line. "He's a jerk."

"What's that got to do with it?"

"He wanted to get in your pants."

She pulled away. "Look, Detective, it was harmless. Whether he wanted to get in my pants or not, it didn't mean anything. Just the way your flirtation with me...the sex we had didn't mean anything."

Oops. Wrong thing to say. His face went solid with rising frustration. Pulling the tie out of his hair, he allowed it to tumble around his neck and shoulders.

Oh, man. Her stomach tightened and stirred as she appreciated how he looked as he prowled the room. Power rippled through his muscles, and she felt the heat of his body even from a distance. She almost trembled with the excitement, unable to resist the heavy arousal that rolled through her body.

"So if you think dumb-ass Damon is all right, I guess there's a chance you think I'm okay, too." He stopped and looked at her. His hands clenched at his sides. "What's happening between us is crazy."

She nodded. "It is." She had to know the answer to one question. "I heard you say you were jealous of Damon. Does that mean you don't want me to get to know him?"

"You know that's what it means." Soft and raw, his voice held a combination of tenderness and exasperation. "It made me nuts...hell just the thought of you in that guy's arms...I don't even want to think about it."

She walked toward him, a newfound elation powering her steps. "At the risk of insulting your friend, and in the interest of telling the truth...well, you don't have to worry I'll get in the sack with him. He's got too much testosterone. Drips off him like syrup."

When she stood right in front of him, he looked down at her with surprise, his eyes widening. "You don't like testosterone, eh?"

"I like it, believe me I do. But not when it's attached to an idiot."

"He's a good cop. But he has shit for brains when it comes to women."

Pinning him with her stare and her presence, she assessed his body with greedy eyes. It didn't seem to matter how many times she ogled Luca. He looked better and better every time. Leashed power rippled from those hard, well-worked muscles. Lean, mean and hot described his body down to a fine point. She could barely get her breath as she looked at his wide shoulders and his broad chest. The way he towered over her made her feel protected and warm.

She swallowed hard to regain a little composure. "I'm a little surprised you feel he's competition."

"Why?"

"Because you're—" What she was about to say could give him the biggest ego in town. *Oh, what the hell.* "Because you are the most gorgeous man I've seen in my life."

Her heart sped up as she watched his pupils widen and his nostrils flare the slightest bit. "I doubt that, but thank you."

"You think I'm giving you a line, Detective?" She grinned, enjoying this repartee more than she thought she would. "Blowing sunshine up your ass?"

His gaze widened yet again at her choice of words. *Aha. Managed to shock him again. I like that.* The transformation she'd felt coming on the last few days seemed to expand, invading more than the sexual arena. She'd never sparred with any man the way she did with Luca, and from the beginning her response to him surprised her. Perhaps she'd always been this woman. Independent. Finding her way. Making her mark with who she was and not what she believed others wanted her to be. *Mouthy as hell and liking it.*

"Yeah, I think you are giving me a line," Luca said.

"Why would I do that?"

He smiled and winked. "To get me into bed."

"Aha. So turnabout is fair play?"

He eased a step closer. "You mean foreplay, don't you?"

She couldn't help laughing softly. If he got any nearer she'd have to touch him. And that would be *such* a hardship.

Luca pinned her with a gaze that glittered with unholy fire. "Bella, you almost died out there today because you didn't follow my orders."

"No kidding." She couldn't help the sarcasm. Nothing seemed real right this minute. Her body felt bruised and her psyche rattled. "Tell me about it again, why don't you?"

He released a hard breath. "Why the hell didn't you stay in the lobby? I'm supposed to be guarding you—"

"Because I wasn't thinking, okay?" She held her hands up in surrender. "Convict me of stupidity. I just didn't think. I wasn't deliberately trying to disobey your directive."

She expect his wrath to last longer, but it faded by degrees. It left his eyes first. "Don't do something like that again." When she said nothing, his tight mouth softened. "You scared me shitless, Bella." His voice went husky as he allowed his index finger to trail over her jaw line. "When I saw you lying on the pavement face down, I thought you'd been shot."

"I'm sorry." She savored the warmth of his touch as he cupped her face again with his broad palm.

The flick of his thumb across her lips caught her by surprise. He swallowed hard, his voice husky with raw pain. "I thought my heart would stop."

Surprise shimmered inside her, foremost led by a shocking desire to sink into the comfort and safety of his arms. She wanted his mouth on hers and his body pumping hot and fast between her legs. She realized with growing wonder that her resistance was crumbling. Without a doubt, she was starting to fall for him.

No more pretending she wanted his body for sex only. Her attraction meant more than physical pleasure and daring a man to make love to her. If she hadn't admired Luca before they'd made love, she wouldn't have had sex with him in the first place. Plain and simple facts hit her in the face. She'd backed away and doubted herself because the idea she could fall hard for him in such a short time shook her to the core. Falling in love this quickly wasn't practical and it shocked the hell out of her.

But it was how she felt.

His thumb did a foray along her jaw line as he shifted nearer. His skin felt callused, and she wanted that thumb teasing other places. Where she longed to be touched and taken. "You are one tough woman, Bella, but you aren't invincible."

"Apparently I *am* invincible. That bastard shot up the whole street and didn't hit me."

His penetrating look made her feeling vulnerable. "This town is going to the dogs."

"Maybe bad luck followed me here."

"Don't give me that."

She didn't speak; a lump grew in her throat that was far too large to allow a sound.

"I think I'll keep you around." His voice dropped a notch, rough with sexual excitement. "You could be good for a man's ego."

She touched his shirt with her index finger and felt the heat of him under her skin. "As my sister used to say when she was a kid, you're not the boss of me."

"As my little sister used to say, you wanna bet?"

Giving Luca a smile filled with the mischievousness of a child, she allowed her palm to trace the hard wall of his chest. "I wanna."

His chest heaved, his breath unstable. "What are you doing, Bella? Trying to get me to pay attention? You've succeeded."

Sliding her finger upward, she reached his left nipple. For a half second, maybe, she hesitated. To touch or not to touch. That was the question.

With a daring born of pure pleasure, she circled her finger over his nipple with a lightning quick touch. Luca twitched, his breath hissing from between his teeth as his nipple tightened into a hard point. She'd do to him what he'd done to her.

A flush centered high on his cheekbones. "You're playing with fire. I said I wasn't going to do this, Bella."

"So burn me."

She touched the nipple again, this time attempting to grasp it between her thumb and finger. Instead she managed to pluck him. But it was enough.

His breath sucked inward again. "After this serial killer thing is over, you'll leave. Don't start something you don't want to finish."

"Maybe I'll leave. Maybe I won't."

"What could I do to make you stay?" His question held a pleading note.

Bella looked away, a momentary wash of shyness making her retreat from her sensual aggression. "I'm not sure."

Both of her hands pressed against the warm, muscled surface of his chest. With a swiftness that surprised her, Luca clasped her hands behind her and began walking her backwards. His predatory expression said he wouldn't let up. She'd done it all right. The man had plans for her. Before she could utter another word, she found her back against a wall just outside the kitchen. He took her wrists in his strong hands and held her arms over her head, pressing them to the wall.

Trapped.

Not hurt and not gripped hard, he held her with a touch that said she wouldn't be leaving any time soon. To say she was aroused by his show of masculine assertion didn't cut it. She desired him with a fire she couldn't extinguish.

The delicious way he looked at her said one thing. He wanted her with a passion she found invigorating. Luca generated chaos inside her; a push-and-pull affect that left her dizzy with breathless anticipation.

"I'll tell you why you'll want to stay," he whispered as he pressed his body along the length of hers. "You'll want to stay because I'll fuck you so well you'll never want to leave. You can't get enough of me and I can't get enough of you. Tell me if that's what you want. Tell me what you want me to do."

Shivers traced along her skin at his raw words.

She wanted him all right. And she would say and do whatever it took to get him.

"Fuck me." The words felt delicious on her lips. Shocking. Forbidden. Absolutely divine. "Please fuck me."

His hot breath brushed her ear as he chuckled in triumph.

"How do you want it?" He nuzzled her earlobe. "Hard and fast...or slow?"

Muscles deep between her legs clenched and released as moisture gathered. *Oh, yes. hard. Yes.*

She moaned softly as he stuck his tongue in her ear. "How about hard and fast?"

Luca didn't need another moment's encouragement. "Your wish is my command."

Pleasure made her smile. She'd bet a thousand bucks this man wasn't used to women steering him in any direction.

Terrified and yet feeling like a goddess, she arched her lower body against him. He stood as still as a statue and for a quivering moment she wondered if he would change his mind. She gave him her most sultry smile. Their lips hovered a scant inch apart. She drew out the tension, relishing her female power to send this man to his knees with desire. Newfound courage rose within her.

He didn't wait for man or beast. His mouth molded to hers, and she relished the warm pliancy as he shaped and stroked. She melted into the kiss with body and soul. Nothing and no one would remove her from his arms until she'd explored the length and depth of sex with him tonight. When they went their separate ways, she wanted to remember him. She might not have his undying affection or love, and she might never see him again. So she would explore and tantalize and take. She would show him that deep inside she had a hot, willing, sexual woman living inside a sedate veneer. Bella would discover the breadth, height, and depth of his sexuality and her own.

For once in her life she would take charge.

With hot attention she caressed his lips with her tongue. She waited for him to take over the kiss, but instead he allowed her full supremacy. Sizzling sensations made her groan into his mouth.

Her body led the way, tutoring her in how to seduce a big, tough man like this one without a hitch. She felt new empowerment as she allowed her inhibitions to bust free again.

She strained against him, but he wouldn't release his grip on her wrists. Bella liked the plundering force of his kiss, and the way he held her against the wall. Primeval desire roared up before she could conquer it.

Why would she want to vanquish this heady sensation of being out of control? Like a bird in flight she soared, ready to fly to any distant shore that would take her to completion. More than anything she wanted to feel his possession again, to feel the steady, hard pumping of his cock between her legs. Just the thought of him thrust high and tight inside her made her pulse flutter and shake.

Warm and searching, his mouth taught her to enjoy kissing for each small step. With each brush of his lips over hers, he gave and took. Although she coaxed him, he refused to deepen the kiss. Then, moments after the giddy torture seemed it would never end, his tongue slid into her mouth. She hummed into his mouth, and he stroked her tongue. Tangling, twisting and pumping, they initiated a sexual rhythm that stated what they must have.

A hot, fast union.

Luca thought he'd go mad if he couldn't have Bella immediately. From the first moment he'd felt jealous, he realized he had to put his stamp on her. She *was* his. He'd never wanted a woman the way he wanted this incredible, smart-mouthed, assertive, amazing creature. The sex goddess in his arms dared him and begged to be taken. He wanted her pleading and writhing with the most incredible orgasm she'd ever experienced.

His breath felt tight as each rapid exhalation pushed through his lungs. Excitement slammed through his cock like a firestorm, demanding instant satiation. The litany rang in his head like a steady drum with each motion of his tongue inside her mouth.

Luca released her wrists and made short work of the top of her sun dress, pulling until the damn thing fell in gathers around her waist. A strapless, hot-red lace bra cupped her. Shit, she looked so sweet he wanted to eat her from one end of her body to the next. Yeah, he wanted to explore her with a torturous, slow desire, but he wanted to fuck her hard and fast even more. With swift movements he released the bra, then he shoved her dress up to the waist. He cupped her ass in his palms, savoring her warm, curved flesh through her panties until he thought he'd come in his pants. Lust slammed into his gut with the force of a bullet and he writhed against her with growing desire. He would have her now.

Bella's eyes blazed up at him, hot and filled with shaking need. Her hands swept through the hair at his temples. "Please, Luca."

He knew what she wanted; she seemed so close to him right now he thought he could read her mind. Visions of what he could do to her danced in his head, tormenting him down to the rock hard base of his cock.

"Yes," he said.

As Luca's mouth came back down on hers, Bella's stomach clenched and her thighs tingled. She'd never experienced sex in a half-clothed, frantic state. Thinking about a quickie made her heart beat like crazy. She knew by the look in his eyes that he wanted her now with a capital *N!*

Seconds later she pushed the panties and the dress down her legs and off. No pausing to tantalize with the hot musk scent of her panties. Bella could feel the moisture between her legs as it escaped and trickled down the side of her leg.

Oh...my...God.

He unbuttoned and unzipped his pants, pushing down his jeans and briefs and freeing his erection.

Wrapped in his big hand, his cock looked thicker, longer and harder than she remembered from their first encounter. Luca's expression held rapt hunger, his pupils dilated, and his breath puffing with the tempo of excitement. His eyes smoldered with secret questions.

Bella wanted to know the answers that lurked behind his dark eyes.

She didn't think, she just did. Reaching out, she replaced his grip with her own and started a smooth stroke. Pre-cum moistened the slide. Each movement, from base to tip, made his breath hiss inward.

He groaned and trapped her hand into stillness. "God, baby. Keep that up and I'll come right now."

She licked her lips. "If that's what you want."

"No. No." He leaned in and captured her mouth under his for a tender kiss. "I want to be inside you."

He disappeared long enough to grab a condom, and within seconds he'd returned. As he walked toward her, she smiled and enjoyed the satisfaction of his admiration. Luca's gaze slid from her shoulders to the top of her thighs. Her gaze snagged on his erection framed by the open fly of his jeans. Everything inside her wanted to ignite. She couldn't recall the last time she'd ever wanted a man this much, if ever. His swagger added to the sexuality that poured off him in waves. She felt his want and his excitement and it piled onto her needs until she felt sure they would find a deep satisfaction they hadn't reached before. Bella moistened with the slickness of a woman stimulated to the maximum. She licked her lips in anticipation.

His arms slid around her as he moved in for a voracious kiss, his tongue finding its way into her mouth and caressing her tongue. Both his hands slid under her naked ass, cupped her, then lifted her up. As her legs came around his hips, she wondered if this would work.

But when the tip of his cock slid between the lips of her labia, she doubted no more. She gasped as he jammed straight into her with one powerful stroke.

Everything seemed to still inside her for one trembling moment.

She couldn't see, hear, or breathe.

Then, sensation upon sensation piled upon Bella. He filled her, thick and as deep as he could go. He stuffed her full, and she thought she'd never experienced anything so exhilarating. Luca moved the tiniest bit, and the abrasion of iron hard sex deep inside her made her cry out. As incredible as he'd felt inside her the first time they'd had sex, this time took her astonishment to another level. He felt like a spike, unforgiving and jammed up as high inside her as he could go.

He tore his mouth from hers and glared down at her, wild-eyed and beyond control. She experienced the beast inside him as a growl issued from his throat. He moaned as he slid out slowly.

He thrust hard with a powerful movement of his hips. She gasped and her eyes flew open again. Daring to stare into his eyes, she writhed as the inner walls of her vagina seemed to swell with an engorgement so profound she thought she might scream with one more stroke. Instead she tightened her pussy around him.

His eyes widened and he gasped. "Oh, shit."

She remembered his words when he'd been dreaming about having sex.

"Oh, shit," he said again. "Oh, baby."

She closed her eyes and echoed his moan, her head dropping back against the wall as she tightened her legs around him and ground her pelvis against him so that he gored her center. The movement teased his cock into a stirring motion. She panted as the incredible sensation trailed up her spine and burst out of control.

Along with the staggering sensations rocketing through her, her emotions slipped through. Heat met with happiness as she realized she couldn't withstand any request Luca wanted to make. If he asked her right now to climb Mount Everest, she'd be tempted to do it to please him.

"Take me." She barely heard the yearning whisper and realized she'd said it. She'd begged and it actually made her hotter for completion. "Please. Oh, God. Please!"

"With pleasure." With a rough noise he covered her mouth with his again, plunging his tongue deep.

One powerful shove jolted her and she gasped into his mouth. Every solid, straining inch of his cock pressed and probed and danced inside her, stroking heated tissues that trembled on the brink of incredible ecstasy. Tiny strokes of his cock worked her into a frenzy, and Bella discovered she could no longer stand the exquisite torture. Spots seemed to cloud her vision, her breathing rapid, and hoarse words of desperate need freed from her lips.

All she could do was beg for the finale. "Please, please. Oh, God, Luca. That feels so good."

Luca made a primitive noise of acknowledgement, aroused and hot. "Anything you want. Anything at all."

She contracted around him. He groaned as he thrust again, then again, building the movement with each hard pump of his hips until he rutted with merciless intensity. Friction inside her built to unbearable levels, and her hands grasped for purchase, holding onto his relentless bucking. His fingers tightened on her naked ass as he jack- hammered. He shuttled in and out until the folds between her thighs trembled around his cock.

Bella couldn't contain the thrill as Luca grunted and growled with every deep plunge. Each earthy masculine sound sent her elation higher and higher. Beyond caring, she started to keen and chant, moaning for release.

Unable to keep a hold on her world, she let the burning deep in her interior rage. Sensations spread, heat and fire and mind-altering bliss. Her vagina expanded and then clamped down on him. Splintering pleasure gathered in her loins and undulated with slow building waves that made her gasp and arch.

Orgasm after orgasm rolled through her body in waves of unbelievable heat until one last rending thrust sent her to the final edge. Ecstasy cascaded out from her womb and burst. Her clit pulsated with exquisite pleasure.

She screamed.

Bella's breath was suspended for a minute as her limbs writhed and her hips bucked. She cried out again and again as pleasure crested, then ended. A loud growl issued from his throat as he came a few seconds later. He ground his cock inside her, his moans of pleasure slowly easing.

Chapter Eleven

Floating on mind-altering amazement, Luca stayed snug inside Bella's body. As the sexual mindless state retreated, awareness brought the scent of sex. He felt an ache in his body and at the same time an elation that came from a good, hard bout of fucking.

As his lungs bellowed with effort, his voice rasped, "Bella."

She buried her face against his neck, her moist, warm breath stirring his hair. "Mmm?"

He looked into her eyes as he loosened his hold upon her. Animalistic feelings coursed through his mind and body. He wanted to howl like a wolf in triumph. He'd put a stamp on his woman.

His woman.

Oh, shit.

He really did have it bad. Whether he liked it or not, some pretty mushy emotions swirled inside him like a tornado. All his talk that he wouldn't do this again split right out the window. He wanted to cradle her close, whisper how much he cared about her, then make excruciatingly slow love to her. He wanted to give her flowers, take her to a fancy restaurant, and even put on a monkey suit for her.

A tie and everything.

Double shit.

Foremost, he realized that he'd taken her deep, hard and insistently. While he'd never experienced anything more delicious than loving her with furious intensity, he knew a man could take a woman too hard, even if she was aroused. The idea he might have hurt her in any way made his stomach roll with sudden nausea.

He drew back and plunged his hands into her mussed hair. Her eyes looked slumberous and well-satisfied, her lips red and puffy. A pink afterglow touched her cheeks and neck.

He caressed her face with his thumbs. "Did I hurt you, baby?"

She smiled and traced her fingers over his jaw. "Hurt? Are you kidding? I'm in heaven."

He smiled, relieved. "Good. You made me crazy. I wanted you so damn bad."

Before she could say anything, he picked her up and carried her toward the bedroom. She laughed. "What are we doing?"

"For once I'd like to have sex on the bed. With all of our clothes off."

"Oh. Sounds wonderful."

She looped her arms tighter around his neck, and his cock started to harden again, eager to take her tight, slick body once again.

In the bedroom he dropped the rest of his clothes and left a trail along the floor. They launched into each other's arms and fell on the bed. Eagerness spread to every point in his body. He wanted her again, hard and fast. Elated by his body's ready reaction, he decided to wallow in the feeling rather than question it. As he looked down on her, she smiled.

"Bella," he whispered, unable to keep need out of his voice. "I've got to have you again."

"Then have me. Now."

Bella smiled, wicked and warm. She reached down and gripped his cock, and the pressure felt just right. He sucked in a harsh breath. "Wait." He launched off the bed and into the bathroom. He came back with a box of condoms. "I think this is going to require an entire box."

Her eyes widened and for a second she looked shy, as if she might retreat from anything extraordinary. "An entire box?"

"I'm so damned excited, I can't wait to be inside you again. But we won't do anything you don't want."

As he lay half over her, she arched against him and moaned. "What did you have in mind?"

He kissed her neck. "Sex in every position we can manage."

"Mmm. Sounds wonderful." She traced her fingers over his cock again and he hissed in a breath.

As she began a slow, steady pumping of his cock, he enjoyed the sensation of heat and pressure. A few seconds passed before he got an even better idea. Gently he peeled himself away from her touch. At her curious look, he smiled and positioned them in a classic sixty-nine position.

Bella enjoyed her new-found boldness, a little surprised at how great it felt to simply let go. She received a new, very intimate view of his gorgeous buns and balls, and realized she'd never done sixty-nine with any man before.

Wonder why later. Enjoy now.

She slid her hands along his thighs, loving the rock solid muscle and the dark hair over his skin. She inched down a little farther. With excitement she latched onto his erection and took him into her mouth.

"Oh, Bella. That's it. Take all of me," he groaned, his hoarse request full of desire.

As she complied, he parted her thighs. She almost held her breath in anticipation. The first sweep of his tongue along her labia made her moan loudly. His encouragements, murmured against her hot flesh, whipped her excitement into a new frenzy. Another languid, gentle lick made her arch and writhe. All the while, she deep- throated Luca, taking him as far into her mouth as she could. She gripped his cock at the base, then her tongue came into play, dancing along the tip. He moved against her, his own control unraveling as his moans grew louder. Luca spread her thighs wider and buried his head deeper between her thighs.

She groaned as he stuck his tongue into her.

He French kissed her vagina with deep strokes, but never once did he take her clit in his mouth. She ached for it, died for it, had to have it. He removed his tongue and slipped two fingers deep inside her. She moaned as sweet sensations rocketed through her. He drew his fingers away and did the most mind-blowing thing of all.

With gentle persuasion, he took her juices and spread it to her anus. As he spread her arousal, creamy and thick, against her puckered entry, she quivered with anticipation.

"Bella?" he asked softly.

Without a moment's hesitation, she decided now was the time to try something she'd never allowed a man to do. "Yes, Luca."

He oh so slowly pushed the tip of his index finger into forbidden territory. Not far, but enough so she could feel a warm pressure.

"Like it?" His soft voice made her shiver in reaction, pleased and warmed by his care.

"Yes."

His mouth latched onto her clit and began to suck.

An exclamation of surprise turned to amazed wonder. Seconds drew out as the draw of his tongue and lips over her clitoris made her arch against his mouth. Sensations piled on one after the other. The gentle presence of his finger, along with the continual stimulation of her clit, made her want more. All her sexual experiences, so white bread and mundane, couldn't have prepared her for Luca's overpowering sexual power, or his determination to make her come.

She needed all the wanton and different things he did to her, and yet a tiny part of her watched from the outside inward, astounded and a tiny bit scandalized. She, Isabella Markham, had a man sucking on her clit and his finger in her ass.

That single, wholly taboo thought did the opposite of what she expected.

She went thermonuclear.

An orgasm slammed her out of nowhere. As she screamed, her mouth still wrapped around his cock, he held her tight and kept his finger inserted. She wanted to scream as he moved that finger and kept the stimulation heightened. Luca snacked on her clit with a relentlessness that swore there was no tomorrow.

Continual heat and stinging ecstasy shot through her loins. Amazed and aroused beyond belief, Bella rotated her butt and skewered herself on that invading finger. Gasps and groans came from her lips as she enjoyed every moment.

When her pleasure faded to intermittent pulses, he removed his mouth and finger from her and turned to face Bella.

Hunger took his eyes, but his mouth held a tender curve that spoke of longing and something she dare not hope for.

"Good?" he asked in a guttural, masculine tone that said man and woman hadn't been out of the cave for that long.

Panting, she reached for him. She slipped her fingers into his long hair, and the silky dark strands fell down along her face. "Are you kidding? Good doesn't even begin to describe that. That's the longest, best orgasm I've ever had in my life."

He cupped her face. "Then let's see if we can top it."

"Is that possible?"

As he leaned over and retrieved a condom, he whispered, "Oh, yeah."

Aching to have Luca inside her, she didn't think about tomorrow or what the future would bring. All that mattered was having Luca's thickness lodged as high inside her as he could get. She didn't have long to wait. Without more preliminaries, he covered himself.

Luca didn't want the feelings that came to him next. Had he ever felt this tender with a need to love a woman? Not screw her mindlessly, but to assure each sexual need she wanted was fulfilled down to the last touch? They'd gone at each other like rabbits, and yet he wanted an encounter where he could show he could be gentle and sweet and —

Oh, hell. Had he just admitted that? Sweet?

If it was possible, his cock hardened even more.

He lay back and threw his arms over his head. "Come on, Bella. I'm yours."

Something he could only call a shit-eating grin covered her pink, luscious mouth. A mouth that had almost made him blow his load down her throat moments ago. Her hair looked tossed and twisted. Her breath surged as she took one deep breath; it made her small breasts thrust out. She looked perfect, and his mouth watered thinking about what he wanted to do to those hard, tight nipples.

She looked totally fuckable.

"Ride me," he said.

Deep inside he felt a tingle, a liquid heat pulse that demanded to be transformed into another breath-stealing orgasm. Without hesitation she straddled him, and seconds later her heated, wet channel slid over him. He gasped and closed his eyes at the incredible sensation of Bella's passage encompassing him. As his fingers clamped down on her hips, she ground herself against him. Her warmth tightened on him, and he sucked in a breath as his cock lengthened and became even harder. His balls felt ready to detonate. He didn't know how much longer he could take it before he filled her with cum.

"Bella, sweetheart," he rasped. "Put me out of my misery."

She leaned on her palms and smiled down at him, then gave him a soft, sensual kiss. "With pleasure."

She tightened and released, tightened and released. With a groan of frustration and excitement, he lifted his hips upward, trying to move inside her. He arched against her.

"Naughty boy." She purred in a silken voice that sounded like paradise to his ears. "Don't move. I'm in control."

She made a circling motion with her hips, then oscillated on him the slightest bit. Luca knew she wanted to prolong his pleasure, and that thought made him wilder. He restrained himself, not daring to thrust. He wanted her to enjoy every last minute of her dominance over him. As she rotated her hips, churning on him faster and faster, he allowed rough growls of need to leave his lips.

Seconds later her eyes closed and her head tilted back. Her panting breaths increased as she quickened the pace, riding him hard and fast.

At last he couldn't endure it any more. He drove upwards, his movements relentless as she rode him and he thrust like a madman.

She gasped, her eyes opening wide, her hips no longer gyrating. They hung together, not moving for several moments. Then Bella began to tremble and he saw the flush of orgasm fill her chest and go upwards. A low, whimpering moan left her throat as she clenched down on him, rippling in powerful spasms. He let it erupt, one last thrust spearing her core and bringing him flood after flood of staggering pleasure.

* * * * *

Bella hated the darkness, and even though Luca's arms held her against his chest, the feeling of terror nipped at her defenses, attempting to wedge into her psyche like a nightmare that never went away. As she launched out of the it, a cry of fear on her lips, she felt Luca's arms tighten around her.

"Bella? What's wrong?"

"Just a nightmare." Her voice sounded puny to her ears, and she cursed the weakness. "It's nothing."

"What was it about?"

"Nothing…I don't want to talk about it."

He cradled her close but said nothing more.

Bella awoke some time later, spooned together with Luca. Darkness edged through the blinds, and she knew they'd slept for some time.

His hands started to move on her, a gentle touch that felt almost chaste. Each slow rub of his fingers across her hip and down her leg made her arch back against him. She wiggled her butt and encountered his cock. He arched his hips and pressed against her, insinuating a rubbing, caressing motion of his cock against the cleft of her ass. With a gesture that said she approved, she reached behind and clasped his head. She made her neck and shoulder area vulnerable, and he tasted the line of her neck with his tongue.

She enjoyed the hair-roughened feeling of his legs against hers, of his —

Oh. Oh, yes.

He lifted her leg up, clasped her thigh and brought it up over his hip so that his cock slid between her thighs. Smooth as silk, before she could take a breath, his cock nudged into her channel. She gasped, not wet enough to take him all at once. Probing her entrance, he edged his way with one small stroke just inside her entrance, two strokes. Three. She helped him, arching against that delicious hardness with shudders of pure enjoyment. She lifted her leg higher over his hip. Her breath quickened, pushed forward by the whirling excitement that throbbed with insistence between her legs.

"Luca?"

"Hmmmm?"

"God, this is so good." Excitement, tenderness and wonder engulfed her, and tears spilled into her eyes. Happiness added to her joy, and she gasped. "So good."

Without a word, he increased her pleasure, dipping inside her again a small distance. His right arm tightened around her, his hand slipping upward until he cupped her left breast. He kneaded her with each slow thrust, maddening Bella with the need to have him completely inside her. In that satisfying need she also found a quiet contentment, brought on by the knowledge that this man wanted her with a passion she'd never experienced before she met him. She felt it in the way he touched her, and in the way he held her. Whatever was happening between them wasn't just a quick slam-bam-thank-you-ma'am.

He reached up, clasped her nipple and pinched. She gasped in pleasure. His other hand traveled from her hip, finding her clit with unerring precision. He fluttered his fingertip over that button, taking her moisture and slicking over her again and again. Sensation upon sensation bombarded her.

The craziness started.

His fingers crimped, tugged, and plucked her nipple. The other hand tormented her clit.

She moaned, undulating against the hardness that refused to penetrate. Then, with one hard plow, he took her. As she cried out in relief, his fingers ruthlessly rolled and tugged her nipple. Her clit throbbed under his demanding strokes. She pushed her ass back against him, grinding on his cock as he stayed motionless inside her. Her moans of need escalated as multiple delights filled her.

He began to whisper into her ear.

"You like it when I stick my dick up your cunt." He didn't ask, he told her in no uncertain terms. "You like it up high inside you."

"Yes," she whimpered, aroused beyond belief by his dirty talk.

"You like it when I pinch your nipples and rub your pussy."

He put action to words and gently clasped her clit between two fingers. He tugged.

A firestorm started to throb in her captured flesh. "Yes!"

He stroked her nipple and made one last tug on her clit.

"Yes!" Drawn out and vibrating with the energy of her pure ecstasy, her answer echoed in the room as she burst into a superheated orgasm.

He pushed her to the limit, prolonging the pleasure by keeping her nipple between his fingers, his finger moving on her clit and swiveling his hips as he kept that hard cock as far up as it would fit.

As her climax faded, he withdrew from her. He rolled her onto her stomach and kneed apart her legs. Before she could even think about what he intended, he drove his cock inside her with a power that made her gasp in surprise. She stayed flat, her arms and legs akimbo as he rutted and groaned. A few movements later and his breath strangled, then a guttural sound left his throat as he shook above her in the final stages.

He pulled out of her and fell to the bed, his breath rasping in and out like bellows.

She comforted him with sweeps of her hand over his back, caressing away the last trembles that still racked his body. They didn't speak for some time, until he opened his eyes and propped up on one elbow.

Alarm filled her, and she sat bolt upright. "We didn't use a condom."

He chuckled. "Look at my cock, sweetheart."

Covered with a now thoroughly used condom, his fading erection lay between his thighs.

Relief replaced worry, and she sank back onto the bed. "When did you put that on?"

"I woke up with this tremendous hard on and got a rubber right away. I knew I wouldn't be able to stop once I got started." His smile faded into a frown as his brows drew together. "Bella, you know I'll always protect you. I don't want to get you pregnant." Understanding flashed across his face. "You do have a lot of trouble trusting men, don't you?"

She didn't want to admit it. "I haven't run into that many reliable males."

"Until me?" His hopeful tone made her smile.

"Until you."

His expression faded to almost boyish concern, like a young man who wanted something but couldn't ask for it. "This is going to sound needy as hell, but I've got to know."

"About what?"

"I know we said we wouldn't do this anymore. I know that things between us in the beginning were dicey. I taunted you more than I should have."

"That's for certain." She sighed. "But I guess I'm equally to blame." Her dry throat almost kept her from speaking again. She licked her lips and looked straight into the darkness of his gaze. "You just drove me so nuts; I couldn't believe how crazy you made me and how gorgeous you were. It turned me on so much."

His grin went to Mount Everest proportions. "Fighting with me turned you on?"

"Yes. Isn't that sick?"

"No way. Same thing happened to me." He laughed. "Obviously."

Secondary relief washed over her, and she sighed. "What did you have to know, Luca?"

He swept his hand over his face and his lips narrowed as if he contemplated reneging. "I've got to know if you feel anything for me." He moved nearer, leaning over her. With a sincere, almost puppy-like pleading look in his eyes, he asked, "Do you care about me? Because if you don't, I really do need to stop this right now before…well, I just need to stop it."

Absorbing his words, she wondered if he wanted to know because he didn't want to get hurt. Her heart pounded with renewed excitement. She felt giddier than a teenage girl with her first crush. She reached up to cup his face. "I may not have realized it at first, but there's no way I could have made love with you if I didn't already care about you. Very much."

An understatement, Bella.

"Good." Like a satisfied animal, a predator savoring the lingering taste of his latest meal with relish, he gave her a cocky grin and stretched like a cat. "Because the sex we had almost killed me."

She lifted one eyebrow. "You? I may not be able to walk tomorrow."

He chuckled. "Three times in a few hours will keep you from walking?"

"Luca, I haven't had sex three times in the last...I don't even remember when."

His mouth dropped open. "Really?"

"Really." Self-confidence ebbed a bit as she thought about the women he'd probably made love to. "Just because you're used to having sex every day—"

"What?" His incredulous expression said she'd hit a nerve. He sat up, letting his legs sprawl out. "I don't have sex every day. I haven't had a woman in a long time."

Maybe her skepticism showed on her face, because he launched into a defense. "Even when I've had a semi-steady relationship, I only slept with the woman maybe once or twice in an encounter. I'm not a sex machine." He drew her closer, sweeping his hand down her back and over her backside. He cupped her butt and kept his hand there, his gaze admiring and shimmering with heat. "Except with you. You make me so hard I...I feel like making love to you every minute of the day."

Sincere surprise and a new desire kept her silent. She'd given him too much credit for fooling around. *Make love?* When had his vocabulary changed? And why? Beyond that, his statements liquefied more of the hard casing around her heart. She wanted something more from him, and now she knew the truth. Because if she'd wanted him for a boy toy, a convenient screw, she could have blown off her growing feelings for him.

Instead, those sweet feelings that grew inside her the longer she knew him, flourished. As he kept his hand on her butt, not moving, she arched against him.

Serious trouble. Yep, I'm in serious trouble.

"Come with me to meet Mom and Dad and my brothers."

This feels serious. Very serious. "Are you sure?"

"Yes." Intent, smoldering, and determined to achieve what he wanted, his gaze said there would be no mercy.

"All right."

"Great."

His state of semi-arousal grew into full hardness. Astonishment slid into heady pleasure. The sight of all that masculinity, muscles, bone and flesh, made her thighs clench together. She rolled over onto her back, anticipation making her needs boil to the surface faster than anything she'd known.

Luca didn't ask, he gently pulled her up and turned her around. Without sugar coating he said, "I want to take you from behind."

As she complied, turning her back to him, she presented him with her ass high in the air and her legs spread wide. She got down on her elbows. He cupped her butt, rubbing over it with tender touches that belied his urgency.

He thrust with excruciating slowness. A little squeak of surprise and pleasure escaped her, and she pressed back against him, driving him up inside her with one slamming motion.

She would never forget what he felt like holding there with maximum control. Refusing to move. Refusing to put her out of her abject misery.

She moved against him as he grasped her nipples with his thumbs and forefingers. Lust, as all-consuming and powerful as the first time they'd loved, made her buck against him and moan. He flicked her nipples, torturing her as he strummed and caressed them into screaming hard need.

Then, as he thrust with short, driving motions, moving inside with merciless intent, she detonated in one glorious, mind-altering second.

Chapter Twelve

"Are we there yet?" Bella turned to smile at Luca, enjoying the teasing banter they'd shared for the last few minutes as they drove toward Luca's home. "Are we there yet?"

He smiled, sexy as hell and heaven together, and her insides almost dissolved into jelly. "Are you tryin' to be funny, doll?"

His voice sounded like a cross between James Cagney and Humphrey Bogart. Bella never would have guess when she first met him that Luca harbored such a droll sense of humor.

She winked. "I was trying to be a smart-ass."

"Well, baby face, you succeeded."

She wrinkled her nose. "Baby face?"

"Okay." His voice went deeper, with a soft, sensual edge that sent pure shivers of excitement over her skin. "How about sweetheart?"

Just the sound of that word made her heart skip a beat.

"Am I your sweetheart?" she asked a little breathlessly.

Silence hovered in the car for longer than she would have expected. His expression stayed serious, and she wondered if she'd stepped in it big time. "Yes. Because of the way I feel about you." He glanced at her for a quick, searing moment. "I said that I care about you, and I'll say it again. You mean a hell of a lot to me, Bella."

If he'd shrugged and played casual, she could have accepted his reasoning. Instead, he made his endearment special. She liked the attention way too much. Who would have guessed that he possessed one tiny romantic bone in his body? Surprise, surprise.

I'm falling hard for him. Down to the hilt, and all the way.

For the last day, they'd spent hours talking and pawing each other in a frantic need to copulate. She'd discovered new and intriguing positions, and she even discovered she liked talking dirty to him.

Most of all she knew her growing feelings reached the edge of no return. The next few days, perhaps, would tell the tale. Either she would realize she'd made the biggest relationship blunder of her life, or she would say the words out loud.

Those words.

Those highly-charged, dangerous, perhaps fatal expressions that so many longed to hear and yet didn't.

I love you.

Yep, there could no longer be any doubt. She didn't want it, shouldn't want it, but there it lay. She'd gone down the hazardous route of falling in love with Luca Angello. She couldn't conjure anger at him for anything. Tender feelings masked her common sense, taken it all from her and promised a few more days of fairy tale romance.

Teetering on the edge of surrender left her restless and unable to make a decision. Instead, she plunged into her relationship with abandon, giving up the restraint she'd approached him with in the beginning. Something about Luca made her lose control. His nearness seemed to liberate her inner-self. She felt lighter than whipped cream, as free as a cloud.

He pulled into the driveway of his one story cream stucco home. "We're here."

Bella removed her attention from her mushy thoughts long enough to admire the house in front of her. He drove the car inside the garage. Once they stepped into the house and he gave her a quick tour, she knew about a dozen more things about him she never would have guessed. The three bedroom home felt cozy and well cared for in every way. To her surprise, the place was clean and tidy.

She gazed with wonder at the rugged leather and old-fashioned looking dark furniture.

"This is wonderful. My type of furniture."

"What did you expect?" He smiled, teasing as he walked toward her. "A dump?"

She allowed a tiny smile to escape as he looped his arms around her waist. "Well, actually, yes."

He made a growling noise and swooped in for a quick kiss. "Wench."

Bella changed to her weak imitation of Mae West. "Why, sir, you have a filthy mouth."

"*Wench* is filthy? Try this." He leaned in and whispered in her ear, all the while moving his hands down to cup her butt. "I want to fuck you. Again."

At his words she felt instant arousal; her insides clenched in reaction, and heat spilled over her skin. His hands kneaded her ass.

She found it amazing how little it took for her to go wild with him. She allowed her hands to rest against his chest. "What did you have in mind?"

He wiggled his eyebrows. "Decadence. Kinkiness. And not necessarily in that order."

She glanced at the clock on the wall. "We're supposed to be at your parents' house when?"

"Not until five."

"That leaves us with several hours." She slid her arms up until she encircled his neck. She kissed his chin. "What...um...do you mean by kinky?"

He shook his head. "It's a surprise. Don't worry, it's nothing that hurts."

She pulled his head down so she could kiss him. "Bring it on." With a whoop, he picked her up and carried her down the hall. "Where are we going?"

"Guess."

"The bedroom."

"You got it."

She grinned. "Oh, goody."

He stopped in the hallway long enough to kiss her senseless. When he released her mouth, he stared, a new awakening in his eyes. "You know how beautiful you are?"

Heat filled her face. She might have gone primitive with Luca, but that didn't mean she believed every compliment. "No."

"You're so damned stunning you make me ache inside."

A new blush heated her cheeks as she smiled. "Flattery will get you everything and anything, Detective Angello."

He pushed open the door to his bedroom with his foot. Shades covered the big windows, so they'd have plenty of privacy to do whatever they desired. By the ravenous look on his face, she knew Luca wanted her with a fierceness she'd never seen on his face before. As he allowed her to slide down his body, she savored every muscular inch. She could feel the storm building inside her, and she knew she didn't want a long, lingering bout of lovemaking. No. She wanted whatever he had to give her right now, right this minute.

Instead of rushing right into love making, as she expected, he stopped and stared at her.

"Bella, there's something I've been wanting to ask you, but you've been distracting me with things like getting shot at and fucking me unconscious."

Laughter burst from her. "Is that all? From the look on your face I thought it was serious."

He sighed, but he kept his arms around her. "It is serious."

Worried now, she almost loosened her grip on him. "What is it?"

"There's something I've got to know before we do this again. Before we lose our heads."

Giving Luca a teasing smile she said, "Well, tell me already before I scream."

"You never explained to me what else happened to make you leave your father's estate. You said you wanted independence and to get back your muse. I've always felt there was something you've held back."

Fess up, girl. You've got to tell him.

Maybe, now that they'd shared so much, it wouldn't be so bad to confess. Bella saw Luca's worry etched in his eyes and the tightness of his mouth.

Gently she pulled from his arms. "Let's sit here." She took a deep breath as he sat down beside her. "It isn't that bad, and most people would say I'm nuts. When I was a little girl I was very afraid of the dark, but my father wouldn't allow me to have a night light. He said I needed to buck up and take it like a Markham. No Markham ever admits to being afraid, according to him."

His eyes darkened with anger. "I can't believe he did that to you."

"He did it all right. Almost every night I was terrified to go to sleep. When I woke up screaming a few times, he told me he'd send me to a shrink if I didn't stop it. I told him that there was a bad man in my dreams. He always came to my bedroom door and stood watching me." She felt a fine trembling skitter over her skin.

Luca slid his arm around her shoulders and took one of her hands in his. Bella saw the concern fixed in his eyes and the tightness of his mouth. "You were dreaming about a man."

She shook her head. "I'm not so sure now that he was a figment of my imagination."

"What?" His arm tightened around her. Another shiver flittered over her skin. He must have felt her goose bumps, because he rubbed her arm in soothing strokes. "Are you saying there was a real man standing in your doorway every night?"

"That's what I'm saying."

"Who the hell was it?"

"I think that it was one of the bodyguards on the estate."

"How do you know?"

She realized the more she told Luca, the better she felt. She wished she'd told him before. But like he said, they'd kept each other pretty occupied in the short time they'd known each other.

"One night I woke up and heard an argument outside my bedroom door. I thought I heard my father say that if he ever caught this guy hovering near my doorway again, he'd have him arrested."

Luca's fingers caressed hers softly, but not in a sexual fashion. Pure comfort flowed between them, and in that moment she felt a budding gratefulness. "Your dreams were reality."

"Exactly. After that I never saw the man in my doorway again."

"Your father fired him?"

"I don't think so. Every day I looked at each of the security men and wondered who it might have been. The same men that were in his employ before the argument were still there."

"At least your father did something."

"At least."

His eyes widened and anger flickered in their depths. "Wait a minute. You said that before you left the estate, you woke one night and a man was standing in your doorway."

"Yes." She spoke softly, as if confirming in a louder voice would make it even more real. "I knew, deep down in my heart, that the man was back."

"Jesus," he rasped. "Bella, this guy could be dangerous. Why didn't you tell your father?"

"Come on. You know why. I've told you about him."

Luca's fingers tightened on hers for a second, but not enough to hurt. "He needs to know."

"That's why I left so quickly. I also knew that it could only be one of the three men in my father's employment, because all of the other men had left or been fired by that time."

He stood and began to pace the room. "At least you've narrowed the suspects." When he stopped walking he looked down on her and shoved his hands in his pockets. "It isn't just your father that's made you wary of men, is it, Bella?"

She shook her head, realizing for the first time something she'd never acknowledged to herself or anyone before. Jamming her fingers in her hair, she absorbed the implications.

"I was so afraid, Luca. He could have been a rapist or something worse. I don't know."

He settled down beside her again and drew her deep into his arms. "It's all right. We'll call your father tomorrow and talk with him about it. You can give me the name of the men still working there and we'll check it out."

She looked up at him, doubt creeping inside. "He won't believe me."

Determination etched a line between his brows. "He'll believe me, even if I have to visit him in person." He brushed his fingers through her hair and kissed her brow. "Nothing like that is ever going to happen to you again. I promise. I'll protect you."

She grabbed his shirt and tugged him closer. "A woman could get very used to hearing all that macho garbage, Detective."

He slid his hand into her hair. When he spoke, the low, husky tone made her toes curl. His eyes held seriousness and exasperation. "It's not macho to want to protect the woman you…"

Stopping in mid sentence, he seemed stunned into silence by a revelation. Her heart screamed in joy that he might, just might, have said that he loved her. She wouldn't be able to resist him if he admitted something so profound and moving.

She lifted one eyebrow. "The woman you…what?"

The Dare

Instead of answering, he kissed her, his immediate ravenous attention washing away questions in a tide of passion. After devouring her mouth, he released her.

With a grin that spoke of one thousand and one delights, he yanked his shirt over his head, then unbuttoned his jeans and shoved them to the floor. He'd worn sedate white boxer briefs, but the way the cotton hugged his muscles to mid-thigh made her heart pick up speed. She reached out and touched his thigh, glorying in the tight feeling of his leg.

He sucked in a breath and laid his hand over hers. "Bella, do that now and I won't be able to control myself."

She inched closer. "Who said I want you in control?"

His expression turned hungry and confident. *Watch out, the beast is on the loose.* He reached for her short-sleeved knit top and yanked it over her head. Then he wrestled with the waistband of her shorts. She helped him, and in a few seconds they both stood naked.

"Take me now." She felt aggressive, and for one second wondered if he wouldn't do as she asked. "Take me where I've never gone before."

He stared at her, allowing his dark gaze to say everything and more. He wanted her, needed her, wished to eat every inch of her with his lips and tongue. "You ever used sex toys, Bella?"

She didn't want to admit it, but the gentle inquiry didn't accuse or condemn. "Yes. I have my own...vibrator. Just a little thing that I haven't used in forever."

"Why not?"

Why indeed? "I guess I had this strange notion that I needed a man to give me sexual satisfaction...real satisfaction."

"Do you think there's something wrong with using a vibrator?"

"No, not at all. I just kept forgetting I had it, and I wanted more."

He brushed his fingers over her hair. "I didn't want to scare you with suggesting something drastic after short acquaintance."

She grinned. "You don't think what we've done already is extreme?"

His unrepentant smile twinkled in his eyes as well. "Then lay back and enjoy."

Excitement gathered in her stomach, pooling molten and pure. He went to the bathroom and returned later with an assortment of toys. A big vibrating dildo he could strap over his own penis. A brand new butt plug in a sterile wrapper. A large bottle of lubricant, and a box of condoms.

Her breath quickened. *"Holy cow."*

He slipped his arms around her. "Is that a good holy cow, or a bad?"

"I've never…I mean…I've never tried those."

"We don't have to if you don't want to."

"I want to."

"Then you're in for a treat."

With gentle persuasion he brought her into his arms, and their mouths met with a blunt invitation to rock and roll without consequences. Within seconds they tangled, rolling along the bed like children wrestling. Tentative kisses led to deep, tongue-thrusting action. Soon she dripped with arousal, her nipples plucked and sucked and kissed into hard points, a need-to-be-filled aching between her thighs.

When he touched between her legs and found her wet and swollen, he drew back. "Close your eyes. Let me do all the work this time."

Glad to be pampered, she lay with her legs parted and her arms akimbo. Oh, yes. She'd let him do anything and everything. She kept her eyes closed, even when she heard him ripping the condom package open. She didn't have long to wait.

She felt him massaging the lubricant around her anus, touching gently.

"Oh." She sighed at the unfamiliar, but pleasant sensation.

He stopped. "You all right?"

"Yes." Seconds later she felt something warm and soft probe her. With extreme gentleness, Luca inserted the butt plug until the wide end stopped its entry. "That feels good."

"Great. Now it's going to be even better."

She opened her eyes to watch him. Instead of strapping the dildo device over his cock, he put a condom on the dildo and added lubricant. Apparently this time would be a hand job.

As the dildo probed her vagina, she gasped. "Oh God, Luca. That feels good."

With slow precision, he slid the big dildo into her until it could go no deeper. Then he turned on the vibrator. She gasped again. The twin sensations caused star bright excitement to tighten her belly. She tightened around the dildo and enjoyed the new sensations.

"Feel all right?" he asked as she opened her eyes.

"Wonderful." She sighed and closed her eyes again. "What now?"

"Wait and see."

Screaming anticipation made her clench her muscles. The vibrating dick pulsed with powerful waves of sensation. The hardness, the thickness, and the length made her crazy to move, to do anything to reach satisfaction.

Luca reached down and parted the folds covering her clit. With one hand he held her open, with the other he gently pulled the dildo out half way. Her eyes popped open as he slid the dildo back in, and his tongue flicked over her clit.

A moan of satisfaction came from her lips. "Oh, Luca."

"Hold on sweetheart," he said huskily. "This is going to be good."

With a smile, she closed her eyes again and enjoyed the triple sensation of tongue on clit, the dildo fucking her, and the butt plug tickling places inside her she never imagined existed.

As he drew the dildo out, then thrust it into her with a slow, continual motion, his tongue tapped, licked, and sucked on her clit. Her vagina clenched again, and she felt both the plug and the dildo being pushed out.

He held the dildo and plug in place, and fluttered his tongue over her clit with non- stop pressure. She began to pant, the pleasure starting to burn deep inside her as she throbbed to life under his assistance.

"Come on, sweetheart." He reached up and latched onto her left nipple, clasping it in his fingers. Very gently he pinched her nipple. "Come on."

Overwhelming pleasure sparked and twitched inside her as his tongue, the thrusting dildo, the plug in her ass, and his fingers fondling her nipple caused her to ignite. As her climax hit her, she screamed in ecstasy.

Luca pulled the dildo and butt plug out of her, and when she opened her eyes she realized he wore a condom. He slid between her thighs and rammed home. His mouth took hers, and without pause he jack-hammered inside her. Bella bucked against him, wanting every inch of him touching all the hot buttons inside her. As he pounded his way to the finish, another incredible orgasm slammed through her, and they both shouted their finale.

She savored the way he shivered in her arms, each pulsating jet of his release making him groan in delight. His powerful body blanketed her, hot and protective. He levered off her and rolled to the side, gathering her in his arms to hold her close. Bella sighed with pure satiation as she slid her arms around him as well.

Luca's hands traced over her back, her butt and then up to her hair. He pressed kisses to her forehead. "Bella, you know what a turn on that was for me to see you enjoy yourself?"

"Glad you liked it." She sighed again happily.

"That's an understatement."

She stayed quiet for awhile after that, taking in the beat of his heart, his slow breathing, his heat and strength.

After a few minutes of silence, Luca shifted and got up from the bed, and she did the same. They made trips to the bathroom, then came back to bed. She propped herself up with pillows, feeling like a giddy, wild college girl that had newly discovered the wonder of sex. Just when she thought she'd felt it all and done it all with Luca, he would surprise her. Half the fun was wondering what would come next.

Luca turned on his side and propped his head up on his hand. He watched her with curious eyes, his attention almost unnerving in its force. She felt like he could see right through her.

"I'd love to see your other paintings," he said.

"I've got four displayed at Portia's Galleria in Cherry Creek in Denver."

As if he sensed her tension, he allowed his warm palm to skim her stomach. "What kinds of paintings are they?"

He slid his leg over both of hers, and the warm roughness of his hairy thigh made her body sit up and take notice once again. Her nipples peaked with new arousal.

"Landscapes," she said softly. "As I mentioned before, I don't like painting people nearly as much."

"Do you think those portraits of me were flukes? Or will you be painting people more from now on?"

Her mouth fell open as she started to answer, then she realized she didn't know the answer. Something akin to anger spiked in her gut, as it always did when someone asked when she'd last painted or why they hadn't seen anything new from her in months and months.

As his arms gathered her close again, the care in his hold and the soft expression in his eyes made her defensiveness dissolve. "I don't know if I'll even paint again tomorrow."

"Any idea why you stopped?"

She shook her head, then changed her mind and nodded. As his fingers continued a warm dance upon her belly, she gave her attention to the washboard quality of his stomach.

"Maybe because the inspiration was gone. When you're dying literally from the inside out...that will crush a lot of creativity. It's one of the reasons I wanted to vacation away from family. I needed that freedom. A new place to refresh my muse and my soul." Heat filled her face. "Maybe I needed an adventure."

He grinned as his fingers continued to tease her belly, then touched the hair below. "I'm sorry you had to be the target of a serial killer to get the inspiration to paint."

She tilted her head to look up at him. "It wasn't the killer, Luca, which inspired me to paint. You inspired me. When I get back to the condo I'd like to paint you for a third time."

He chuckled. "Whoa, I don't know about that. I'm one of the least photogenic people I know."

She allowed her hands to trace rock-hard muscles. "Do you realize how just looking at you gives me serious, stomach twisting pleasure? You're a perfect artist's model."

He made a growling noise as he tightened his arms around her. His blatant arousal pressed against her thigh. "Woman, stop saying things like that to me or we're never gong to get out of here."

She craned her neck trying to see the clock. "What time is it?"

"Too damn late. Let's get a shower and head out."

She groaned in disappointment. "Shoot. And here I was hoping we'd have time for another round."

His eyes widened at her blatant request. "Shameless hussy." He leaned in for a deep kiss that made her senses reel. When he let her go he said, "There's always time for a shower *together.*"

Once hot water pounded their well-worked bodies, Bella soon discovered why a shower together could be ecstasy.

Chapter Thirteen

"What a pretty home," Bella said as they stepped out of his car in the driveway of his parents' house nestled in the foothills of Denver.

Luca placed his hand on the small of her back as they proceeded down the flagstone walkway. "They love it. It's an older house, but it fit in their budget and it's nice and big for when they have guests."

Sharp pangs of excitement mixed with apprehension in her stomach. She didn't know whether to be terrified at meeting his parents, or excited about meeting them. They sounded like neat people. A man had never taken her home to meet mom and dad before, and she found she wanted to make a good impression.

Damn it. Now you know you're in love with the man.

Lush grass carpeted the yard, with a profusion of colorful flowers in beds near the porch. She guessed the blue and white house was built sometime in the thirties or forties.

The screen door opened with a squawk, and a smiling, late middle-age woman with grey, short hair appeared at the door. Her casual blue floral dress looked wonderful with her peach complexion. "Luca!"

"Momma."

Luca's answering grin and exclamation touched something deep in Bella's heart. This big, sometimes macho guy called his mother "Momma" with a sweet, tender smile on his face. She never would have believed it if she hadn't seen it for herself.

As his petite, slim mother ushered them inside, it took about three seconds before the Angello family descended on the large family room. Two young men, obviously well-built and handsomer than any group of men had a right to be, sauntered into the room. An older man rolled his wheelchair into the area, his smile welcoming.

"Miss Markham," Mrs. Angello said with a huge grin. She shook Bella's hand. "We're pleased to have you here."

"It's nice to meet you," Bella said. "Please, call me Bella."

Luca introduced his father. Marcello, or Mark as he preferred to be called, smiled and offered his hand. "Luca's told us all about you."

Luca frowned. "Dad."

His father laughed. "Don't worry, Bella. He only told us that you're involved with one of his cases." He winked. "And you're one of the good guys."

Bella smiled back, then slanted Luca a look of mock disapproval. "That's good to know."

With a sheepish grin Bella never expected to see on his face in a million years, Luca introduced her to his brothers. Tall, dark-haired and knee-knocking handsome, Carmine and William Angello possessed the vigorous charisma of strong, good-looking men with huge smiles. Good heavens, did any one family have a right to possess such gorgeous children?

Carmine Angello, a muscled man with bold green eyes, had short wavy hair the same color as Luca's. He wore a red polo shirt and dark slacks that made him look like a million dollars. She liked his easy going friendliness.

William, dressed in jeans and a polo shirt, appeared a little more wary. His physique, honed hard by construction work, would impress any woman with half a libido. Dark brown eyes similar to Luca's assessed her as if she might pose a threat to the happy family.

Luca even appeared a bit nervous, and that made Bella wonder if he regretted bringing her here to meet part of his family. "Where's Diana?"

"Getting the children up from their nap," Mr. Angello said as he led the way into the casual living room. "She'll be out soon. Come on in. Momma's getting the meal ready."

Warm, delicious scents of pasta cooking filled the house. On top of that tantalizing scent, Bella could almost taste fresh bread, too. "It smells wonderful."

Carmine grinned. "My specialty."

Seconds later the house erupted in activity. William, Luca, and Mr. Angello settled in to the den to watch some sports, and Carmine and the ladies headed for the kitchen. Bella offered to help, and Mrs. Angelo led her into the cozy room where sauce bubbled on the stove and the oven heated the area. Peppered with country-style decorations, the huge kitchen had a homey feel Bella instantly liked. Though not partial to the country look, Bella appreciated Mrs. Angello's tasteful arrangements.

As Bella cut fresh bread, Carmine arranged the table and Mrs. Angelo chattered about her family. A sense of belonging and easygoing acceptance slipped over Bella and she began to relax.

Moments later a young blonde woman stepped into the room with two blonde, chubby toddler boys walking alongside her.

Slim-bodied, her face a study in elegant bone structure, the woman moved with a grace that held refinement and quiet regality. Her smile, though, said she held no airs. Even the pale pink broomstick skirt and pink short-sleeved top she wore looked candy sweet.

She put her hand out to Bella before Mrs. Angello could introduce them. "Hi. You must be Isabella?"

Returning the younger woman's smile, Bella nodded. "That's me. You must be Diana."

"Pleased to meet you." The woman's grin broadened. She gestured to the children. "This is Jack and Danny."

Bella squatted down to the children's level and greeted them. Jack grinned and giggled. Danny smiled but looked a little more wary.

"Luca's told us a lot about you," Diana said with a conspiratorial grin.

Mrs. Angello laughed. "She's heard that once already. We're going to make the poor girl nervous."

"Me? Nervous?" Bella asked as she straightened up. "Not at all." Then she laughed, her breath coming out in a shudder. "And I'm lying."

Mrs. Angello and Diana laughed with her, and Bella felt their acceptance down in her heart. She went back to cutting bread.

Mrs. Angello fumbled in a drawer for a utensil. "Luca explained over the phone what happened." She sighed. "I don't mind saying his job worries me on occasion, but you must be terrified. The possibility that a madman may be targeting you..."

Bella realized she hadn't thought about the killer much lately, but she could blame Luca's brand of distraction for keeping her mind off danger. She also felt one hundred percent safe whenever Luca was near.

Diana reached for a mug and poured herself coffee. "Maybe she doesn't want to talk about that right now."

Bella put all of the bread on a platter. "No, it's all right. Luca's assured me the guy won't try anything while I'm under protective custody."

Diana poured cream in her coffee and stirred. "You can be sure of that. Luca will keep you safe."

"Yeah," Luca's big, deep voice interrupted the conversation as he strode into the room. "But who is going to keep her safe against me?"

Diana opened the big stockpot and laughed. The scent of a delicious marinara sauce filled the room. She added some fresh mushrooms and stirred again. Her bright eyes danced with playful teasing. "Big brother strikes again. Many a woman's heart has fluttered at the sight of him."

Bella didn't think she liked the idea of other women's hearts palpitating over Luca, especially if those women thought they'd get a piece of him.

Luca slipped his arm around Bella and hugged her to his side. A thrill darted through her, mixed with a simmering lust she couldn't avoid. She didn't know whether to be embarrassed or happy that he showed affection for her in front of his family.

Mrs. Angello pinned her eldest son with a mock glare. "Are you trying to tell us something, son?"

Carmine changed the subject. "Mom, I'll bet the sauce is ready. The animals are getting restless." Carmine's distinctive New York voice held strong, unlike Luca's softened accent. He grinned at his family like he knew a secret. "The human animals, that is. Did you guys introduce Bella to Hitchcock?"

"He's outside," Mrs. Angello said.

Carmine grinned and gestured. "After dinner we'll show you Hitchcock."

Bella winced. "With a name like that, I'm not so sure I want to meet him."

Luca slung his arm around her shoulders and steered her toward the dining room. "You're gonna love the monster."

She groaned in mock terror.

* * * * *

During dinner Bella fell in love with Luca's family. As the sound of crystal pinging, utensils clanking, and conversation mixed into a noisy soup, she watched each member of the group with dawning inspiration. A smile broke over her face.

She wanted to paint the whole bunch.

"I'd love to paint this family."

Silence. Everyone stopped in mid chew, mid bite, or mid sentence and gazed at her.

"A portrait?" Mr. Angello asked, his face altering the slightest bit into skepticism.

"Of us?" Diana sounded like she didn't believe a word of it.

Bella took a deep breath and then a sip of her wine. "That is, if you want to. I'm offering my painting services for free. I recently did a couple of portraits of Luca. I'm not charging him a dime."

William gave his brother a teasing look. "That right, bro?"

Luca winked at his family, taking them in with one glance. "You got it. She did a great job."

"Sounds fantastic," Carmine said with enthusiasm. "In fact, if you did a portrait of the family we'd put it up in the restaurant."

Mrs. Angello said, "Excellent idea. I love it."

Bella realized that she'd made a commitment. A solid pledge to keep in touch with Luca and his family long after police protection was no longer needed. A painting of this family, displayed in their restaurant, would make her happy in a way she'd never felt before. She didn't know why or how, but she knew keeping contact with them would be one of the best decisions she'd made. The Angellos cast light through the darkness. She needed that sunshine in her life.

More than that, she enjoyed the Angello family's sincerity. She'd been around so few people that shared honesty and good humor. She savored this family's genuineness like a kid with a new toy.

They didn't always hold back disagreement, and yet loving respect laced the conversation between them. Carmine's hysterical sense of humor almost made her choke on her Chianti. Diana's precocious children were so cute they made Bella smile, and Luca's sister owned personal warmth that few women could boast. William's reserve thawed a little and revealed a man with a quiet goodness Bella felt down to her soul. Mr. and Mrs. Angello treated her like an honored guest, and before long any nerves she'd anticipated about meeting Luca's family disappeared under their genuine kindness.

Did Luca realize he was the luckiest man on earth to have a family like this? Bella's heart ached as she contrasted her family with Luca's situation.

Luca dug into the pasta with relish. He loved his mom's marinara sauce. But as he ate, the savory taste of his mother's cooking couldn't erase a building worry.

Now that Bella saw that his family didn't bite, she seemed to have settled into a comfort zone with them. He wanted to smile with pure satisfaction until he remembered the last time he'd brought a woman home to meet his parents over ten years ago.

Maria Concita Dominquez had been a fireball of the first order with a sexuality that sparked like a live wire. At first she seemed to like his parents, then later on she'd belittled them in subtle terms. When he'd told her he didn't appreciate her derogatory comments about his family, she blew him off. That had been the end of the relationship.

But not before he'd fallen one hundred percent in love with Maria.

Okay, so he'd tried to tell himself repeatedly that he'd never really loved her. After all, he couldn't afford the time it took to maintain and work at a relationship that involved something as intense as love.

Being here with Bella felt akin to déjà vu, even though he possessed no reason to think Bella would disparage his family. A mini panic wave overtook Luca as he recognized that he desperately wanted her to like his family as much as he hoped they liked Bella.

He saw the looks his brothers and sister threw him, and the twinkle in his mother's expressive eyes that said she appreciated Bella's wit. He barely recognized Bella.

Hell no. She'd transformed. Gone was the acerbic, defiant woman he'd met a few days ago. Still mouthy on occasion, but softer, warmer, more —

More maddening.

Watching her smile, relax, and joke with his family turned him on because he liked that side of her. The one that went all mushy and womanly when she didn't think anyone noticed. Heady, longing feelings stirred in his gut, and he realized that Bella stared at him across the table.

In that moment he allowed his apprehensions to build. He pulled his gaze away from hers and concentrated on dessert.

After a sumptuous helping of apple cobbler, Bella leaned back in her chair and groaned. "I'm never going to eat again." When they all laughed, she said, "Until the next time, anyway."

Luca put his hand on the back of her chair as he stood. "Want to come outside and meet Hitchcock?"

"I see how it is." Bella rose from her chair. "Fatten me up and feed me to the monster."

Another round of laughs ensued.

"Better watch out, Bella." Mr. Angello pushed his chair back. "Hitchcock is about the most ferocious creature in the neighborhood."

After she agreed, Luca opened the sliding glass door. Carmine followed as they stepped onto the small concrete patio. Light washed over her as the sun spilled over the area. Fragrant roses, daisies and a variety of other garden plants filled the brick lined flower beds.

A roly-poly, yellow-coated, mongrel puppy waddled their way. If she thought great looking men could do things to her heart, she hadn't thought about precious little dogs with big brown eyes and lolling tongues. The creature was just about the cutest thing she'd ever set eyes upon.

She hunkered down on the grass. The little guy worked his way toward her, pausing here and there to sniff the ground. "This is the ogre everyone warned me about?"

"That's him. Don't ask me where Carmine got the name."

"Actually, he's Mom and Dad's ogre," Carmine said.

By this time the adorable, small dude decided walking wouldn't cut it. He ran, his piercing puppy barks ringing in her ears. She laughed and as his little paws landed on her shin, she gathered him up in her arms. He licked her chin. She held him at arms length, and his legs dangled. Hitchcock snuffled, whined, and kicked his legs.

She held him close again, and he snuggled, his sweet eyes conveying that he'd found heaven. "All right then. But no more licking." He licked her face again. "He's not listening."

Luca and Carmine laughed, and soon she joined with them. Hitchcock made sure to wipe her chin again, determined to have her full attention.

"He's notoriously naughty." Mrs. Angello said from the doorway. Her voice held a gentleness that said she adored the animal. "We think he's a yellow lab and German shepherd mix. Several mongrel pups were found abandoned by the road side two weeks ago, and we decided we had to adopt him."

"Oh, he's so sweet." Bella almost blushed at the gushing sweetness in her own voice. "It's been so long since I've cuddled a puppy."

"You don't have a pet?" Carmine asked.

An unusual sting of regret passed through her. "I've never had a pet."

Luca reached over and stroked the pup's head. Hitchcock sighed in contentment and closed his eyes. "Not even a gerbil?"

Bella shook her head. "Are you kidding? My sister hates animals of any kind, and my father is just indifferent."

Diana stepped out of the house and onto the patio, curiosity written on her pretty features. "Why does your sister hate animals?"

"She was bitten by a bulldog when she was three." Bella watched Luca continue to pet Hitchcock. "She never got over it."

Luca frowned. "Too bad."

Bella wondered how many things in her life she refused to get over. Not many. She tried, whenever she could, to let go of the past. *You're holding onto a certain fear, and you know the truth.* If she went back to her father's estate, a man might enter her room and harm her.

Bella sank down into the grass and let the puppy go. Hitchcock stumbled, then righted himself. He sniffed around Luca, his inquisitive nose tracking every scent. He leapt into her arms again and painted her chin with kisses. This sent her into a giggle, and she released him before he could lick her to death.

Carmine shook his head as he observed the proceedings. "Hitchcock, you are a nut."

Diana laughed. "My kids love him, and of course they want one of their own. We just can't afford a pet right now, so we'll have to wait."

After chatting about dogs for a considerable time, Mrs. Angello said, "As much as I'd like to stand here in wild kingdom, I think I ate too much. I'm going to flop on the couch."

While the others went inside, Luca and Bella sat on the cool grass. She wanted more time with this young dog. She adored the petite guy, and his eyes pleaded for love. With a sense of loss, she put him down on the grass and he waggled his way toward the water bowl near the porch.

Luca reached over and tenderly pushed her hair back from her face. "Why don't you get a dog, Bella? It's clear you love them."

She pondered a short while. "Maybe I will now that I'm away from Father and Madeleine." She came to an impulsive decision in that instant. "In fact, I'm pretty sure that I want to move away from Denver." She dared a glance at Luca. "Make a home for myself away from their interference. Maybe if I'm lucky I won't have to see them other than at holidays. Does that sound cruel?"

Denise A. Agnew

He brushed his finger over her cheek. "Not at all. I think you're learning what you want to do with the rest of your life. Isn't that why you went on vacation in the first place?"

Sweet understanding burst inside her. "I've learned a lot lately." A grin parted her lips as she realized how suggestive that could sound. "Most of it's because of you, Luca."

"Me?" Soft and almost unsteady, his voice went husky. His eyes turned hot and searching. "Why?"

"Because you've freed me. I can paint now." She looked around to see if anyone was within hearing distance. The coast looked clear. "You're one hell of a man. A smart aleck and a pain in the ass sometimes, but you're also hot."

His eyebrows twitched. "Hot, eh? I think I like the sound of that. But I'm not sure I like just being a sex object." She smacked his thigh. "Ow!"

Leaning toward him, she whispered in his ear, "Turnabout is fair play, Detective. Women have been treated as sex objects forever. Don't you think it's time for a little payback?"

He lay back in the grass, his arms thrown above his head. As he stretched he let out a groan that sounded similar to the ones he made when he first sank deep inside her. Her face flushed hot. As he flexed his powerful arms and legs, she remembered how each inch of incredible musculature felt against her. Like a flash fire, her emotions and her lust came together in a blast of heat and need. She swallowed hard, her mouth dry.

"That," she said, "is not an answer."

He lowered his voice to a whisper. "If you're going to start talking dirty to me, I might have to do something about it."

Anticipation rose inside her. "Such as?"

"Find somewhere secluded and fuck you."

Her face burned. She wanted to make love with him all right. In that one second, in a blinding flash of lust, she pictured lying right down on this grass, totally naked, and enjoying a hard round of lovemaking. Just the idea made her squirm in anticipation of getting him alone.

She looked around, half certain someone heard their spicy conversation. "Maybe this isn't a topic of conversation we should have here."

A teasing grin touched his lips. "What should we talk about?"

"Your family. You know, they're an interesting bunch. Very unique."

Instead of the smile she expected, he frowned. "Unique, how?

"Your siblings are all very different. Carmine's obviously made things work for himself despite his past history. William is a little stand-offish, but he's nice enough. Diana seems a little insecure around the edges. But you are the most unique at all." She arched her eyebrows and flirted with her gaze. "A hot bod and a cock to die for."

She expected him to laugh. Instead his frown grew and anger flashed in his eyes.

Worry gathered inside her like an approaching storm. "What's wrong?"

"Is that how you really think of me?" He sounded disappointed. "Am I just a good fuck?"

His hard words made her stare at him in open-mouthed astonishment. "You've got to be kidding me."

"Are you looking at this like a little adventure?" His voice lowered, getting softer and more intense. "Is it a game?"

Hurt by the total change in his attitude, she took a slow, steadying breath. "Maybe I did see it as an adventure at first. We said we'd keep our relationship professional and then look what happened."

Something in his face looked sad. A hollow expression so unlike the man she thought she knew. What on earth had changed?

"When this serial killer case is all over, you're going to go back to your father's estate or off to your own new house and forget what happened here."

He didn't ask her, he told her.

Resentment rose like a black tide. Her insides trembled, her happiness rolling downhill as she wondered why he put distance between them when everything felt so right. "Why are you saying this, Luca?"

"Because you know and I know that this thing we've got going isn't reality. I saw you here today with my family and its all cozy and warm, but it isn't normal."

"Isn't normal?" Her voice rose even as she struggled to lower the volume. "I thought we were having a nice, simple get together and all of a sudden you're rejecting me? You have a rotten sense of timing, *Detective*."

"Yes." He sounded so sure her heart began to break into a myriad of pieces. "Because your world is different than mine. Rich girl and cop. Not always a good combination, right?"

Astonished by his change in mood and attitude, she glared at him. "You invited me, remember? Not the other way around. If you think I'm playing a game then you really don't know me very well, do you?"

Without warning he stood, his face a hard mask so unlike moments before when they'd shared the puppy's antics. "You can fuck me all you want, but don't fuck with my family."

Pain speared her like an arrow in the heart. Everything she thought she knew about their relationship went straight into the toilet. She might be in love with him, but if he felt this way she'd better cut ties while she could still salvage a bit of her heart. His unmitigated attack burned like a brand.

Fine, you arrogant, manipulating...hard-nosed rat! The words almost escaped her mouth, but she allowed them to remain unspoken. "How dare you? How could ever think I'd want to hurt your family? And what the hell does your family have to do with our relationship?" On a roll, emotions boiling, she continued like a steamroller. "I resent your attitude and the implication that I'm shallow." Swallowing hard, she decided she didn't care if anyone heard them. She'd lay it on the line right now. "I also resent you spoiling this beautiful moment with this puppy because you're a...a self-absorbed, arrogant bastard."

With that parting shot, she went back into the house.

Chapter Fourteen

Bella ached inside as she walked into Luca's condo ahead of him. After a silent, tense ride from his parents' home, she wanted to lie down and sob her eyes out.

They'd left his parents' home immediately. She claimed to have a headache, and Luca didn't try to make her stay. Although his family looked puzzled and acted concerned, a tiny part of her didn't care.

If she wouldn't be seeing his family again, she couldn't afford to invest any more in what they thought. She was done with them and with the man she'd fallen hopelessly in love with. Luca couldn't be trusted with her heart. Too bad she hadn't figured that out before she'd committed some deep feelings for him.

She ached like she'd come down with the flu, and part of her wondered if maybe Luca knew what was best. Maybe the little rich girl and the tough cop couldn't have a life together.

So this is what it feels like to have a broken heart.

As she stalked toward the bedroom, Luca said, "Bella, wait."

Ignoring his plea she went into the master bedroom and retrieved her things. She went into the guest bedroom and closed the door with a click. Leaning against the wood, she drew a deep, shuddering breath. Time to cut her losses. She inhaled again and fought against more tears. She wouldn't give into this pain, even though the bite of it nipped at her with cruel teeth. No man, least of all a cop with attitude, would reduce her to a sobbing mass of misery.

Wrung out from the day's stress, she slipped out of her clothes and into her flannels. She crawled into bed, curled into a ball and jammed down the tears once again.

* * * * *

Bella woke about five thirty the next morning with a sickening feeling of something being unfinished or left hanging. She didn't know which emotion bothered her more. She rolled over in bed and stared at the ceiling without really seeing it, and knew what she must do to remove some of the mental pain carving a hole through her gut.

The man she loved didn't love her. Would never love her. He cared about her and didn't want to be treated like a piece of meat, but he obviously hadn't given her his heart.

Why on earth had he reacted so strongly to her simple words about him being a sex object? Disgusted, she climbed out of bed and took a shower.

After she dressed, she opened her bedroom door and tip-toed her way to the den so she wouldn't wake Luca. She didn't feel like having it out with him at the moment. No, she needed a therapy far more soothing. She would paint to start the morning, letting frustration and pain transform the canvas.

Then she would pack up her stuff, head back to her condo, and get ready to move. Not to her father's home, but a resort where she could bury herself in a sea of faces. Anonymous and carefree she would contemplate her future without the most gorgeous, exasperating man she'd ever met.

In time she'd get over him. But she'd never forget him.

Bella went into the den and realized other paints she needed were still over at her condo. It would take only a minute to run over there and retrieve them. After grabbing her keys, she slipped out the back door and traipsed through the gate between their properties. A stiff cold breeze battered at her T-shirt and jeans as she opened the door to her condo. She heard a sudden rattling noise and it stopped her cold. Listening, she waited to see if she would hear it again.

Nothing.

Shrugging, she stepped inside her darkened condo and headed right for her bedroom. She made it just into the bedroom when she heard another sound, this one light and chilling. The flap of the soft curtains over an open window.

An open window.

A low, hollow laugh came from nearby.

Bella's heart froze with a stab of unholy fear. Before she could react, a sharp pain exploded in her head. She staggered as waves of pain and dizziness made her totter on her feet. Then everything went black.

* * * * *

When the alarm clock rang at six thirty in the morning, Luca almost knocked it off the bedside table as he jammed his hand over the button. The first attempt didn't work, and the instrument went right on shrieking. He cursed and sat bolt upright. He slapped his hand onto the clock and glared at it as it stopped ringing. With a sigh, he flopped backwards onto his pillows.

He felt like hell. With dry mouth and throbbing head, he sat up again. After a night of tossing, turning, and contemplating what a total ass he'd been, he realized that he might have screwed the pooch forever.

Bella would never speak to him again.

Way to go, Angello. He'd created a one hundred percent bum fuck.

Groaning, he stumbled out of bed. He couldn't remember the last time he felt this stupid. He'd done a few ignorant things in his life, as everyone did. This time he'd hit an all-time low for ignorance. When Bella started listing his family's qualities yesterday, Maria's ugly specter arose and he reacted without thinking. Fear had driven him to say things he didn't mean.

If Bella did think of him as a sex object…well, for a lot of men that would be fine. At the beginning of their association he only wanted to make love with her and protect her. She might think he could fuck mechanically without emotions involved, but he'd discovered differently since the time he met her. No matter what, he'd always remember that Bella fed his mind and his body in a way no other woman could.

The thought left him with a hollow ache in his gut.

After he showered and dressed, he left his bedroom in search of her. A few moments later, with worry prickling the hairs on the back of his neck, he realized she was not in the house.

A horrible premonition of danger rose in his gut, so sharp and certain that he knew he must act. He reached for the phone and called for emergency backup.

Seconds later he found his weapon, checked the clip, and went for the door.

* * * * *

Sounds registered in Bella's mind first. A whisper soft chuckling. The clank of something indefinable.

Pain lacerated her skull, and she moaned. She put her fingers to her temples and pressed, as if the gesture could remove the crunching agony. Where was she? What happened?

Someone in the house. Someone —

She jerked into total consciousness with a gasp and her eyes opened. Her wooly brain cleared faster than a dash of cold water in the face.

Watery sunlight filtered through her bedroom curtains, giving the room an eerie half-darkness. She lay on her bed covered with a blanket, the soothing warmth of the fabric against her naked skin.

Naked. Oh, God.

"Don't even think about trying to escape, darling." A cultured English accent filled her ears. "You are right where I want you. As much as I love you, if you try anything it will all go very badly for you."

She looked around for the voice but didn't see anyone. Her breathing quickened, her heart pounded.

Another chilling laugh, deeper and more sinister, slipped from the figure's lips.

Almost afraid to move, she reached up to touch her aching head. She found the injured spot, a tender area on the back of her head. Her fingers came away sticky. When she glanced at her hand, the dark streaks betrayed her situation. No wonder her head hurt like fire.

Nausea curled inside her. "Oh, God."

"Blast it." She heard a grunt. This time the voice sounded unsteady, almost as if they, too, suffered an injury. "If you get the sheets all mucked, I'll have to hurt you again."

When she looked up, the dark figure came closer. Her throat felt so tight she almost couldn't squeeze the words passed her lips. "I can bandage my wound. Then I won't bleed any more."

A dark figure loomed up from her right, and she jerked in alarm. The English voice belonged to a big man. He must have been sitting on the floor against the far wall. As the man came toward her, the last fuzziness cleared from her vision, replaced with the knowledge she might have little time to live. Her breathing came hard, spurred by a gut-wrenching dread that tore at her body. She tried to take a deep breath to gain perspective, but it hurt. Tremors, uncontrollable and constant, began to coast through her.

"You do know me, don't you, luv?" the man asked as he hovered near her bedside. "It wasn't so long ago that we met."

Her gaze latched onto his face, and for one stunning moment she couldn't believe her eyes. Deep in her soul she'd been terrified of him since childhood without knowing who he could be. Instead he'd remained the shadow man who stood at her doorway and gazed at her night after night, a massive shape in dark clothing that made his huge form more menacing.

She recognized his unrelenting silver stare, as hard and unforgiving as an executioner. He stood about six feet, six inches, even taller and bigger than Luca's well-built form. Brick solid, the man's robust frame held muscles toned by years of pumping iron. She knew that she didn't have a chance in hell of escaping him without a good plan.

In dim light she saw his smile framed in a wide jaw. His teeth, yellowed by endless cups of coffee in the morning, gave him a used look. Nearing his mid-fifties, he did have crow's feet forming, and his jowls seemed looser than in his youth. Cut military short, his almost totally gray hair had once been coal black. His cold eyes held the inexorable essence of a man intent on attaining what he wanted, no matter the cost.

His persistent attention, when she was a child, had cost Bella her sense of security and a confidence she'd wanted all her life. He'd been the monster under the bed, in the closet, in her dreams.

The man Father had threatened to fire, but who never left the household service.

Elias Peterborough, born in a slum in England, was a nightmare come to life. He'd immigrated to the United States at twenty-five and worked his way through several security jobs before latching onto one at her father's estate.

"It was you watching me all those nights when I was little. You stopped because my father told you to. Then you started again two months ago." Revulsion made her skin ripple with goose bumps. "I should have known it was you. I should have—"

"Shut the fuck up, darling."

Her heart jumped. A tremor ran through her again, and Bella tugged the blanket closer. Her nakedness left her feeling impotent. She almost glanced around the room to look for a weapon, but she also didn't want him to realize that she had command of herself. Her head continued to ache, and she wondered if the nausea in her stomach came from fear or a concussion.

He brushed one hand over his hair. "Certainly I watched over you. Your father misunderstood. He thought I was doing something strange looking at you. But I'd never hurt a little girl in a million years. Only grown up bitches deserve to be hurt."

Edgy and tight, his voice made her stomach tighten with new fear. She heard the unwavering certainty in his voice and knew the man teetered on a fine boundary of psychosis. Bella knew his mental illness didn't mean he was stupid.

"And why are you here now?" she asked.

"The cop. I've been watching both of you, and it's clear what you've been doing. Anyone can see it." His voice sounded as calm as a tour guide explaining how Anne Boleyn lost her head in the Tower of London. "I'm here to finish what I started all those years ago and to keep on protecting you even when your father doesn't see that you need it. You're just like the other bitches. I watched over you. Kept others from hurting you when you were just a child. You know, you're so much like Emily. But then even Emily betrayed me."

"Emily?"

"My daughter. She was a sweet, gentle girl until men corrupted her."

"What happened to her?"

He laughed, the soft noise like a ripple of sound at a cocktail party. Certainly not the chuckle of a man ready to commit murder. "She allowed them to use her and so I had to put her down. What else? She should have stayed pure and untouched until marriage."

Put her down. Like an animal.

Horror started a surefire path through Bella. Her forehead wrinkled in pain as her head continued to throb. A stomach-churning thought came to life. "Is that why you've been killing women in town?"

"Of course. But this wasn't the only place I've cleansed of evil bitches. They've paid with their lives for their sins."

"Before...you've killed—" Her voice cracked, and she swallowed around the dry lump in her throat. "You killed women somewhere else other than Piper's Grove?"

"Of course," he chuckled, throaty and almost normal in tone. Only a hint of madness lay in the rumble of sound coming from his chest. "I used to take trips out of Denver on weekends, and sometimes found some useless whore no one would miss. The police are bloody stupid. They never found the women I executed. I buried the little cunts where no one could find them. You didn't think I'd waited all these years just to kill bitches in this ridiculous town, did you? When I was in England last, I managed to kill a bitch a month for three months."

Her brain tried to recall when Peterborough had taken vacation, but her head hurt too much. "When were you in London?"

He slapped her, hard. Bella's head snapped to one side under the blow. A gasp of astonished pain left her lips.

Peterborough's eyes glittered with a strange mixture of hate and love, a parody of emotions that shouldn't be stirred together. "You don't remember?"

"No." Her voice came as a whisper of sound, fear keeping her voice softer than she meant it to be.

"It was a long time ago, when you were a girl. When no one had corrupted you or fucked you, or made you a whore. " He paused, his eyes filled with all the insanity in the world. "When you went out with all those men, I knew all of them were fucking you."

"No. Not all of them. I—" He slapped her on the other cheek, and a soft whimper escaped her mouth. "Please, stop."

"You deserve it and desire it. Those men wanted your money and status and your body along with it. You were strong and told the bastards to get out of your life. But I helped it along. I told them all if they hurt you I would kill them."

She understood in a blinding flash why the men she'd dated always left her life without a whimper. Elias Peterborough threatened them with injury or perhaps even death.

Another heavy shudder wracked her body. Bella wanted to scream, but instead her mouth opened and nothing came out. She swallowed hard to ease the dryness and tightness in her throat. This monster had killed all those women because of her. "You followed me here."

"Yes. I thought you were different, but you need protecting like they did," he said as he shifted slightly. "I watched and waited for them to do the right thing and dump their lovers. But they never did. And I saw you and the stupid cop together and knew that this one was different than the other fornicators you knew. This man wants to screw you until the sun doesn't rise ever again. We can't have that, can we?"

Shuddering with a bone-deep cold fueled by horror, she struggled to make her mind work. She couldn't give into panic or he could subdue and murder her. It would take him mere seconds to kill.

I know the serial killer. I knew him all along.

The idea sickened her down to the depths of her soul.

He sat on the edge of the bed, and she fought the urge to cringe. He smelled dank and musty, like a long closed-up closet.

"Fate says you're to be mine, because I'm the only one who can save you."

"You followed me in that sedan, didn't you?"

"I wanted to protect you. But then that stupid cop decided he would sully you."

"Why did you hurt me just now if you want to protect me?"

"Because I know you've been sleeping with that low-life cop. Don't you know he's not for you? He isn't class, just the way the other men weren't class."

How long would it take Luca to realize she'd left the house and come looking for her? She wanted him to save her with everything inside her, yet the idea of him being killed by Peterborough made her blood freeze. "May I get dressed?"

"No." His fingers passed over her neck, then slid with fish-cold flesh down to her left breast. She shivered as he plucked one nipple. "Don't try anything, or I'll have to punish you. You are a ripe little cunt, aren't you? I wondered."

She almost gagged, revulsion making her stomach rumble and pitch. The stark coldness in his words made her obey. She wouldn't allow this man to hurt the one she loved. One way or the other she'd escape and make her way back to Luca and safety.

"Do you repent?" he asked as he looked down at her with cold eyes. He trailed his index finger over her other nipple, and she shuddered again in distaste. "Do you realize what sins you've committed?"

"Tell me?" she asked in the quietest voice she could muster. Let him think she'd gone submissive. "Tell me so I can repent."

A grim smile cracked his face, and as she dared in that one moment to look into his eyes, she felt the iniquity inside him reach for her. With poison-like consistency, it rolled over her in a wave, cold as ice and as pitiless as a murderous beast stalking a meal. She'd always heard you could see evil in someone's eyes if you knew what to look for. Now she knew it was the truth. Bella saw it, and it wanted her, needed her, and would consume her in fire if she didn't escape.

Flee.

How? Oh, God, how.

Tears prickled at the back of her eyes, and she held them back, knowing that if he saw them, she would receive another punishment.

Finally, he answered her. "Your sin is that you aren't obedient. That you allow more than a husband to take you, and that you flaunt your body and opinions in ways you shouldn't. You know, when you were a little girl I wondered what type whore you might turn out to be. I dare say it was worth the wait to find out."

Her heart thundered and fright started to wear away at her strength. If she made any sudden moves, Peterborough might kill her on the spot. On the other hand, if she didn't do something, she would die anyway.

She had one opportunity.

Now.

Now.

Determination banished her pain, and she reached for the lamp on the bedside table and yanked with all her might. She heaved the heavy ceramic lamp toward his head. Alarm and wild-eyed anger didn't make him fast enough to avoid the lamp.

The lamp cracked him in the face, and he screamed as he lost balance and fell backwards. "No!"

She slid off the bed and ran, bursting out of the bedroom with fear giving her feet swiftness. She tripped and fell flat on her face on the hard floor. Her breath whooshed out of her, making her gasp for air. Forcing herself to her feet, she scrambled toward the living room.

He was right behind her.

Run.

Run.

"Bitch! Bitch! Bitch! Come back here! You can't escape punishment!"

She knew if he caught her this time, there would be no getaway.

The back door burst open, wood cracking. Luca rushed through, holding his weapon ready, his crouch that of a warrior.

"Luca!" she gasped, her relief mingling with tearing fear.

Another wave of dizziness made her legs wobble, but she staggered toward him.

He spied her and in that second Peterborough ran from the bedroom. Luca grabbed her arm and shoved her behind him. "Police! Don't move asshole!"

Instinct made her back up until she bumped against the wall. Her legs quivered, but she forced herself to stay standing.

Peterborough's face held the determination of a man at the end of his cares, at the last drop of humanity. He came at Luca with a roar.

Luca's weapon fired, the noise jolting through Bella as if she'd been shot herself.

Blood spread over Peterborough's shoulder.

Like a mindless beast, the madman kept coming.

Luca fired again, this time hitting the raging man in the chest. Peterborough flew backwards, hitting the coffee table. Wood cracked and split and the dead man lay among the fractured remains, his eyes wide open.

Bella's legs gave out and she slid down the wall.

Sirens wailed in the distance.

"Luca?" Bella's weak voice sounded childlike to her own ears.

Luca turned toward her, his eyes filled with vestiges of glittering rage and the desire to protect. His gaze cleared, concern replacing anger as he squatted next to her. He cupped her cheek.

"Bella, you're hurt." His voice cracked, his lips trembling. "Did that son-of-a bitch touch you?"

Tears began to cascade down her face. "He hit me in the head. I don't know…"

"Shhhhh, baby. It's all right. You're all right." He holstered his gun and then reached for her, gathering her in his arms. He looked deep into her eyes, then cursed. "There's blood everywhere. Shit, shit, shit."

She sank into the haven of his arms, but couldn't stop shaking. Power and tenderness surrounded her. Luca murmured reassurances, his hand brushing over her back.

"Are you hurt anywhere else?" A new horror covered his face. "Oh, Jesus, Bella, did he—"

She shook her head. "No. No." She sobbed. "He killed all those women because of me!"

"No, sweetheart." His voice went husky with emotion, and she thought she saw moisture in his eyes. "He was insane. Don't blame this on yourself."

She tried to speak again, but sobbed instead as she lost control of her strength.

"Easy, sweetheart. Easy. I've got you." He released her and stood up.

"Don't leave me." A sob escaped her throat.

"I just need to get you something to put on."

After he found her clothes and helped her into them, he picked her up and carried her toward the ruined door. "We've got to get you to the hospital."

"He was—I knew him. He was the man in the shadows." She drew back slightly to look at Luca. "He's been near me all that time. Since I was a little girl." Shivering uncontrollably, she laid her head on Luca's shoulder and wept. "Those women died because of me."

Luca cursed again, a string of harsh words she barely heard but understood. Then, he softened his voice again as he carried her around the side of the house. "Help is here, Bella. Just hang in there with me. You're safe, now."

Three police cruisers and an ambulance screeched to a halt in front of the residence.

Tired, hurt, and relieved despite the fear that continued to roll through her in waves, she looked up at him through eyes blurred by tears.

It didn't matter if Luca didn't love her.

She knew in that moment she would love him until the day she died.

Epilogue

Luca strode through the hospital corridor. Flowers and card clutched in his hands, he knew that the next few minutes might establish the course of the rest of his life.

He couldn't remember the last time he'd been so nervous. Less than ten hours had passed since he'd blown away Elias Peterborough. After the knee-buckling moments when he'd carried Bella out of the condo and toward emergency help, he'd wanted to go with Bella to the hospital. Instead he knew he must stay behind as required for the investigation.

He knew that after this visit to Bella, Captain O'Hara wanted him back at the office to clean up details about the case.

The nightmare concluded the minute the bullet struck the serial killer in the heart, but now the questions would come and the answers would have to be found. He felt almost as if he'd been the one hit in the head and terrorized. Done with the preliminary nut-roll required by Internal Affairs and ready to see Bella, Luca had told Damon he was heading to the hospital. Other than finding out that she had suffered a concussion and would be hospitalized at least overnight, he hadn't been able to get to the hospital and tell her what he needed to say with all his heart.

Before Luca left the office, Damon's eyes had gleamed with an unusual understanding. "Go get her, buddy." Damon had clapped him on the shoulder and winked.

Maybe his partner wasn't such a terrible son-of-a-bitch after all.

News media had descended on the police department, and Luca had fought his way through the frenzied reporters with the firm statement of, "No comment!" At the hospital he went through the same routine. Hospital security chased the reporters away when they saw him plunging through the crowd outside.

Right now, with Bella safe, he should feel on top of the world. Instead his entire body ached with the worry that she would reject him. He didn't have a care in the world most days, and now his stomach felt hollow and his mind whirled with doubts.

Luca tried to remember the last time he felt this torn up and this uncertain. He couldn't. Even his big breakup with Maria hadn't hurt this bad. No, he didn't plan on leaving Bella's life, but he worried she would tell him to get the hell out of her sight. More that that, he wondered if any amount of apologizing could fix the damage he'd done.

Damn it, I'll get down on my knees and beg, if I have to.

His heart lurched as he thought about how close he'd come to losing her forever.

He paused at the door and realized that Bella's family didn't know what had happened since he hadn't called them. Luca doubted Bella would have called them. Perhaps they would have caught the story on the news. He took a deep breath and sighed. Perhaps she'd been alone with her demons for hours.

As he eased open the door, it creaked.

Bella's eyes snapped wide at the sharp sound, her nerves remaining ragged and jumpy.

When she saw Luca, looking worried and a little disheveled, her breath left her in a rush of relief. "Luca."

"Hey, sweetheart."

God, she loved it when he spoke endearments in soft, tender tones. It melted her defenses and brought grateful tears to her eyes. She could be dead right now. Instead, the man she'd fallen for stood there, hesitation written on his face.

"Come in," she said, her voice raw with emotions.

He entered quickly at her invitation, uncertainty hovering in his eyes. His gaze snagged for a second on the flowers gracing her bedside table. He frowned a little and she read his expression; he had to wonder who gave her the flowers. Not only did he look used up and weary, a strange sadness gave his eyes a darkness she'd never noted before.

New apprehension filled her soul, a strangling sense of being out of control, battered, and depressed. She was alive, but she felt like something worse could happen—Luca could walk out of her life.

She hated feeling weak, but right then she did feel worn and vulnerable. Tears seeped into her eyes again, and not even the joy of seeing Luca could hold them inside. As the tears released, she wiped at them.

With typical male horror, he stood stock still for a second with his mouth open. It would have been funny if she didn't hurt inside, and her head still didn't feel heavier than a bowling ball.

He put the flowers down near the other vase, and the card, too. Reaching out to stroke her face, his gaze coasted over her face with rapt attention. "Doctor says you're going to be all right, but I'm still worried as hell. Why are you crying? Are you in pain?"

Under the gentle caress of his fingers, some of her trepidation left. "My head aches, but I'm all right. It's actually a mild concussion."

"Thank God it wasn't worse." His voice was hoarse, as if he might be the one in pain. "Bella, I have so much to say." He swallowed hard. "So much that I don't know where to start."

Here it comes. The part where he says goodbye.

He held out the flowers and card and she took them. "First, this."

She sniffed the gentle fragrance of pink carnations. "Thank you. They're pretty."

Luca reached for her shoulder and pressed gently. He explained about how things went at the police station. "I thought I would never get away from there."

"I understand. It's your job."

He didn't look any happier. "Yeah, but you're a hell of a lot more important than a job."

Bella decided not to take what he'd just said to mean undying love.

He cleared his throat. "Have you talked to your family?"

She sighed. "I called them and they got here as fast as they could. I insisted they get something to eat, so they're down in the lounge. Besides, I needed a break from my father's ranting and Madeleine repeating over and over that she told me coming to Piper's Grove was a bad idea." She gave him a watery smile. "Um...your mother is a sweetie, you know. She called the hospital after she heard a news report, and she and Diana came over about an hour ago. It was interesting watching our families together."

He glanced at the additional flowers in a vase on the table. His expression lightened. "I'll bet that was fascinating to watch."

Bella shoved back more tears, appalled at her inability to stop crying. "I'm sorry. I don't know what's wrong with me."

Luca's eyes softened, chocolate-warm even in their darkness. He came closer and slid his arm around her, bringing her head down to his shoulder. He kissed the top of her head.

"It's all right. No one's going to hurt you again."

"I know. I know." She gulped. "I'm just trying to think how to say what I feel."

He turned her face toward him, his fingers a caress along her jaw line. "If you're trying to tell me I'm the biggest asshole on the planet and I should go fuck myself, go right ahead. I deserve it."

"What?" She slipped from under his shoulder as she pulled back. "Why would I say that?"

Looking grim beyond words, he sighed and reached for her hands. He drew them to his lips. "I'm going to kiss these before you slap me with them."

He touched excruciatingly tender kisses to her knuckles. She shivered with sweet delight. Why would a man who planned to tell her to get out of his life kiss her hand? He was acting like she was fragile and needed the utmost care.

"Why would I slap you?"

He retained his gentle grip on her hands. "There are three things I've got to apologize for. I shouldn't have spoken like that to you when you were at my parents' house. I knew better than that. I let my past get in the way of my present. I panicked." He explained about Maria and how she'd ridiculed his family. "When I started thinking that you and I run in different circles and the fact we've known each other about a week, I let myself believe we couldn't be together."

She nodded. "It hurt, Luca. I won't deny it."

His took another one of those deep breaths, as he closed his eyes for a minute. When he opened them she thought his eyes looked moist. "It was damned immature of me. It's eating me up right now thinking that by being the biggest jackass on the planet, that I may have ruined every last chance I have with you."

He still wants to be with me.

Again he nestled her closer, his face near hers. The heat and power of his body made her long for more. He cupped her face and kissed her forehead. "I'm sorry I hurt you. When I realized that bastard Peterborough had you, I had to admit the truth to myself. I'd never been so scared in my life. I told you I'd protect you, and I failed."

"No," she said softly, hating to see the excruciating pain in his expression. "No, you didn't fail me. You saved my life. I'll never forget that. I was stupid, Luca. I was so ruffled from our argument last night that I didn't think. Going to the condo by myself was dumb...and it almost got me killed."

"It was my duty to protect you. You wouldn't have been ruffled if I hadn't started that ridiculous argument."

She smiled, feeling better by the moment. She ran her fingers through the white strands of hair at his temple. "So we're both idiots. What are we going to do about it?"

Luca grinned, and she cherished that smile and absorbed it into her heart. He pushed her hair back from her face. "If he'd — " He closed his eyes again, and when he reopened them, not all of his pain vanished. "If I'd lost you, I couldn't have lived with it."

As his arm tightened around her, he kissed her.

Her world swayed as his tender caress showed passion mixed with gentleness, an exploration that asked for her understanding. She met that need, opening her lips and thrusting her tongue inside his mouth. Determined to show him how much passion she held for him, she caressed him. When he pulled back she felt breathless and more alive than she could ever remember.

"Say you forgive me," he said.

She caressed his jaw. "Oh, Luca, there's nothing to forgive. You know, when you walked in here I thought maybe you were going to say goodbye forever. I was terrified. That's one of the reasons why I was crying. And I can't seem to stop."

He brushed the tears away with his thumb. "No, I don't want to leave you." His voice went husky. "I love you so damned much." As he pressed fevered kisses on her face and lips, he said those sought after words again. "I love you. I love you."

As his words sank in, she slipped her arms around his neck and hugged him with everything inside her. "Oh, yes. I love you, too."

Oblivious to where they were, she responded and initiated several hot kisses that held nothing back. Injury or not, she knew if she wasn't lying in a hospital bed, Detective Luca Angello would be in very big trouble. She would have stripped him and made love to him right then and there.

This time his smile held joy and a promise she knew would never be broken. "Stay with me. We'll make a new life together. Marry me."

As she pulled his head down for another kiss, she said against his lips. "Yes."

A brilliant grin touched his mouth when he released her. "You've just made me the happiest bastard in the world." After another mind-altering kiss, he said, "You realize our families are going to flip. Yours won't approve, and mine will be ecstatic."

She shook her head, even though it hurt. "It doesn't matter. We're together and that's all that counts."

And she proved it with another kiss.

The End

Enjoy this excerpt from:
WINTER WARRIORS
MANEATER
© Copyright Denise A. Agnew 2003

Chapter One
Date: Christmas Eve
Place: Special Investigations Agency
Location: Top Secret

"You've got to be kidding?" Cora Destiny Tremayne asked the tall, thin man as she stomped across the huge marble and glass lobby of the United States branch of SIA, Special Investigations Agency. Anger heated her blood. "You know I work alone on most missions, and you want me to team up with the biggest hard-ass in the agency? I don't think so."

The Brit, Controller Quinton Maybrick, gave her a patient sideways glance. "He's not that bad."

She gave an unladylike snort and glared. "Uh-huh. Right."

Cora felt his stare and realized he'd waited until they reached his office before answering. His eyes, enormous behind thick glasses, made him look like an owl. A very intelligent, blinking, curious bird. He palmed one big hand across his curly blond hair and looked a little nervous around the edges. Today he wore a beige suit that fit his skinny body to perfection; his navy blue tie held designer flair. She doubted he'd paid much for the ensemble. Quinton could negotiate a juicy rodent out of a python's mouth if need be. Bargaining might be the Englishman's forte, but she wouldn't be pushed on this point.

No way.

As she walked faster, her sensible low-heeled boots echoed across the tiles. For once she'd like to have a decent Christmas. But *noooooooo*. She'd set foot in the building maybe three minutes before Quinton nabbed her and said she must go on emergency assignment. Her blood filled with instant excitement until she heard her partner would be special agent Mac Tudor.

Absolutely, positively *not*. She wouldn't do it. "You're going to have to fire me."

Quinton didn't reply as he opened his outer office door and they walked passed his secretary. "We'll be in my office, Cheryl. Hold my calls, please."

With her usual aplomb, Destiny barged forward and opened his inner office door before he could get there. She charged through and turned toward him as he came inside and closed the door. Tinsel and glass ornaments hung around the sides of the door moved in the sudden breeze.

She planted her hands on her hips. "Now, I'd like an explanation. You know I've always agreed to every assignment you've sent me on, but not with a mega-bastard like Tudor."

Quinton slid into the black leather executive chair behind the desk. "Please, have a seat."

She almost refused, then realized that would be too dramatic. Despite being pissed, Destiny knew Quinton didn't make assignment pairings lightly. Whether she liked it or not, he somehow thought putting her with Tudor would be a good idea.

She sat in the chair, perched on the edge, razor-fine tension in her muscles. She could feel her jaw aching and tried to relax.

Mac Tudor. Just his name set her teeth on edge. She didn't want anything to do with the man. One encounter, at last year's holiday party, solidified her dislike for the agent once and for all.

Her face heated as she recalled in painful detail how fellow agents teased them about being wallflowers until Mac took her into his arms for a slow dance. One touch from his hands, one look into his gorgeous, melting-chocolate brown eyes, and she'd felt a quivering sexual awakening shocking her down to her designer shoes.

Mac had looked down on her as he'd brought her body up against his rock-hard, muscled frame. Undeniable need had eased through her as he'd palmed her back and spoke in that husky, velvet-rich deep voice. She'd seen something hot in his eyes as they'd danced. Consuming, as a matter of fact. No man before or since made her feel on the edge of a cliff, ready to jump into dangerous sexual territory. He'd possessed the gall to whisper in her ear a few sensual possibilities for them later that evening.

She'd told him in no uncertain terms she wanted nothing to do with a man who slept with every woman within a twenty-mile radius.

"Destiny?"

She snapped back to reality, disturbed by the memory of Tudor's arms around her. "Sorry. Go on."

"There are two reasons why you've been paired with Mac." Quinton held up his hand and started to count off. "One, you're both single and don't have families to worry about this Christmas. Many other agents have time off for the holidays. Two, you both have wilderness survival training and are in excellent physical condition. This case is particularly tough."

She shrugged, not convinced. "SIA takes on all the gnarly cases. That's why we're here."

Quinton blinked behind those gold-rimmed glasses, then smiled. His narrow, forty-something face always looked like a patient professor. "Destiny, this is of the utmost importance. The President of the United States ordered us to take care of this problem directly."

Wonderful. Use the old "You would never let down the Commander-in-Chief" ploy.

"Just listen to what I have to say," Quinton said.

She heard a new hard-edged tone in his voice, and when Quinton Maybrick spoke like this, she knew he meant business. She sat up straight. "All right."

He opened the file on his desk and drew out an eight-by-ten glossy black and white photograph. He slid it along the desk until she could see it and pick it up.

When she recognized the older woman in the photograph, her insides tumbled. Fifty-year-old agency veteran Phyllida

Cuthbert smiled back at Destiny from the photo. Pretty, blonde, and one of the best agents in the business, Phyllida was a legend.

"Why am I holding her photo?" Destiny asked.

Quinton rolled his chair closer to the desk and leaned on it. He clasped his long-fingered hands together.

A lump rose in her throat, her heart beat quickened. "Cut to the chase, Quinton."

"Very well. Phyllida's gone missing."

"What?"

"For three days. She supposedly disappeared at the same time as Dr. Bayou LaCroix, the director of the research complex."

"Maybe she's off getting some nookie with the good doctor."

Chagrin entered his expression. "Destiny—"

"Missing isn't as bad as dead. Especially not for an experienced agent like Phyllida." Her mind tumbled with possibilities. "She's the best agent you have."

"Nonetheless, she was on assignment at the time of her disappearance from a high-mountain experiments lab."

"Oh, crap," Destiny murmured.

His pale face became a study in concern and frustration. "Since she went into the lab undercover last week, she's maintained steady contact with SIA. Until three days ago, that is. Satellite surveillance shows there is still activity there, and we have the heat signatures of several individuals at the complex."

Destiny stuffed her hands in her hair, running her fingers through the toss of long curls. "She wouldn't leave the complex without making contact and telling us her plans."

"Exactly." If the look in his pale blue eyes hadn't told Destiny he feared the worst, the resignation in his voice would have. "She needs our help."

Destiny's animosity dropped a full degree. "Of course. But Tudor won't want to work with me. He hates my guts."

A smile exploded across Quinton's face. "He doesn't hate you."

"He does."

"Does not."

"Does—" She stopped. "This is ridiculous."

"That's why I need you both to get over it. This agency is relying on you and Tudor to bring your fellow agent home safely."

Never one to cover up the truth, no matter how painful, she said, "If she's still alive."

He nodded and stood. As he walked to the window and looked at the snow beginning to blanket the parking lot, his voice went soft. "There's more to this case than rescuing her."

Oh-oh. Here it comes.

He turned back to her, hands behind his back and imperial British written all over him. "You and Mac will receive a full dossier on the situation, but I need to warn you. Even if Phyllida is alive and well, she may need assistance. Situational Development Corporation is a huge facility. We're talking a couple of football fields long and three stories high."

She shrugged. "So it's a big building. What's the problem?"

"Several Situational Development Corporation employees have gone missing over the last few months, and that's why the SIA got into the investigation in the first place."

"How many is several?" Incredulous, she stood and joined him at the window. "Are we talking about a serial killer?"

"Maybe. This year several strange things have occurred around the world, and there is worry in some circles it has to do with a conspiracy. You're not the only investigations team we're sending out this winter."

She hadn't spoken lately with two of her close friends, other female agents assigned in Europe and Canada. "One of those agents wouldn't happen to be Nur Aydan?"

Quinton looked uneasy. When Destiny met the agent some years ago, she knew there was something different about the woman, but she couldn't say what. She got along well with Nur and liked the woman very much. Quinton wouldn't tell her what made Nur different, so she'd dropped the subject long ago.

"Yes. And we planned to send out Jenna MacDonald, but she's on holiday right now," Quinton said.

"Well, Nur won't let you down. She's one of the finest agents around for any situation."

Quinton smoothed a hand down the lapel of his suit. "Frankly, even if there were other agents available, you and Mac are the best operatives we've got for a situation like this."

She smiled. "Go ahead, try buttering me up."

He didn't smile back. "Mac is in top physical shape. He can do just about anything we ask. You'll be in rugged territory. If anything should happen to your SUV, you will need the skills you've been taught by the agency, and more. Mac can mountainclimb—"

"I know, I know." She stood up, and then sat on the edge of the mahogany desk, well aware how cheeky it was. "Every time I see the section secretary, she's extolling his many virtues."

Probably getting fucked by him, too.

Whoa, Destiny. Where did that little piece of venom come from?

"You've always gotten along with the other agents, Destiny, what's so different about Mac?"

She started to speak, then sputtered. "He's…well, he's so arrogant." She couldn't remember the last time she'd acted like a petulant two-year-old, but right now she didn't care. Working with Mac would be like grinding sand in her teeth all day. "He's infuriating. Always smiling like he knows what you're thinking, and damned smug about it. And here's the kicker. He dared to call me a maneater. Can you believe that?"

A smile parted the Englishman's mouth as he tried to stifle a laugh and failed.

She glared. Never mind that other people called her Destiny Cora "Maneater" Tremayne behind her back. She wore the nickname with pride. She'd chewed up and spit out more male chauvinists in her career than any other female agent at SIA.

And God forbid if anyone called her Cora.

Quinton rolled his gaze to the ceiling and exhaled an annoyed sigh. "If you can't come up with something better than the objection that he's arrogant, then I really am surprised at you."

Destiny felt it down in her bones. She was sunk.

"I didn't want to do this, Destiny." He walked to his desk and picked up the file. He handed it to her. "You're ordered to work with Special Agent Mac Tudor, whether you like it or not." He glanced at his watch. "You're going to meet with him in a half hour in the gym and talk out your differences."

Apprehension slid over her skin. "Why the gym?"

He smiled, conspiracy written in his grin. "About this time every day he works on his martial arts. I need you to talk ASAP. And by the way, I'd dress the part if I were you."

She sighed. After a slight pause she said, "Mac and I can't pretend we don't hate each other's guts."

"Well, then, you're going to dislike this assignment more than you anticipated."

Oh, brother. What now? She looked at the file in her hand. "I'm afraid to open this."

"You'll have to read it before you see Mac."

As she read the file, heat rose in her face. "You've got to be kidding. Who thought up this crazy cover story?"

Quinton didn't look the least repentant. "I did."

"What if I still refuse?"

"Then you'll be looking at a transfer to the upper reaches of North Dakota."

She grimaced. "Well, shit."

About the author:

Suspenseful, erotic, edgy, thrilling, romantic, adventurous. All these words are used to describe award-winning, best-selling novelist Denise A. Agnew's novels. Romantic Times Magazine called her romantic suspense novels DANGEROUS INTENTIONS and TREACHEROUS WISHES "top-notch romantic suspense." With paranormal, time travel, romantic comedy, contemporary, historical, erotica, and romantic suspense novels under her belt, she proves her gift for writing about a diverse range of subjects. (Writing tales that scare the reader is her ultimate thrill.)Denise's inspiration for her novels comes from innumerable sources, but the fact she has lived in Colorado, Hawaii, and the United Kingdom has given her a lifetime of ideas. Her experiences with archaeology have crept into her work, as well as numerous travels throughout England, Ireland, Scotland, and Wales. Denise currently lives in Arizona with her real life hero, her husband.

Denise welcomes mail from readers. You can write to her c/o Ellora's Cave Publishing at 1337 Commerce Drive, Suite 13, Stow OH 44224.

Also by Denise Agnew:

Why an electronic book?

We live in the Information Age—an exciting time in the history of human civilization in which technology rules supreme and continues to progress in leaps and bounds every minute of every hour of every day. For a multitude of reasons, more and more avid literary fans are opting to purchase e-books instead of paperbacks. The question to those not yet initiated to the world of electronic reading is simply: *why?*

1. *Price.* An electronic title at Ellora's Cave Publishing runs anywhere from 40-75% less than the cover price of the <u>exact same title</u> in paperback format. Why? Cold mathematics. It is less expensive to publish an e-book than it is to publish a paperback, so the savings are passed along to the consumer.

2. *Space.* Running out of room to house your paperback books? That is one worry you will never have with electronic novels. For a low one-time cost, you can purchase a handheld computer designed specifically for e-reading purposes. Many e-readers are larger than the average handheld, giving you plenty of screen room. Better yet, hundreds of titles can be stored within your new library—a single microchip. (Please note that Ellora's Cave does not endorse any specific brands. You can check our website at www.ellorascave.com for customer

recommendations we make available to new consumers.)

3. *Mobility*. Because your new library now consists of only a microchip, your entire cache of books can be taken with you wherever you go.

4. *Personal preferences are accounted for*. Are the words you are currently reading too small? Too large? Too…**ANNOYING**? Paperback books cannot be modified according to personal preferences, but e-books can.

5. *Innovation*. The way you read a book is not the only advancement the Information Age has gifted the literary community with. There is also the factor of what you can read. Ellora's Cave Publishing will be introducing a new line of interactive titles that are available in e-book format only.

6. *Instant gratification*. Is it the middle of the night and all the bookstores are closed? Are you tired of waiting days—sometimes weeks—for online and offline bookstores to ship the novels you bought? Ellora's Cave Publishing sells instantaneous downloads 24 hours a day, 7 days a week, 365 days a year. Our e-book delivery system is 100% automated, meaning your order is filled as soon as you pay for it.

Those are a few of the top reasons why electronic novels are displacing paperbacks for many an avid reader. As always, Ellora's Cave Publishing welcomes your questions and comments. We invite you to email us at service@ellorascave.com or write to us directly at: 1337 Commerce Drive, Suite 13, Stow OH 44224.